THE DEAD TEACH THE LIVING . . .

What indeed, Dody thought, other than the lack of any other specialist surgical positions available to her. She remembered all too well the revulsion she'd felt for the dissecting rooms as a raw medical student and how those feelings had returned during her first few weeks in Edinburgh. But it was amazing what one could get used to, especially when there was no choice. Of course she would rather be working with the living than the dead, but she had soon discovered that her talent for detached observation put her in good stead for such a profession. Irrespective of the gore in which she was sometimes steeped, the wonder of the science and a natural inclination to solve a mystery had soon put an end to the horrors she once had. After a while, even the odors ceased to bother her. *Mortui vivos docent*—the dead teach the living. She wondered what the dead bodies awaiting her below would teach her.

The Anatomy of Death

Felicity Young

BERKLEY BOOKS, NEW YORK

THE BERKLEY PUBLISHING GROUP
Published by the Penguin Group
Penguin Group (USA) Inc.
375 Hudson Street, New York, New York 10014, USA
Penguin Group (Canada), 90 Eglinton Avenue East, Suite 700, Toronto, Ontario M4P 2Y3, Canada
(a division of Pearson Penguin Canada Inc.) • Penguin Books Ltd., 80 Strand, London WC2R 0RL,
England • Penguin Group Ireland, 25 St. Stephen's Green, Dublin 2, Ireland (a division of Penguin
Books Ltd.) • Penguin Group (Australia), 250 Camberwell Road, Camberwell, Victoria 3124, Australia
(a division of Pearson Australia Group Pty. Ltd.) • Penguin Books India Pvt. Ltd., 11 Community
Centre, Panchsheel Park, New Delhi—110 017, India • Penguin Group (NZ), 67 Apollo Drive,
Rosedale, Auckland 0632, New Zealand (a division of Pearson New Zealand Ltd.) • Penguin Books
(South Africa) (Pty.) Ltd., 24 Sturdee Avenue, Rosebank, Johannesburg 2196, South Africa

Penguin Books Ltd., Registered Offices: 80 Strand, London WC2R 0RL, England

This is an original publication of The Berkley Publishing Group.

This is a work of fiction. Names, characters, places, and incidents either are the product of the author's
imagination or are used fictitiously, and any resemblance to actual persons, living or dead, business
establishments, events, or locales is entirely coincidental. The publisher does not have any control over
and does not assume any responsibility for author or third-party websites or their content.

PUBLISHING HISTORY
Berkley trade paperback edition / May 2012

Library of Congress Cataloging-in-Publication Data

Young, Felicity, 1960-
The anatomy of death / Felicity Young.—Berkley trade paperback ed.
p. cm.
ISBN 978-0-425-24729-7
1. Women forensic scientists—Fiction. 2. Suffragists—Violence against—Fiction. 3. Murder—
Investigation—Fiction. 4. London (England)—Fiction. I. Title.
PR9199.4.Y674A53 2012
813'.6—dc22
2011051705

PRINTED IN THE UNITED STATES OF AMERICA

10 9 8 7 6 5 4 3 2 1

ACKNOWLEDGMENTS

I am very lucky to have a team of supportive friends and colleagues behind me. First, I'd like to thank Patricia O'Neill, Carole Sutton, and Christine Nagel for their literary skills and valuable friendship and Janet Blagg and Deonie Fiford for ironing out the editorial creases. Many thanks also to Emily Rapoport from The Berkley Publishing Group for believing in this project; to my agents, Sheila Drummond (Australia) and Lisa Grubka (U.S.), and to my cousin Peter Stone for passing on our grandmother's memoirs.

To Mick and my father, Nial, with love

Prologue

The protesters marched under the bare winter trees, the smoke of a thousand London chimneys spiralling above their heads. Motorcars jostled for right of way with carriages, and petroleum fumes overpowered the sweeter odour of horse manure.

A three-wheeled motorcar slowed to take in the sight, and its occupants, male and female, leaned out of the car and cheered the marching ranks on. Violet waved back. Violet and her friend Marjorie were no longer schoolgirls; they were part of a victorious army marching into a newly taken city to liberate the women of Britain from slavery and oppression. It was less than a mile to the Houses of Parliament, but she wished it were longer; she wanted this glorious moment to last forever.

As the Houses of Parliament neared, however, the atmosphere began to change. There were fewer motorcars on the street and more pedestrians, roughly dressed people who shouted and heckled. Near St. Stephen's entrance, the marchers were jeered and pelted with rotten fruit by groups of men and woman carrying placards saying A WOMAN'S PLACE IS IN THE HOME and GO BACK TO YOUR FAMILIES. The marchers waved back their own banners and chanted, "No more shuffling, carry the Bill! There is time if they've the will!"

"Can't you see we're doing this for the good of all of us? Women have got to be given the vote!" Marjorie cried to a woman who stood amongst the hostile mob, shaking her fist.

"Go home and make your husband's tea," the woman shouted, her face red with anger.

"Perverted lesbians, the lot of you!" a man yelled. Marjorie and Violet exchanged looks; the expression on the man's face suggested he meant something lascivious by the remark. Violet made a mental note to look the word up when they returned to Marjorie's house.

At the steps of the House of Commons, lines of police were waiting for them. They were big men with hard faces, not at all the type of policeman Violet would approach if she were lost. She had not thought of there being policemen present and felt cold with the thought, the stamping hooves of the mounted policemen making her especially nervous. The other marchers seemed uneasy, too.

The banner bearers, grouped at the head of the march, presented an irresistible target, and the police made a sudden charge at them. There was an immediate scattering as banners were snatched and hurled to the ground or shredded like sails in a storm. A working-class woman linked her arm through Violet's as they all surged forward toward the Commons steps. There were people everywhere, and Violet noticed crowds of rowdy men wearing rough clothes join the police lines, many of them armed with clubs and bricks. She looked around for a means of escape, but found none. The crowd was hemmed in on all directions.

The men and the police shoved into the line of marchers and women began to scream. The effect upon the men was like the cries of a distressed animal to a hungry predator. A bobby lunged at Marjorie and forced his hand up her skirt, tearing at her drawers. Another went for Violet's breasts. As he twisted her flesh, she felt his gin-drenched breath upon her face and caught a tirade of foul words. "You've been wanting this for a long time, haven't you, love?" and then she heard that word *lesbian* again.

She knocked the helmet off his head and broke free, turning in panicked circles as she tried to find Marjorie in the mêlée. Amongst the chaos she glimpsed a woman she'd spoken to earlier, then in a wide-brimmed hat with purple plumes—now hatless—flaying out at a bobby who was beating her about the head with a truncheon. Violet felt sick; policemen should not behave like this. She tried to enlist the help of a young gentleman marcher, but he shook her off and ran away with panic in his eyes. Then she spotted Marjorie, sprawled on the cobbled street, in danger of being trampled by a policeman's horse. For a moment she panicked, not knowing which way to turn. She found herself running towards her friend first. As she was about to haul Marjorie to her feet, however, she felt herself grabbed roughly by her hair from behind and flung to the ground. Then someone kicked her in the ribs. She had never felt such physical pain before, and desperately hoped she would not faint. "Asked for this you did, disgracing yerself in public, you orta be ashamed of yerself," a coarse voice shouted, as if she were the most hateful thing he had ever laid eyes upon.

Violet turned on her side and drew up her legs and pressed her cheek into the greasy cobblestones. As she gritted her teeth and waited for the next blow, she glimpsed the broad-brimmed hat with its spray of purple plumes crushed into the cobbles by a pair of hobnailed boots.

Chapter One

Dody McCleland was the last passenger to alight from the Edinburgh train. After hauling her luggage from the railway carriage, she remounted the step and scanned the milling crowds. She did not spot him immediately. And then, in a gap through the hissing steam, there he was, one of the few figures not engaged in the mad scurry that Euston Station seemed to demand. He stared right through her, then turned towards the exit.

"Rupert!" she cried, waving wildly, "Don't go, I'm here!"

The tall figure stopped, swivelled. The Honourable Rupert Sotherby took off his cloth workingman's cap as if he might see better without it. Dody smiled to herself; had he not changed at all in the last year? With the looks of Adonis (a widely held opinion) and the bearing of an Officer of the Guard, he would have looked less incongruous in the station if he had dressed in white tie and tails.

Then he was rushing across the platform towards her, wrapping his arms around her and lifting her from the ground. "My dear," he said, beaming, "I thought you must have changed your mind and decided to stay on in Edinburgh."

"I'm sorry," she gasped through his bear hug. "It took me a while to gather my things together." When he finally put her down, she pointed with her rolled umbrella to the trunk, portmanteau, Gladstone bag, and assorted hatboxes strewn upon the platform floor. "You see?"

"You should have called a porter," he said.

"I lugged it on myself, I was quite capable of lugging it off myself."

"Well, I hope you don't expect me to do the same, it looks far too heavy." He winked at her, replaced his cap, and looked around vainly for an unoccupied porter. "So, are you home for good this time?"

"For the time being. How are Mother and Poppa? Have you seen them recently?" She already knew the answer. He adored her literary critic mother and had been practically living at her parents' home in Sussex near Tunbridge Wells.

"They are both in fine fettle. Your mother is all for purchasing a new Daimler, and your father is against having anything to do with motorcars, all resulting in a series of somewhat lively conversations around the dining table."

"I would expect nothing less."

"But I'm afraid they are united in their worry about Florence."

Dody laughed. Her parents were hardly conventional members of their class; some even saw them as radicals. So the fact that the rebellious Florence was giving them cause for concern was an irony Dody could not help but find amusing—her sister was only following in the family tradition. "Why, what has the young madam been up to this time?" she asked with a smile.

But Rupert's expression was serious. He nodded towards the paperboy standing next to a *Times* billboard. "You haven't heard?"

"Rupert, I've been on the night train from Edinburgh; I haven't even seen a newspaper—what are you talking about?" As she spoke, she got out her purse and moved towards the boy, handing him threepence for a paper.

"Page ten, I think," Rupert said, taking the paper from her. He riffled through the pages. "Here it is: 'Disorderly Scenes and Arrests at Westminster . . .'"

"Oh, no—is Florence all right? Has she been arrested? No? Thank heavens. Rupert, you must take me to her at once! Is she all right?" Hastily folding the paper, Dody slid it into the pocket of her portmanteau. She would read it later in the comfort of her own home.

"Don't worry, she's fine, although quite a few aren't, so I've heard. But as for going home, I'd better warn you that, since you left, your home has become less of a townhouse and more of a military headquarters."

Dody sighed. "I hope she hasn't let any of her rabble into my rooms. When I was last home, I found my microscope slides covered in sticky fingerprints."

But Rupert wasn't listening. He had caught the eye of a porter who'd just returned to the platform with an empty trolley. He beckoned the man over with an impatient wave. "Come on, Dodes, let's get your things stowed away."

They followed the porter merging with the crowds under the coffered ceiling of the Great Hall. Outside the shelter of the station the wind was bitter, the warning pricks of an imminent cloudburst cold upon Dody's cheeks, and she pulled her cape tightly around her shoulders.

Hansom cabs rattled up and down Drummond Street, jostling for space, and more motor taxis than she'd seen during her whole year in Edinburgh. As Rupert seemed in no hurry to hail a driver, she raised her own hand, eager for the comparative warmth of a cab. She was tired. She never slept well in strange beds, and the bunk on the train had been narrow and hard. All she wanted to do was get home, kick off her travelling boots, and settle in front of her hearth in her own private rooms. Much had happened in the year she had been away; decisions had to be made and she needed time to think. Alone.

Unfortunately it appeared that Rupert, one of her chief decisions, had other ideas. To her consternation, he waved away the slowing hansom and took her hand. "Dody, we need to go somewhere and have a long talk. Speaking across the country over the telephone just isn't the same."

Dody squeezed his arm. "Rupert, I . . ."

"I have exciting news. Your mother thinks my new play has great potential—she wants to show it to Mr. George Bernard Shaw. This could make my name, Dody, set me up as a writer. It will need funding, of course, and your father seems a bit reluctant. But with you and your mother's encouragement, I think we might be able to turn him around. I told your parents we would be seeing them next weekend."

"That's wonderful, Rupert. I'm very excited for you," she said as she scanned the street for another cab. "I intend on seeing my parents soon, of course, but I don't know if it will be next weekend. You will have to give me a few days to settle back home first."

"Well, there's something else, too, and it doesn't involve

travelling down to Sussex. Dody . . ." Rupert loosened his coarse wool scarf and cleared his throat. "I was hoping we might take tea together this afternoon. Now that I am getting established, there are other matters to discuss that are of equal importance. There's a new teahouse opened down the road from you, the Copper Kettle, they make a splendid teacake. I could pick you up at about four—does that give you enough time to rest and unpack?"

Dody tore her gaze from the street, back to his pleading puppy eyes. How could she refuse? She swallowed down a sudden feeling of trepidation. "Certainly, if that is what you wish."

He looked delighted, and very much as if he might attempt to kiss her. *Oh Lord, please don't try*, she willed silently as she drew back. A year ago she'd have been eager for his attentions, and the strength of her feeling now surprised her; but this was a good sign, she decided. Now she knew how she felt. Really, her decision was made. It just had to be told. She looked again for another cab; there was one drawing near.

"Oh, I almost forgot," he said, patting the pockets of his threadbare overcoat and reaching into one of them. "I was asked to give you this note. It was delivered to your house this morning and Florence forwarded it to me."

Her name on the envelope—Dr. Dorothy McCleland—was written in the unmistakable scrawl of Dr. Spilsbury from the Home Office. Her breath caught in her chest, her search for a cab temporarily forgotten. She removed her gloves and handed them to Rupert, the trembling in her fingers having nothing to do with the cold now. After reading the note, she attempted to speak, but it was as if she had been struck mute. How could she explain its content to Rupert?

"I say, Dody, you've become quite flushed. Not bad news, I hope?"

He attempted a glance at the note, but she dropped the hand that held it, pulling it into the warmth of her cape.

"No, not bad news, it just came sooner than I expected. I need to go directly. Would you mind seeing that my things are delivered safely home?"

"Of course not, but what is it, where are you going?"

"I won't be long. I'll tell you all about it this afternoon at tea."

Had Rupert ever shown the slightest bit of interest in her work, she would have told him long ago the nature of the post-graduate course she'd just completed. Reluctantly, it is true, but she would have told him. Although if he had known the precise nature of what she had been up to in Edinburgh, he might not have been quite so eager to meet her upon her return.

Chapter Two

"He's late," Superintendent Shepherd grunted, returning his watch to the voluminous folds of his mackintosh. Detective Chief Inspector Matthew Pike stepped further back into the portico, partly to shelter from the mud-splattering rain and partly to distance himself from the dank odours exuding from the mackintosh. Pike indicated the peeling door to the mortuary with a tilt of his head. "When I last checked the basement, sir, they hadn't finished setting up."

"Huh, just as well. Still, I won't stand for poor timekeeping. Spilsbury should have impressed that upon him. I have enough to do and so do you."

"I suppose there was a lot to sort out before he went on leave, and Dr. Spilsbury was left exhausted by the Crippen case."

"But not you, eh, Pike? You ex–military men are made of sterner stuff."

Pike had learnt long ago to ignore the digs of his superior officer. "My role in Crippen's conviction was administrative only and not as demanding as that of Inspector Dew or Dr. Spilsbury."

"Yes, obviously," the superintendent said, fixing his small eyes on Pike's walking cane.

I set myself up for that one, Pike thought.

"Indeed," the superintendent went on, "so demanding that the forensic surgeon's chuffed off to the Lake District for a holiday, leaving us with some stranger to hold the fort who probably can't tell an arse from an elbow."

"The new man might not be as eminent as Spilsbury, sir, but he cannot be as incompetent as many of the coroner's medical appointees." A hacking cough from the mortuary anteroom reached them through the closed door, as if someone were trying to dispute this claim. "He's an experienced medical practitioner," Pike went on, "with a qualification in forensic autopsy."

Superintendent Shepherd answered with a snort. Pike knew that he had little time for the new forensic sciences and in this he was not alone at New Scotland Yard. Even Pike, who was more open than most to new ideas, found some of Spilsbury's methods questionable. Pike could still picture the bespectacled Hawley Crippen as he had last seen him, awaiting his execution date—head in hands, sitting on his narrow prison cot, sick with worry for the fate of his lover, Ethel Le Neve. The man was guilty of something, Pike did not dispute that, but he had reservations about whether it was the deliberate poisoning and subsequent dismembering of his wife as Spilsbury's forensics apparently proved.

He tried to push away his doubts. "Well, like it or not, we have need of specialist help," he said to Shepherd. "The cause of two of the deaths is self-evident, the signature of the Home Office pathologist a mere formality. But we do require the autopsy surgeon's detailed opinion on the third lady."

"We're under a magnifying glass over this—you appreciate that, don't you, Pike?" Shepherd said.

"If you mean we are being accused of unnecessary brutality in the suppression of the women's riot, yes, sir. And of course, the lady was a prominent member of society. The press will be watching our every move."

"We can deal with the press, to some extent at least. You weren't there, naturally"—another glance at Pike's cane—"but I heard all about it. It was pandemonium, utter chaos. Insane females scratching and spitting like wildcats, yelling like Red Indians. Our lads did their best, though I have to admit, it sounds as if there were a few who were overly zealous."

"I will be interviewing several officers from the Whitechapel Division this afternoon, sir. Am I permitted to deal with them at my discretion?"

Pike caught the look of relief in Shepherd's eyes. Having risen through the ranks to become deputy head of Scotland Yard's Detective Division, Shepherd preferred to pass the more distasteful jobs to his underlings so he remained in favour with the men. Pike, on the other hand, had little to lose. Not only was he resented for never having walked the beat, but many envied the apparent ease with which he exchanged the role of army captain for that of plainclothes inspector, followed rapidly by promotion to chief inspector.

"Yes, yes, Pike, deal with them as you will, though I doubt you will find much to concern you. They are good men, just a trifle zealous."

"And the roughs," Pike went on. "It's more than a

coincidence that there were so many armed layabouts around the place. I think they might have been organised troublemakers."

Shepherd pulled at his moustache. "There is an odour of the Fenians about this, Pike, I can smell 'em."

The fact that Shepherd still called the Irish Nationalists by their old name, the Fenians, showed how steeped in the past he still was. In an attempt to distance themselves from their own atrocities, the Fenians had changed their name to Sinn Fein. They were still desperate for the end of British rule in Ireland, but at least for now, their violent tactics had been tempered.

"Special Branch are asking questions in known Sinn Fein hangouts, public houses, et cetera, though personally I feel Sinn Fein involvement unlikely," Pike said. "They've gone very quiet since the Queen Anne Hotel bombing." Pike ignored Shepherd's quick glance at him. "And I do wonder why they would involve themselves in a women's riot."

"To foment unrest, of course, get that damned Home Rule Bill passed. If it can be proved that an Irish Nationalist bludgeoned the lady to death, we can all breathe a sigh of relief." He kicked a muddy boot at Pike's foot. "And you'd rather like that, too, I imagine, eh?"

Pike kept his body rigid against the door, his face blank. Whatever Shepherd might think, he was not seeking vengeance against the Irish. The Queen Anne Hotel bombing ten years earlier, in which his wife had perished, had been a terrible end to a distressing period of his life and was well behind him now. His wife's lover had died with her. There was no one left alive who knew quite how much of a sham his marriage had been.

Silence hung like a tainted mist between the men. They

stirred only when a clopping cab halted in the road adjacent to the mortuary house.

"Good, he's here at last." Shepherd pulled the hood of his mackintosh over his head and stepped from the portico into the rain. Within seconds he'd rushed back under the shelter. "Dash it all—it's only a woman!" he said through the water dripping down his face. "Where can the bloody fellow be?"

St. Thomas's mortuary was a dilapidated two-level struc-ture, for reasons of hygiene situated as far away from the main hospital buildings as the grounds would allow. There were two entrances: the front portico, to which Dody now headed, and an underground passageway where corpses from the hospital were discreetly wheeled.

They all introduced themselves. Dody spent some time shaking out and folding her umbrella to give the policemen the chance they needed to regain their lost composure. They stepped into the sputtering gaslight of the anteroom where the wheezing mortuary attendant, Alfred, instructed them to hang their coats and hats upon the pegs provided. Dody hung up her travelling cape and hat, but chose to retain her jacket. It was cool in the anteroom, but it would be colder than an icehouse downstairs. She wished she'd had the chance to go home and change. When working, she favoured tailored skirts and jackets, butterfly-collared blouses, and men's ties. The lace blouse and tweed travelling suit she wore now were hardly appropriate.

The superintendent slid his eyes down her body and let out a low sigh, which did nothing to alleviate her self-consciousness. She resisted the temptation to mimic his sigh back. He was hardly a paradigm of professionalism himself in that dreadful mackintosh. A juggernaut of a man with moustache and side-whiskers, he had a bulbous nose and a florid face that suggested a fondness for strong liquor. When the attendant offered to hang the mackintosh up for him, he declined, quipping that when he descended the stairs, he would need all the waterproof protection it offered.

The other man, Pike, seemed his complete opposite; smaller, clean-shaven, and finer featured. He leaned heavily on a cane as he walked the few steps to the coat pegs. His physique under the worn but well-cut overcoat appeared straight-backed and trim—he had not yet surrendered to the portliness of middle age—yet the antique blue eyes with their dark pouches spoke of a weariness beyond years. Standing next to the anteroom wall, he seemed almost to blend into it. If not for the cane, his unobtrusive appearance and mild manner would have rendered him the perfect invisible policeman, or "defective detective," as her sister, Florence, was wont to call men of his kind.

The elderly attendant sat behind his desk and slid a leather-bound register towards them. His request for them to enter their names was interrupted by a fit of painful coughing. Unable to speak for a moment, he rapped himself on the chest and pointed with a crooked finger to the place they were to sign. Upon his recovery, he cocked his head and read aloud the string of initials Dody had written after her name. The policemen, neither of whom had said a word to her beyond that first introduction, looked at each other. A small glow of satisfaction melted Dody's earlier feelings of trepidation. She could, and would, go through with this. She had the training and she would prove to them that she could do the job as well as anyone.

"This can't be a healthy environment for someone with as

delicate a chest as yours, sir," she said to the attendant as she
passed the pen on to Pike.

Alfred gave her a toothless smile. "Goose fat and brown
paper, miss, that's what keeps the chill away."

"Well, it doesn't appear to be working very satisfactorily,"
she said, and withdrew a glass bottle from her Gladstone bag.
"Here, try this camphoric lotion; you will find it much more
effective than goose fat. Rub it on to your chest and the soles
of your feet, too. It will tide you over until you get the chance
to purchase a carbolic ball from the chemist, which will be
better still. You can carry the ball around with you and inhale
its fumes whenever the need arises."

The old man took the bottle from her, got to his feet, and
clasped both of her hands. "Why, thank you, miss, thank you
very much. But I'll 'ave to owe you for this medicine, I—"

"Please don't worry about it." Dody smiled.

"Then if I can ever be of any extra assistance, you'll find
me 'ere six days a week and sometimes into the night, too."

The superintendent had finished signing his name and was
pointing to a bleak stone staircase. "Time is of the essence;
lead on, if you please, Alfred. After you, miss."

"It's Dr. McCleland, Superintendent," Dody reminded him.

His mumbled response was lost on her.

Dody followed Alfred down the stairs, the two detectives
clumping behind.

Halfway down Shepherd stopped. "You don't say much,
Pike"—Dody caught Shepherd's loud whisper—"but I can
tell you're as unhappy about this as I am. Impudent creature,
answering me back like that. What in God's name do you
think would induce a woman to get herself involved in the
Beastly Science?"

What indeed, Dody thought, other than the lack of any other specialist surgical positions available to her. She remembered all too well the revulsion she'd felt for the dissecting rooms as a raw medical student, and how those feelings had returned during her first few weeks in Edinburgh. But it was amazing what one could get used to, especially when there was no choice. Of course, she would rather be working with the living than the dead, but she had soon discovered that her talent for detached observation put her in good stead for such a profession. Irrespective of the gore in which she was sometimes steeped, the wonder of the science and a natural inclination to solve a mystery had soon put an end to the horrors she once had. After a while, even the odours ceased to bother her. *Mortui vivos docent*—the dead teach the living. She wondered what the dead bodies awaiting below would teach her.

At the bottom of the stairs she looked around the small autopsy room. It was a far cry from the facilities in Edinburgh. No amphitheatre here with raised seats on which craning students sat and observed; no benevolent pedagogues and powerful electric lighting, ventilation, and decent drainage. Here she would be a one-woman show, performing in a primitive environment for sceptical men who didn't believe women should be engaged in the practice of medicine, let alone the Beastly Science. The sudden weight of it hit her as she stepped into the icy cold room.

Exposed pipes clung to the chipped and dingy white-washed walls. A stained porcelain sink rested against the far wall between shelves of books and specimen jars. Above the sink there hung a portrait of King Edward VII, black mourning crepe still wound about the frame. There was no portrait of the yet-to-be-crowned King George V. It seemed appropriate somehow: a dead king to rule over the kingdom of the dead.

The tap over the sink dripped and gaslights spluttered from their brackets on the walls. In bygone years, Dody reflected, autopsies would have been conducted in police stations or public houses; either would have been preferable to this dank, foul-smelling cave.

A bowler-hatted gentleman in a suit of loud checks stepped forward and introduced himself as Mr. Bright from the coroner's office. He gave Dody a little bow, doffing his hat to reveal a skull as bald as an egg. Another mortuary attendant, marginally younger than Alfred, appeared from the cadaver keep and told them everything was ready.

Shepherd fumbled in the folds of his coat and produced a fat cigar. He bit the end off it and spat it onto the sawdust-strewn floor. After lighting up, he gulped down the smoke like he was slaking a thirst. Pike took a silver case from his inside pocket, offered a cigarette to Bright and the attendants, took one for himself, and snapped the lid closed.

Dody gave him a quizzical look, which he did not appear to notice. From her Gladstone bag she removed the velvet pouch containing her own smoking paraphernalia. Five pairs of eyes converged on her as she expertly packed her clay pipe, swiped the match across the rough wall, and coaxed the tobacco to a gentle glow.

"How many bodies are there, Superintendent?" she asked between puffs.

Shepherd was staring at her in undisguised disbelief. *A most unbecoming habit in a lady*, she could imagine him saying to his colleagues later in the station house. But what did he expect her to use to combat the stench—lavender water?

"Superintendent . . ." she repeated.

"Three, miss, all from yesterday's riot at Westminster."

Good God, the women's march! Spilsbury's note had made no mention of that. Now she wished she had allowed Rupert to read her the whole of the article from *The Times*. She bit hard upon the pipe stem. She would be fair and professional; of course she would. But if these policemen were to find out that her sister was a prominent suffragette and had also been present at the riot, would they have faith in her impartiality? What a way to start a new engagement. But it was too late to back down now; they might think she had no stomach for the job.

With their combined smoke swirling around the room, she removed her jacket and replaced it with an apron she found hanging on a peg near the sink. Some nurse's cuffs also rested near the sink, and these she slipped over the sleeves of her lace blouse.

"The first body, if you please," she said.

Shepherd snapped his fingers and Alfred appeared from the cadaver keep, pushing a wooden trolley with a sheeted body upon it. A parcel of personal effects rested at the body's feet. Dody glanced through them while the attendants heaved the body onto the marble slab.

She read aloud from the victim's file. " 'Seventy-year-old Miss Jemima Jenkins. Witnesses say she was complaining of shortness of breath before the riot, then later they saw her clasp her chest and fall to the ground.' " Dody spent another minute reading the case notes provided by Miss Jenkins's physician and the police surgeon, respectively. She noticed Pike had found himself a spot leaning against the far wall, puffing on his cigarette and apparently listening to a murmured conversation between Mr. Bright and the attendants. Superintendent

Shepherd seemed unable to stand still; he glided about the room in his oversized mackintosh like one of Count Zeppelin's airships.

But when she drew back the sheet covering the body, the men stopped what they were doing. *They are probably expecting me to faint,* Dody thought. *I have never fainted before in my life and I will not start now.*

There was no need for dissection; the oedematous ankles backed up what she had already read in the notes. Evidence of pink froth on the lips, since dissipated, but reported by the police surgeon soon after the woman's death, also assisted her with her conclusion.

"Death due to heart attack, the result of longstanding congestive cardiac failure," she dictated to Mr. Bright. She stared at the body for a moment longer, wondering what force of passions, now extinguished, had compelled this frail old lady to participate in such a vigorous demonstration.

The cause of death of Mrs. Margaret Baxter, age forty-five, was also self-evident, but required some thoracic dissection to discover the precise nature of the injuries beneath the gaping chest wound. From the row of autopsy instruments on a nearby bench, Dody took a heavy anatomist's scalpel and with a few deft strokes performed a Y-incision from armpits to groin. What blood there was—the women had been on ice since yesterday and there wasn't much—was directed by Alfred into the runnels of the slab, and from thence to the blood bucket below. Dody peeled back the skin, then set to with the bulky rib-cutters, snipping through the bone to reveal the heart where the bulk of the blood had pooled.

Superintendent Shepherd watched over her shoulder, spilling ash from his cigar into the thoracic cavity. She waved him

away with a flick of her scalpel, then used the chest spreader
to part the lungs. There was no need to remove the heart; a
cursory glance revealed all that was necessary. The railing
upon which Mrs. Baxter had impaled herself had penetrated
the thorax and diaphragm at a forty-five-degree angle, pierc-
ing the left ventricle and the descending aorta. Death would
have occurred within seconds. Small comfort to her family,
Dody mused, as she finished dictating her findings to Mr.
Bright. She rinsed the scalpel and her gory hands under the
tap while Alfred repaired the damage to Mrs. Baxter with
needle and thread.

The other attendant wheeled in the next body from the
cadaver keep and Dody refilled her pipe.

"Now this death has to be regarded as potentially suspicious," Shepherd said as the attendants exchanged one body
for the other on the slab. "We are obliged to perform a full
medico-legal autopsy, though I'm sure you will be able to
confirm accidental causes. We don't need to take too long
about it."

Dody riffled through the items in the effects parcel: an
expensive walking outfit, gloves, boots, stockings, silk blouse,
assorted linen, and a somewhat crushed wide-brimmed hat.
Under this, something metallic glinted against the brown
paper packaging. She picked it out and turned it over in her
hand. The silver medal of a hunger strike survivor gleamed
back at her—her sister Florence had one just like it. For a
moment Dody ceased to breathe. At once she dreaded what
she might find under the sheet.

But Florence was alive and unharmed; Rupert had told
her so. Drawing a lungful of pipe smoke, she pulled back the
sheet and found herself looking upon the familiar face of Lady

Catherine Cartwright, one of her sister's close friends. Closing her eyes, she prayed her vision was playing tricks on her. She opened them again. It was not. She felt herself grow dizzy.

She must not faint.

To steady herself, she reached for the dissecting slab. With the other hand, she replaced the sheet.

"Doctor? Is something the matter?" Pike appeared from nowhere, moving to her side.

"Fetch some smelling salts, Alfred, the lady is going to faint." Shepherd made no effort to hide the glee in his voice.

"I am not about to faint, Superintendent," Dody managed. "Alfred, stay where you are if you please, I am perfectly all right. But I regret to inform you that I cannot proceed with this autopsy. I know this woman; she was a friend of my sister. It would be unprofessional of me to continue."

Shepherd smacked a heavy fist into his hand. "Damn it, this is all we need. Are you quite sure? It is most important we ascertain a cause of death immediately."

"Sir," Pike cut in, "Dr. McCleland is correct; she can't be expected to continue." He spoke with a peculiar emphasis, and Dody looked up to see him giving his superior a meaningful glance, as if he was trying to signal something to the superintendent that should already have been self-evident.

Chapter Three

Pike held Shepherd back from following Dr. McCleland up the mortuary stairs. "McCleland, sir, do you not recognise the name?"

Shepherd turned. "Should I? Not a bad-looking filly," he said, as if to himself. "But marred by intelligence and overly wilful, I suspect."

Pike hadn't paid much attention to the woman's looks; he had other things on his mind. "Florence McCleland is an associate of Emmeline and Christabel Pankhurst, the leaders of the militant suffragettes," he said. "She runs the Bloomsbury Division of the Women's Suffrage and Political Union. Presumably she is the sister Dr. McCleland was referring to."

Shepherd slapped the side of his mackintosh. "You mean that woman is one of those godforsaken Anglo-Irish-Russian-Socialist McClelands from Sussex?"

"I believe they call themselves Fabians, sir."

"Fabians, socialists, what's the difference?"

Pike allowed a faint smile. "Despite their close ties with the Labour Party, Fabians tend to be better bred than most socialists. They believe in gradual reform through education rather than sweeping, revolutionary changes. The simple way of life is important to them, though some are absurdly rich and often artistic—Mr. Bernard Shaw is a Fabian I believe, sir."

"Intellectual poppycock."

For a change Pike was inclined to agree with his superior. "But it would have been useful to have Dr. McCleland conduct the autopsy—should the result fall in our favour, sir," he said. "If a suffragette sympathiser could prove we had no involvement in the death, then no one could accuse us of falsifying the results. Assuming, of course, that, like her sister, she is a sympathiser."

"Yes, but if the results aren't in our favour—if one of ours is accused of dealing the fatal blows—how could we trust such a woman to give an unbiased account? We need someone totally neutral on the job." Shepherd called out to the assistant coroner. "Bright, you've conducted autopsies before, haven't you?"

"Yes, sir, a fair few, but that was a long time ago, before they changed the regulations."

"Sir," Pike cut in. "Law requires that a medical practitioner conduct—"

"And the coroner's office has the legal authority to appoint one." Shepherd all but sneered. "Bright will find us a medical man, won't you, Bright?"

"Dr. Mangini is usually available, sir," Bright said.

Pike yanked the cigarette from his mouth. "Mangini? The man's a soak. Probably only available because no one will employ him!"

"We don't have the time to rustle up someone else through the Home Office. I want this off my plate today. Mangini's a medical practitioner and his rooms are close by; that's all that counts. We'll make sure he does the right thing, won't we, Bright?" Shepherd slapped the assistant coroner on the shoulder.

Just then Sergeant Walter Fisher, Pike's assistant, stepped into the frigid basement. "Sorry to disturb you, sirs," he said, waistcoat buttons straining across his giant belly, bowler hat deferentially twisting in his hand. "I've assembled the officers outside your office, Detective Chief Inspector, and they're waiting for their interviews." Fisher had a flattened nose and missing front tooth—he'd been a fistfighter in his youth—but he was a gentle giant, and a man Pike was glad to have in his corner.

Pike hesitated. He wanted to stay for the autopsy, especially now that he knew who was to conduct it.

"I'll stay and supervise Mangini, Pike," Shepherd said with an air of magnanimity. "You'd better get going. Can't have the men kept waiting indefinitely. Rest assured Bright and I will see the doctor does the right thing."

The right thing, Pike mused, the right thing for whom? He didn't doubt that Shepherd would have conducted the autopsy himself if he thought he could get away with it.

Situated on the Embankment, the New Scotland Yard building looked like a cross between a medieval fortress and a French château. The top half of the building was red brick and included a turret overlooking the Thames. The ground-floor walls were made of granite quarried by inmates of Dartmoor Prison. Rooms of all shapes and sizes were linked by a tangled maze of stairwells and corridors. To avoid putting them to any unnecessary exertion, senior officers were situated at ground level. Many considered this a dubious privilege, for it meant missing out on the views across the Thames from the top floors and the cooling river breezes in summer. Pike, though, appreciated the ground-floor location with its private waiting room and exit, and not only because of his gammy knee. It meant people could enter and leave his office with few of his colleagues being any the wiser. They didn't understand him or the way he operated, and he was happy to keep it that way.

Pike gave the cringing constable standing in front of him one last steely look before pointing to the rear door of his office. He didn't want to give the man any chance of talking with the others in the waiting room. "That way, Excel," Pike said, handing the man his papers of dismissal. "Collect your pay and arrange the return of your uniforms with the Whitechapel quartermaster."

Once the man had gone, Pike stretched his leg out from under his desk. It felt like a block of wood today—in the cold of the autopsy room it had frozen up completely. He rubbed it vigorously for a moment before cautiously pushing himself up from his chair and reaching for his cane. By the time he'd crossed his office, it had loosened up. If time permitted, he would take a long walk this evening to perhaps improve his chances of getting some sleep.

He stopped at the small window in the wall dividing his office from the waiting room, drew the curtain, and looked beyond his own blurry image. This was no ordinary pane of glass, but an observation window, appearing as a plain mirror on the waiting room side. He'd had the innovation shipped from America and installed at his own expense. Few officers in the building, other than Fisher, were aware of its true purpose.

Peering through the curtain now, he saw the two men he had yet to interview, both sitting on the bench in silence, arms folded, legs splayed, brooding upon their fate, no doubt. Pike opened the door and signalled Sergeant Fisher to show the next constable in.

He allowed the man to stand at attention in front of his desk, beehive helmet under his arm, while he examined the paperwork before him. Only when he could hear the man's breathing and sense his figure beginning to sway did he slowly look up into the battered and bruised face. With some difficulty, Pike cracked his lips into a smile. "Dykins, Constable 358, Whitechapel?"

"Yes, sir."

"Pull up a chair, Dykins, you look done in."

"I am at that, sir, thank you, sir." The chair looked no more substantial than a bundle of matchsticks in the constable's hamlike hand, and it creaked as he settled his bulk into it. Pike's transfer from the army into the metropolitan police at officer level had meant he was exempted from the usual height requirements. Sometimes when confronting men such as this, he felt like a midget. He opened his cigarette case. "Care for a cigarette, Dykins?"

"Yes, thank you, sir." The cigarette shook in the constable's hand as Pike lit it for him.

Pike drew in smoke, leaned back in his chair, and regarded the man across his desk. "I hear you had a rough time yesterday, Dykins. Did you get your injuries adequately attended to?"

"Just a few bruises, sir, nothing very serious."

"And what about a look at the person who attacked you?"

"There were several, sir, all of 'em women."

Pike shook his head. "Bloody women, eh? And you let them get the better of you? I'm surprised a big chap like you would let himself be subdued by a gaggle of hysterical females."

Dykins relaxed into his chair, smiled. "Well, it wasn't quite like that, sir. I did manage to put a few of 'em back in their place, if you know what I mean."

Pike met Dykins's eye and shot him a wink. "But not with undue violence, I hope."

"No, sir, but let's just say some of 'em might think twice about taking to the street again."

"A woman's place is in the home, eh, Constable?"

"That's what I always say, sir. If they got 'urt, it was because they asked for it. They'd no business being there."

Pike measured his words carefully. "Some of the women claim they were indecently assaulted by the police. Did you see any evidence of that?"

"Not at all, sir, most of us was just defending ourselves. I think if there was anything not quite right going on, it was probably from all them roughs that was 'anging about, following the marchers. I reckon in the confusion, a woman could easily be mistaken about 'oo it was 'ad touched 'er up."

"And one of the women who died, Lady Catherine Cartwright, can you remember seeing her in the crowd?" Pike pushed the postmortem photographs of Lady Catherine over to him, along with a picture of her wide-brimmed hat.

Dykins studied the photographs for a moment. "No, sir, can't say that I remember seeing that woman at all."

Pike opened a file on his desk and fanned out another series of photographs. "Do you know what these are, Dykins?"

Dykins leaned forward. "More photographs—pictures of the riot, sir?"

"Yes, that's right, but more than just pictures." Pike kept his tone conversational. "These photographs were taken without the subjects' knowledge—we call them surveillance photographs. No one posed for these. The camera operator was concealed in a motor wagon using a special long-focus lens. Some of the images are quite astonishing. Here, have a look at this one." Pike slid a large photograph across his desk.

Dykins rested his cigarette in the ashtray and picked up a photograph of a police officer ripping at a woman's bodice and exposing her breasts. He paled under his bruises.

"Do you recognise that police officer, Dykins?" Pike's tone was no longer conversational.

Dykins put his hand to his mouth as if to cough. The high neck of his tunic moved as he swallowed. "It looks like me, sir, but it must be some mistake, some trick of photography."

"No trick, I assure you. I supervised the setting up of the equipment myself. The idea behind it was to capture the women in the act of breaking the law so we could show proof of their behaviour to the courts." Pike paused. "I had no idea just how useful this surveillance technology would be."

He glanced pointedly at Dykins. Removing a magnifying glass from his desk drawer, he took the photograph back from Dykins and read aloud the enlarged serial numbers on the policeman's collar. Then he left his desk, bent over the seated Dykins, and made a show of inspecting his collar. "No mistake, it's your number: 358."

Dykins jumped to his feet. His face had reddened; his mouth moved without sound. Pike moved back to his side of the desk to sign the dismissal papers. With an impassive expression, he handed the papers over, repeating what he'd said to the three previous interviewees. "Collect your pay and hand your uniforms in to the Whitechapel quartermaster."

He was indicating the rear door when Dykins caught him off guard. With surprising speed, the man grabbed the front of Pike's waistcoat and almost lifted him from the ground one-handed. "You fucking officer toff," Dykins said through a spray of spittle. "You've no bloody idea what it's like out there on the street. I been in the force over fifteen years now, and doing me duty, spat at, 'urt, abused, and you reckon you can judge me by one fucking photograph? We was told to stamp on them women. I was just following orders . . ."

With a swift chop, Pike brought the edge of his hand down on the man's bicep. Dykins lost his grip and cried out in pain.

"Sergeant Fisher," Pike called, pulling down his waistcoat and adjusting his collar. Upon the sergeant's speedy entrance, he said, "Please escort this man from the premises."

Of even greater height and weight than Dykins, Fisher had no trouble restraining the burly man and hustling him out the back door. The sound of the man's curses and threats continued to be heard down the street.

"Another one who said he was following orders," Pike said when Fisher returned, dusting his hands.

"Well, there's orders and orders, ain't there, sir? That Whitechapel mob are a rough lot, they wouldn't need much encouragement."

"Will no one rid me of this meddlesome priest?" Pike mused. Fisher looked back at him blankly. Pike wondered what was troubling the man; he was usually quicker than that. "I want you to speak to the Whitechapel sergeant," Pike said. "Find out what he said to his men. But wait, don't go just yet."

They both needed a break. Pike had noticed the fatigue in the eyes of his sergeant, the paleness of his usually ruddy skin. The final constable could wait a little longer. "How are things at home, Walter?" he said. "Is Mrs. Fisher any better?" Fisher's wife had been diagnosed with tuberculosis, though Pike would never have known had Fisher not recently requested a day off work to take her to the doctor.

"Much better, sir; she was—we both were—very grateful for the hamper. The doctor says she needs as much eggs and fresh milk as we can get."

And a rest cure in Switzerland, no doubt, Pike thought bleakly. "Have you tried for the Policeman's Hardship Fund?"

"No, sir, and I don't intend to neither. A man's got to look after his own, else it's the beginning of a long slippery slope down—don't you think so, sir?"

Pike nodded; pride was something he could understand. He asked Fisher to send the next man in and lowered his head once more to the photographs with their sickening images of animalistic violence. This was only the first batch to be developed, and he had seen no sign yet of Lady Catherine. He wondered what secrets the others might reveal.

Chapter Four

The leadlight door opened in a kaleidoscope of glowing reds and greens. "Miss Dody! I sensed it was you ringing the bell. Welcome home!"

"Hello, Annie, how have you been?" Dody smiled. She was determined not to let the incident at the mortuary mar her homecoming.

"Oh, busy as always," the maid said. "Miss Florence has had ever so many visitors lately." Dody stepped through the porch into the black-and-white-tiled hall, removed her hat, gloves, and cape, and handed them to the parlour maid.

She glanced around her at the stacks of boxes, typewriter cases, and other assorted office equipment. The potted palms, her sister's pride and joy only last year, could barely be seen above the clutter.

"Is my sister alone now?"

"Yes, in the morning room, miss. Would you like to be announced?"

"First, I would like a bath and a change of clothes. I'm afraid I'm dreadfully smelly. Please go to the kitchen and see if Cook can spare me some lemons. The juice is a powerful odour eliminator, and from now on, I'd like her to keep plenty in stock. And see that the clothes I am wearing are washed separately and also rinsed in a weak solution of lemon juice." At the sight of the young maid's wrinkled nose, Dody said, "This is something you're going to have to get used to, Annie."

Annie sighed, "Yes, miss—would you like me to help you wash your hair?"

"No, thank you, I can manage that."

"Very good, miss." Annie took Dody's damp outer garments to the cloakroom.

Dody climbed the stairs to her third-floor rooms. Her suite consisted of a bedroom, a dressing room with attached bathroom, a small sitting room, and an ample study. The furnishings were minimal and the paintwork a soft buttery yellow, further enhanced by the pure light of the new electric system. Large sash windows added to the light, breezy ambience of the suite, and gave extensive views over the green velvet lawn and shrubberies of Cartwright Gardens.

Annie unpacked the bags, drew Dody's bath, and then left her alone. As she eased herself into the hot bath and inhaled the fragrant steam, Dody let out a sigh of contentment. Removing the odours of the mortuary was one sure way of putting the death of Catherine Cartwright behind her. Time enough for that later.

Refreshed and feeling human again, she sat at her dressing table in her silk kimono and brushed out her damp hair. Upon brush stroke number twenty-three she heard rapid steps on the stairs. By stroke number twenty-eight her door was flung open after a knock of such brevity it might not have happened at all.

"Dody!" Florence exclaimed, rushing to her sister's arms. Dody stood up and clasped her tight, marvelling not for the first time at the enormous personality that exuded from a frame even more petite than her own. Florence held her at arm's length and inspected her. "You look lovely and you smell delightful, not at all ghoulish. I must say, Annie got me quite worried when she said she found you on the doorstep smelling like a rotting whale."

"How very creative of her," Dody said. "I doubt she's ever smelled a rotting whale in her life."

Florence threw herself across Dody's bed and lay on her stomach with her chin propped in her hands, her eyes unnaturally bright. "Tell me all about it then—what are your plans?"

"Nothing's really changed," Dody replied as she returned to her dressing table. "I'm going back to my old post at the women's hospital, but with my new qualification, I'll be employed now and then by the Home Office for autopsy consultation."

"On the dashing Dr. Spilsbury's recommendation, I take it?"

Dody felt the heat rise in her face. She turned back to the mirror so that Florence would not notice. "He's married, you know, Florence," she said quietly.

"That won't stop him, from what I've heard."

"But it will stop me. I can't see the harm in admiring him from afar; he is quite easy on the eye. But goodness, Florence, when I told you what I thought about his looks, it was just a passing comment, the result of one too many glasses of hock—you might care to forget I ever said it."

"Very well, I will pretend you only spoke about him professionally."

"As I did, if I recall; perhaps you were too squiffy yourself to remember. They say he's the real-life embodiment of Sherlock Holmes. You should read about how he solved the Crippen case; it was quite brilliant."

"I have been—one can't get away from it. The papers are having a field day with the wretched man due to hang next week. Anyway . . ." Florence paused.

"What is it?" Dody asked.

"Well, I'd be worried about Dr. Spilsbury if I were you, Dody; that kind of life-and-death power can only go to a man's head. I do think he sounds awfully conceited."

"Really, I have never thought of him as conceited. Anyway, he is merely the cipher. It's the science that convicted Crippen."

Dody was disappointed; it was not the reaction she had expected from her younger sister. When had Florence become such a cynic? Unwittingly, she found herself continuing in a defensive mode. "And despite what you might think, Spilsbury hasn't given me any preferential treatment at all. A young male doctor on my course was also granted similar privileges with the Home Office. We are both being employed to share some of Dr. Spilsbury's load when the need arises. We don't have his expertise in the laboratory, naturally, but we can perform the less demanding autopsies for him."

"I'm glad to hear it." Florence's tone made Dody prickle. It seemed she couldn't win. Opportunity was either denied to her because of her gender, or given because of it. It annoyed her that Florence of all people could not see that sometimes merit was also taken into account. Dody loved Florence more than anyone in the world, but it didn't mean they always shared the same opinions. Sometimes she wondered if they shared any at all. Perhaps this was because of Dody's time spent in an English boarding school while the rest of the family still lived in Moscow. Their parents, expecting to move back to England sooner than they had, had sent her ahead of them, hoping to ease her into the English education system. Florence, seven years younger than Dody, had been a child of eight when the family returned to England. She had been schooled at home and remained under their parents' influence until she came of age and moved to London.

Dody continued with her hair, counting the brushstrokes from where she had left off, regarding her sister in the dressing table mirror. With her graceful features, large violet eyes, and abundance of dark hair, Florence had proved irresistible to young men. Her stand on moral purity and her aloofness in male company seemed only to make her all the more alluring to them. When Dody had left for Edinburgh, there had been many hovering in the wings for the first indication that the ice maiden was beginning to melt. Dody was not sure if the thaw would ever happen. Florence had declared vehemently that she would never marry, that this was the only way a woman could gain even the smallest amount of power over men.

Her uncompromising stance was due, Dody had no doubt, to the influence of Christabel Pankhurst and other extreme suffragettes. Dody had sympathy with the suffrage movement—how could she not? She had experienced for herself the slings and arrows when she dared to storm the bastion of men's learning, the subtle and not-so-subtle attempts to put her in her place as she rose to the top of her year in medicine. Still, she preferred the quieter approach, to put her head down to the work and carry on regardless of opposition or obstacles, making herself invisible where she could. The stridence of the militant suffragettes with whom Florence had cast her lot was not at all to her taste.

Florence chatted on: Was it time they invested in a motor-car, or should they continue to make do with the coach and pair? What sort of hours would Dody be working? Would she be able to accompany her on a visit to the new Selfridges department store? And, "Dody, now you're home, we'll have to employ a lady's maid again; Annie can't possibly cope with the two of us as well as her parlour duties."

Dody observed the wrinkle on Florence's brow, the way her fingers worried the edge of the coverlet. It was clear her sister had a lot more on her mind than domestic arrangements. "I managed perfectly well without a lady's maid in Edinburgh," she said. "All I require from Annie is that she sees that my clothes are properly laundered."

"But what about your hair?"

"I have to wash it so often these days, a loose bun is the only style practical for me and I can do that myself—the alternative is to get it all chopped off."

"Next you'll be joining the Rational Dress League."

"Oh, I haven't the time for leagues and such. I'll still get Annie to help with my hair on special occasions." Dody smiled. "Don't worry, I won't let you down."

"Oh, very well then," Florence sighed. "We should set an example, prove that we are a lot more than just wealthy young ladies with too much time on our hands—not that you fit into that category, of course, but that's what some of the news-papers are saying about us. They say if we want to change the world, we can't continue to live the idle life of the upper middle classes and employ other people's daughters to be our servants. Well, at least we're making a start. As Poppa says, social change always takes time."

Dody swivelled on her stool to face the bed. "You've been very brave, darling, asking me about my plans, telling me things that I know must be of little consequence to you right now." She leaned over and took her sister's hand. "But I know all about it, Florence. I know about Catherine's death, and the riot, what you've all been through."

For a moment Florence couldn't answer. She buried her face in the coverlet. "Don't make me cry, Dody. I feel as if I've only just stopped. It won't be long before the others arrive and I don't want to appear all red and blotchy. Everyone's upset; it's not only me. Anyway, you shouldn't call it a riot, as if that's what we set out to do. It was an orderly march. The police and crowds of hoodlums who seemed to be acting with them began the trouble."

Dody got up from the dressing table, leaving her sister to collect herself. She would finish her hair when it was thoroughly dried and she was dressed. She moved into her dressing room, leaving the door open, and gathered her undergarments. After examining her corset for a moment, she shoved it into the back of her wardrobe. If Florence saw her struggling to get into that unaided, she would only start on again about their need for a lady's maid.

"The note you passed on to me through Rupert," she said, slipping into her combinations, "was a summons to the mortuary. When I got there, I discovered they wanted me to perform an autopsy on Lady Catherine to determine her cause of death." Dody quickly buttoned her camisole and pulled up her knickers. Selecting a trumpet skirt and high-necked blouse from her wardrobe, she returned to the bedroom to finish dressing. She found Florence tracing the patterns on the bed's floral coverlet with her finger.

"The police killed her," Florence said softly. "That's what you found out, isn't it?"

Dody hesitated, silk stocking halfway up her leg. "No, I'm afraid I didn't. I had to tell them I knew her. The coroner needs to find someone else."

It took a while for Florence to register what Dody had said. She swung into a sitting position. "What?" She slapped her hand against the bed. "You allowed Catherine's autopsy to be conducted by someone else? A police toady? Do you realise what you've done? You've thrown away a God-given opportunity of proving police brutality. We may never have another, because they'll be doing their damnedest to keep their results squeaky clean. Do you realise some newspapers didn't even report her death? Why is that, do you think? The government is suppressing the truth, that's why."

"Florence, please, that's enough." Dody was taken aback. She hadn't expected Florence to react quite so violently.

"No, Dody, just whose side are you on?"

Dody stepped into her petticoat, and quickly finished dressing. She chose her words carefully. "It would have been unprofessional of me to continue, Florence, I couldn't, I . . ."

She was saved from further explanation by a tap at the door. Annie came in to announce that the first of the visitors had arrived, a Mr. Hugo Cartwright.

"That's Catherine's nephew," Florence said, looking at the fine gold watch on her wrist. "He's early."

Hugo Cartwright's early arrival was a godsend. Florence managed to compose herself in front of Annie, giving her instructions to see that tea was prepared for the guest. When Annie had left, Florence was back in command of her good temper. "I'm sorry, Dody, my nerves are quite shot," she said. "I'm sure you did the right thing. The committee will be interested in talking to you, though—do you think you can manage them? It might be a bit of an interrogation, especially when they discover your connection to the Home Office. Everyone's upset, blaming each other for what went wrong at the march. Sometimes I think there are more factions in the WSPU than in the parliamentary Liberal and Conservative parties combined."

"Don't worry, Florence; the ladies of your committee don't frighten me one bit."

Florence smiled. "My fearless sister."

"But I'm not sure if I'll be able to see them for long, if at all. I have another engagement: tea with Rupert at the Copper Kettle."

Florence paused to regard her sister. "You don't sound exactly thrilled at the prospect. Did he tell you he's endeavouring to become left-handed? He thinks left-handed people are more artistic. He feels that with constant practice he will be able to change the circuits in his brain."

"Oh Lord." Dody laughed. The eccentricities she had once found so entertaining in Rupert now seemed little more than affectation. How quickly the heart changes its tune once it has decided.

Florence shrugged. "Ah well, you got yourself into it, you'll have to get yourself out." When it came to matters of the heart, one thing Dody could always rely on was cool-headed advice from her sister.

The plain cream blouse she'd selected needed some colour.

She reached into her satin jewel box for her Fabergé brooch with its pattern of tiny white, blue, and gold flowers, and pinned it to the high collar.

"That's a very pretty outfit," Florence said. "I'm relieved to see you don't always wear a suit and tie."

"Hardly a suit and tie, just my professional clothes."

"Yes, but some people seem to think we should make an extra effort to dress in a feminine fashion, and I tend to agree. We don't want to give the WSPU a bad name, or let the opposition think that we are . . . well, you know, *that* kind of women."

Dody couldn't help but laugh. "But the union contains umpteen numbers of *that* kind of women. Why, Emmeline Pankhurst's chauffeur is *that* kind of woman—I've never seen her in anything but men's clothing!"

"Yes, but she's not in the Bloomsbury group, is she? We at least try and maintain some standards."

"Is this one of the factions you are talking about?"

"Now you mention it, I suppose it is, although I was mainly thinking about the militants and the nonmilitants. Which reminds me, Mrs. Fawcett was around earlier. She came to give me a reprimand—a severe reprimand—said it was all our fault that the march got so out of hand. You remember her, don't you? She calls herself a suffragist, not a suffragette, and she's been trying for twenty years to convert politicians to our way of thinking over cucumber sandwiches and tea and, of course, has got absolutely nowhere for her pains."

Because of her sister's involvement in the WSPU, Dody had not been able to distance herself from it in the way Millicent Fawcett had. Though she had not expressed her opinion to Florence in so many words, Dody agreed with Mrs. Fawcett. The WSPU's militant actions were harming the chances of female suffrage by alienating the MPs who would be voting on the issue. She had little time for the whip-wielding suffragette who had attacked Mr. Churchill of the Home Office while he stood on a station platform with his wife. Those acts did nothing to endear the suffragettes to the general public, previously the source of their greatest supporters. Public opinion was turning against them.

"Of course I remember Mrs. Fawcett; she's Elizabeth Garrett's sister. The woman lives in the past—won't use a telephone or a motorcar and still dresses like the old queen. When I last saw her, she was wearing a ridiculous lace hanky on her head."

Florence laughed. "It wasn't a hanky; it was a mantilla."

"It looked like a hanky to me." Dody smiled back, pleased with her sister's return to good humour. "Give me a chance to do my hair. I'll be down in ten minutes."

She found Florence and Hugo Cartwright in the drawing room, drinking tea. Hugo looked to be in his mid-twenties, the child of Catherine's older brother. His fair hair and Teutonic cheekbones bespoke the German blood on his mother's side of the family, a distant cousin of the old queen's, if she remembered correctly. A pair of crutches leaned against the side of his chair.

"Pardon me for not getting up, Dr. McCleland," Cartwright said.

Florence pointed to his bandaged foot. "Poor Hugo was hurt in the fighting. He actually saw Catherine being attacked by a policeman, but could do nothing to help on account of falling in the way of a mounted policeman who was charging the crowd."

"It's nothing, really," Cartwright said, miserably shaking his head.

"You told the police what you saw?" Dody asked.

"I tried to, but they paid me no attention. I swear they didn't even write my name down."

Dody gave his arm a sympathetic squeeze above the mourning band. "It must have been terrible for you. Has your foot been examined by a doctor?"

Cartwright pulled a spotted handkerchief from his top pocket, blew his nose, and responded in the negative.

"Well, now's your chance. Come on, Hugo," Florence said. "Let's get that bandage off so Dody can have a look at it."

Hugo tried to push Florence away, in so doing knocking one of the crutches to the floor. "Really, Florence, I—"

"Dody doesn't mind, do you, Dody? It might be broken, and if it's not treated, it will become deformed. Come on, silly, it's only a foot; it's not like she has to pull your trousers down to get to it."

Cartwright's fair skin flamed, and Dody's heart went out to the poor young man. "I'd be happy to examine your foot, Mr. Cartwright, if that is what you want, but I can't force you to let me."

"Of course he wants you to—don't you, Hugo?" Once Florence's mind was made up, nothing would make her change it. Hugo gave in with a resigned nod.

Dody stooped in front of her reluctant patient. She unwound the dressing and examined the foot, gently running her fingers along the red crease marks caused by the clumsy bandaging. She could see no sign of swelling or bruising. When she asked Cartwright to wriggle his toes, he did so with no apparent difficulty.

"Where does it hurt?" she asked.

He waved his hand vaguely over the whole foot. Dody spent a moment running her fingers along the fine bones. "I can't see much sign of injury, but that doesn't mean there's none there. Damaged tendons sometimes don't show swelling at all. If you wish, I can organise transportation to St. Mary's to rule out the possibility of broken bones. The new X-ray department there is supposed to be good . . ."

"No, please, that is quite unnecessary."

"Then when you get home, soak the foot in water as hot as you can stand and that should give you some relief. Meanwhile keep it elevated as much as possible."

"Dody wanted to be a bone surgeon, you know," Florence said as she fetched a stool for Hugo's foot. "But no one would take her on because she's a woman."

"Damned shame," Hugo said, eyes fixed upon Dody's swiftly moving hands.

"There now," Dody said, patting the neat figure-of-eight bandage. She hoped Florence would elaborate no further upon her career; she doubted this emotionally fraught young man would cope well with it at all. "Keep the bandage on as long as you can."

Florence attempted to lift his foot to the stool, but Cartwright protested. "No, Flo, I don't think I can stay. I came early only to see you. Seeing all those women after yesterday, going over what happened to Aunt Catherine, will be too much. I think I might just go home now. Will you pass me my crutches?" He struggled to his feet. "And do give everyone my apologies."

"That's quite all right, darling, we understand." Florence helped him from the drawing room and into the hall, where

Annie handed him his topcoat and silk hat. Dody couldn't help notice how, as he struggled with his coat, he seemed to favour one foot and then the other, as if he were confused as to which was paining him the most. She was muddling this over in her mind when the front doorbell rang. It was still too early for the other guests, surely?

Oh Lord, she remembered—Rupert!

Chapter Five

So much for the "fearless" Dody McCleland, she thought wryly on her way home from the teahouse. She had proved herself as incapable of telling Rupert that their farcical romance was over as she had been of informing him of her new position with the Home Office. She hadn't even seized the opportunity when he leaned over the table to inhale her scent and murmured, "Mmm, lemons."

To be fair, though, he had been making a fine job of anticipating and forestalling any such announcement, playing the wounded puppy if she so much as failed to smile at his endearments. What was she to do? His family were old friends of her family's, and she could forgive him the self-centredness which made him oblivious to so much about her, or her thoughts—unless they pertained to him.

But his behaviour had puzzled her; she was sure he was no more in love with her than she was with him. They had been playing an elaborate game, and now he was building up to a marriage proposal which she was not ready to cope with. She fended him off with questions about the march. She had still not read the *Times* article.

Rupert told her the march was a response to the government's rejection of the Conciliation Bill, a lukewarm compromise to female suffrage. Even if the Bill had been passed, it would give voting rights to female property owners only, ignoring the vast majority of women in the land. But it was a start, and its consideration had for a while given the suffragettes room to hope that the government was at last beginning to listen.

The street fighting lasted for several hours. "I was damned disappointed at missing out on it," he said, battling to crush a knob of hard butter onto his teacake with his left hand, "but I had an appointment with the director of The Playhouse. Heaven knows whether I'd get another crack at it—it's a fickle world, the theatre." From there on, he'd spoken about his play, the theatre, Mr. Shaw, and Dody's mother. Dody had her reprieve, at least until the following weekend, when they would meet at her parents' house.

Only a handful of Florence's Bloomsbury Division were still in the drawing room when Dody returned from the teahouse. She recognised Jane Lithgow and Olivia Barndon-Brown, and Florence introduced her to others she did not know. Several responded to her with a distinct chill, which made her suspect that the events of the autopsy room had already been discussed.

"My sister has just returned from Edinburgh," Florence announced to the group, "to where she was forced to flee after her application to study bone surgery was turned down because she was a woman."

Flee to Edinburgh? *Lord, Florence*, Dody thought, *why do you have to make everything sound so dramatic?*

"I won't tell you what Dody specialised in at Edinburgh," Florence went on, although she had clearly told them before Dody's arrival. "It might put you off Cook's delicious smoked salmon sandwiches."

The laughter was soft and polite except for one of the factory women present. Molly Jenkins, legs splayed beneath her patched skirt, let forth a gusty roar that spread around the drawing room like a contagion, infecting even those who only moments before had acted so cool and disapproving towards Dody.

Dody immediately warmed to the woman with the ruddy cheeks and easy smile. The likes of Molly Jenkins were often missing in the nonmilitant groups. The WSPU understood that a group of differing social classes could foster an important sense of female solidarity. Dody heartily approved.

Dody remembered one of Florence's lengthy telephone calls to Edinburgh in which she had spoken enthusiastically of Mrs. Jenkins's innovations, such as the tying of string to stones and holding on to them when they were thrown as if they were yo-yos. Thrown in this way, the stones would maximise damage to property, but minimise injury to people. It was also economic on stones, which were sometimes in short supply on the London streets. At this, Dody had been forced to cover the receiver to prevent her laughter from escaping down the wire.

The other working-class woman in the room was Daisy Atkins. Dody had already heard her story. A waiflike creature with large blue eyes, Daisy had been orphaned at the age of thirteen and had been adopted by a group of wealthy WSPU women, who taught her to read, write, and type. She had recently been transferred to Bloomsbury, where she held the position of secretary. Her devotion to the movement was complete; this was the family she had always craved. "She doesn't seem to think for herself, though, Dody," Florence had confided. "It's almost as if she's been mesmerised." The comment came as no surprise to Dody. Daisy had spent considerable time living with the Pankhursts; a more mesmerising family one could not imagine. But the women in the group were fond of Daisy and she brought out their maternal instincts.

Dody accepted a cup of tea from Annie and settled herself in a chair next to a handsome, regal-looking woman in her late thirties wearing a fox stole. Miss Jane Lithgow looked at Dody with a steady gaze. "I'd like to know where you stand, Dr. McCleland," she said. "How far would *you* go to support the union, or are you allied more to the likes of Mrs. Fawcett?"

Everyone else in the room stopped talking. Dody knew she would have to choose her words carefully. "I am not in favour of extreme militancy," she replied, "but the cause will always have my moral support. I believe that the emancipation of women is the most effective way of bringing about true social reform to man, woman, and child—"

"You *are* involved with Mrs. Fawcett's group?"

"No, I am still trying to establish my career, and I do not have the time—"

"Mrs. Fawcett's sister, Dr. Elizabeth Garrett, seems to find time for the cause. She was a participant in yesterday's march," Miss Lithgow said.

"That may be, Miss Lithgow, but she is considerably older than I and her career firmly established."

"And she would never have condoned the violence that

erupted yesterday," a sparrow of a woman named Mrs. Slow-croft put in. "Like me, she believes in nonmilitant tactics."

"We didn't start the violence; it was a peaceful march," Molly Jenkins said, but her words were lost as Miss Lithgow, her fair skin emblazoned with passion and her eyes as accusing as those of the fox around her neck, cried out, "How, may I ask, can we be expected to peacefully bring about change when we don't have the political rights to do so? You and your like have had more than twenty years to get us the vote, Mrs. Slowcroft, and where has your nonmilitancy got us? Nowhere! We need to act now: deeds, not words!" Then, turning to the other women in the room, she said, "I propose we launch some kind of counteroffensive. We need to let the authorities know we will not allow ourselves to be trampled in the street!"

"I'm with you," Molly Jenkins called out, and the rest of the room, barring Dody and Mrs. Slowcroft, stamped their feet and rang teaspoons against cups in agreement.

Florence raised her hands to silence the din. "Whatever counterattack we decide upon, we must discuss it with Christabel Pankhurst first."

"I don't think Christabel would be averse to blowing up the Houses of Parliament itself," Miss Olivia Barndon-Brown said with a chuckle. Olivia was a rotund, jolly woman who wore a Moorish kaftan of brilliant hues. When not involved in suffragette activities, she could be found working in the East End soup kitchen funded by her wealthy parents. She was second-in-command of the Bloomsbury Division and her earthy humour had proven a useful antidote to the petty tensions that tended to undermine other groups.

"Then, in the event of any such measure, Miss Barndon-Brown,

I am leaving." Mrs. Slowcroft climbed to her feet. She gave Dody her hand. "It was lovely to meet you, my dear. I'm glad to see you have more sense than your young hotblood of a sister."

"Mrs. Slowcroft is a visitor to our Bloomsbury Division," Florence explained to Dody almost apologetically. "She's a member of Mrs. Fawcett's group, the National Union of Women's Suffrage Society." She shot Mrs. Slowcroft a frown. "I invited her here as a courtesy."

"None of us asked for the trouble yesterday," Molly Jenkins said to Mrs. Slowcroft, more moderately this time. "The Pankhursts told us to be'ave and be'ave we did. It was the police what caused the problems. And this 'ere"—she indicated the seated ladies with a reddened hand—"is exactly what they want—they want us to start bickering and fighting among ourselves so they can smash us up—divide and conquer, that's their plan."

"Quite right, Molly," Florence said. "Mrs. Slowcroft, please sit down, do. Why don't we all have another cup of tea and be friends?" Her sister reminded Dody of their mother breaking up a childish argument. "Although we work through different means," Florence continued, "we are all fighting for the same cause." She pulled the bell for Annie.

Mrs. Slowcroft let out a martyr's sigh and sat back down again.

A slender young woman in a plain office suit, with muddy boots and a sodden hem, accompanied Annie into the room a few minutes later.

"I'm so sorry I'm late, I've had the most dreadful time," she said. Her sudden burst of tears interrupted any kind of formal introduction to Dody, but as the other women fussed around her, repeating her name, Miss Treylen, Dody was able to gather that she worked as a clerk at the docks. She had been using her afternoon off to sell copies of *Votes for Women* until she was accosted by a group of men, who snatched her bundle of newspapers and threw them into the gutter. She didn't know what to do and the papers were quite ruined, she'd had to leave them where they fell—would Miss McCleland like her to collect more newspapers and return to the same street corner or should she try another?

"You will do no such thing; you've had enough for one day," Florence said, her expression torn between anger at the ignorant men and sympathy for the bedraggled victim. "You'll catch your death of cold. Annie, another cup and saucer, please."

"Apropos of the police, dear," Miss Lithgow addressed Florence once Miss Treylen had been settled into a chair by the fire and plied with sandwiches and cake. "Isn't it time we informed your sister what it is that we require of her?" Florence glanced at Dody. "Dr. McCleland," Miss Lithgow continued, her voice calm once more, "seeing as through no fault of your own, you have fallen onto the side of the opposition"—she eyed Dody over her pince-nez—"would it be possible for you to at least find out the results of Lady Catherine's autopsy?"

"I don't see why not," Dody replied, looking Miss Lithgow levelly in the eye. Her acquiescence had nothing to do with the other woman's attempts at intimidation. Having been unable to perform the autopsy, a follow-up was the least she could do, for Florence's sake. "It would be a professional courtesy for them to inform me anyway. I imagine I will be hearing from them soon."

"I'm not sure soon is good enough," Miss Lithgow said.

"We need to know now, Dody," Florence added. "The Division wants me to accompany you to Scotland Yard to make immediate enquiries before the officers leave for the evening."

Dody could see no problem with that. "Very well, I am as eager as you to find out the results."

"Can you tell us the names of the policemen you were dealing with?" Miss Lithgow asked.

"There was a Detective Superintendent Shepherd—"

"The deputy head of the Detective Division—as big a tub of lard as ever I did see," Molly Jenkins cut in, provoking a smile even on the glacially beautiful features of Miss Lithgow.

"And a Detective Chief Inspector Pike," Dody added.

It seemed none of the ladies had come across this name before. But after a few moments, Mrs. Slowcroft said, "Actually, I believe I know the name. Miss Hobhouse has spoken of him. An unusual type for a policeman, if it is the same fellow."

At the mention of Miss Hobhouse, the highly respected welfare campaigner, all eyes became fixed on Mrs. Slowcroft. "There is quite a story. It was during her campaign to expose the appalling conditions inside the British camps in South Africa where the Boer women and children were imprisoned," she said. "Mr. Pike was an army captain then, a bit of a war hero—received the Distinguished Conduct Medal or something or other. Then he was injured and sent to supervise the running of the Bloemfontein camp. He resigned his commission over what he saw there. Miss Hobhouse approached him hoping to use him in her campaign, but he refused, saying his resignation was all he needed to say on the matter."

Deeds, not words, the suffragette slogan—Dody barely managed to keep the thought to herself.

The women exchanged glances. "I think we could suppose he has some sympathy towards the women's movement, and a sympathetic police officer is worth cultivating, surely," Mrs. Slowcroft finished.

"It sounds as if he has some principles at least," Florence said.

"He's still the enemy," Olivia Barndon-Brown said, with no trace of humour at all.

Chapter Six

A plainclothes officer showed Dody into the chief inspector's office. Pike got to his feet and positioned the visitor's chair in front of his desk for her. Dody looked around the room. There were no pictures on the walls, no photographs or mementos on the shelves. A framed photograph stood on his desk, but of whom she could not tell, as it faced away from her. A tidy row of legal tomes stood on a shelf near a small curtained window set into the internal wall. A bicycle leaned against a heavy filing cabinet. Dody wondered how he managed to ride the old boneshaker with his leg as stiff as it seemed. Observing his gait, she deduced the problem to be his right knee; must be the war wound Mrs. Slowcroft had mentioned. He sat down once she had assured him that she was comfortable and had just had tea, and that no, her sister in the waiting room would probably not want tea either.

"I imagine, Doctor, you would like to view Lady Catherine's

autopsy report?" he said before she'd even expressed the reason for her visit. "I anticipated as much, and have it here for your perusal." His voice, which she hadn't paid much attention to in the mortuary, was refined for a police officer, softened with but a trace of a northern accent. His suit was well cut, if slightly dated, his cravat pinned with perfect symmetry. A dandy he was not, but he had a pride of appearance that Dody took to be a legacy of his time in the military.

He pushed the report across the desk. "This is the only copy. I'm afraid you'll have to read it here. The notes were dictated by Dr. Mangini to Mr. Bright, the assistant coroner."

Two photographs had been pinned to the autopsy report. The first was a grainy shot of Lady Catherine lying like a rag doll next to her crushed hat on the cobbles outside St. Stephen's. Litter and debris were strewn about her person; Dody made out a single boot, bricks, and a piece of four-by-two timber. She pointed to a discarded wooden club. "What manner of weapon is that?" she asked.

"A belaying pin, Doctor—a large club used to tie ships' halliards to."

"A common weapon of sailors?"

"Or anyone from the docks."

Dody thought for a moment. "Any of these objects, other than the boot, could be the instrument of death. I assume they were all tested for human blood?"

"The evidence around the body was collected, but not tested. With the autopsy results as conclusive as they seem to be, I doubt such tests will now be authorised. I'm afraid the budget allocated to forensics is limited." Dody directed a look at Pike that told him exactly what she thought about his department's competency. Dr. Spilsbury had told her the police often used the budget as an excuse. If Spilsbury had been in attendance, Dody was sure he would have insisted upon these basic forensic tests.

The other photograph was of Lady Catherine lying naked on the slab. Neither of the pictures showed the head wounds with any clarity.

The autopsy report was brief and didn't take long to read.

"You have finished with the photographs?" Pike asked, reaching out to gather them up.

"Yes," said Dody, "thank you. But I'll just read through this report again if you don't mind."

Pike put the photographs in a drawer then rose from the desk and limped to the waiting room. Through the open door, Dody heard him address Florence. "It's marginally warmer in my office, Miss McCleland, why don't you join us?"

Indeed, the cold bleak day had turned into a colder, bleaker evening. Dody glanced up from the report and noticed through the office window the rising river mists, tinged an eerie blue from the line of police lamps along the building's exterior. As Pike pulled up another chair, Florence caught Dody's eye. She raised an enquiring eyebrow.

"May I share this with my sister, Chief Inspector?"

"By all means," he replied.

Dody read the report's conclusion aloud:

Death believed to be the result of blunt force trauma to the skull. Four separate wounds on the head were discovered, all depressed fractures containing inverted bone fragments and all the result of considerable force. Any one of the blows could have caused coma followed by cessation of life. The indentations of all wounds were of a triangular nature, approximating those that may be caused by

the corner of a brick. Brick dust found after combing the victim's
hair further supports this supposition.

Florence jumped to her feet. "What nonsense is that? She was beaten about the head by a policeman with his truncheon!"

Pike said nothing but observed Florence with his hands folded loosely on the desk, his expression unchanged. He had surgeon's hands, Dody noticed—long, elegant fingers with neatly trimmed fingernails, not the meat cleavers one would expect of a policeman.

Dody tugged the side of her sister's dress until Florence dropped back to her seat. "I don't see your signature here as a witness, Chief Inspector," Dody said.

"Regrettably, I was called away."

Florence pursed her lips. "I have a friend who saw with his own eyes Lady Catherine being beaten about the head by a policeman."

"That is a serious accusation, Miss McCleland. May I ask who this friend might be?"

"The Honourable Mr. Hugo Cartwright, Lady Catherine's nephew," Florence said haughtily.

Pike leaned back in his desk chair. "Ah yes, and the heir to her fortune."

The sisters exchanged glances.

"You were not aware?"

"Now you mention it, I suppose it stands to reason," Florence replied. "He is her only living blood relative. But this is all very convenient for you, isn't it, this autopsy result? The police are off the hook and you think you have licence to throw mud around at whomsoever you wish. You are now saying that Hugo took advantage of the chaos and bludgeoned his aunt to death with a brick in order to receive his inheritance."

"People have been murdered for less, miss, and this wouldn't be the first murder committed under the cover of a public disturbance."

"I'd like to be present when you accuse Hugo of this to his face. He won't stand for it, you know. I hope you have a good solicitor, Mr. Pike," Florence said.

It was hard to imagine the pathetic, grief-stricken creature Dody had bandaged in the drawing room having any such fight in him at all. Antagonising Pike with wild threats would get them nowhere. She pressed her foot into Florence's shin.

"If Mr. Cartwright did indeed witness events as you describe them, he did not report it," Pike said. "That in itself is a punishable offence."

"Indeed he *did* report it, *Mr.* Pike." Florence retorted, her chin raised. Dody knew that by addressing him with his civilian title, Florence wished Pike to know she considered him not worthy of his rank. "But the beastly policeman refused to take his statement or write his name down, even. Hugo tried to stop the attack on Lady Catherine but couldn't move fast enough on account of his injured foot, which had been callously stamped upon by a charging police horse."

Dody detected a hastily suppressed flicker of amusement in Pike's face. Florence must have noticed it, too, for she bristled. "Mr. Pike, you need—"

Pike cut her off. "I have every intention of following the incident up with Mr. Cartwright, and I will personally go through the witness reports again, looking for his name."

Florence frowned, not reassured at all.

"Then in the meantime, sir," Dody said, "I would like permission to examine Lady Catherine's body for myself."

Florence drew a breath and appeared surprised; this was not something they had discussed.

"Is there something in the report that prompts you to make this request, Doctor?" Pike asked.

"Yes, as a matter of fact, there are several things.

"First is the evidence of the brick dust. When a body comes to the slab straight from the ice chest, the hair is always damp. Combing it for dust would be difficult, if not impossible."

"But if the hair had dried?"

"It would also be stiff with blood—how can one expect to remove brick dust from that?" As she spoke, Dody pictured a case she'd studied in Edinburgh in which London police had laundered a victim's shirt before examining it for bullet holes—a prime example of the lack of cooperation between the forensic and police departments. It would have been no surprise to hear that Lady Catherine's hair had also been washed before examination.

Pike's gaze wavered for the first time since the meeting had begun and she wondered if he, too, was reflecting on similar police bungles.

"I'm afraid I didn't notice her hair. Like you, I had only a brief glimpse of the body before the sheet was replaced," he said.

Florence had turned quite pale, Dody noticed. Hearing Lady Catherine spoken about in this manner must be distressing. Perhaps it would have been best if she'd remained in the waiting room.

"In any case," Dody said, "the wounds themselves, not the dust, are what need the most careful observation, and in

Dr. Mangini's report, they received only a cursory mention. It also surprises me that he makes no mention of the scalp being shaved—how else could the head wounds be thoroughly examined? I need to shave the hair, take measurements of the wounds, and then conduct some tests. A conclusion cannot be made instantaneously in the mortuary." Dody flicked the document with her finger. "Furthermore, this illustrates to me that Dr. Mangini is one of those old-school medical practitioners who treat coroner's inquests much too lightly. If he has not assessed the victim's general state of health through adequate dissection, how can it be proved without a doubt that these blows were the cause of her death? She may have had a long-standing ailment of the brain that the blows merely hastened to conclusion. A defence barrister would make a meal out of Dr. Mangini if he were called upon as an expert witness."

Pike didn't respond for a moment, and Dody looked around her as she waited. Her eyes settled on a file lying closed on his desk with the name *Hawley Crippen* inscribed on it. Had he been working the Crippen case with Dr. Spilsbury, too? The flamboyant Inspector Dew was the only member of the police department Dody had remembered the pathologist mentioning.

Pike must have followed her gaze, for he picked up the file and placed it in a desk drawer. Finally he spoke. "I would be the first to agree that coronial enquiries are not infallible, but I will have to ask Superintendent Shepherd's permission. I'm afraid I don't like your chances at a second attempt, seeing as you turned down the initial opportunity. But I understand your argument and I will do my best on your behalf. Excuse me for a minute."

He lifted the telephone receiver, cranked the handle, and

asked the operator to connect him to Shepherd's office. The sisters listened intently as he stated the case to his superior. Upon replacing the receiver, he told them, grim faced, that the coroner had already released the body and that the funeral parlour would be picking it up first thing in the morning. Dody may have been mistaken, but she thought she saw a reflection of her own thoughts in Pike's eyes: that he was as doubtful of Mangini's work as she was, and disappointed that there would be no second autopsy. Perhaps there was a glimmer of hope after all.

He took his watch from his pocket and let out a low sigh. "I'm afraid I'm running out of time, ladies. I have an engagement to attend. But before you go, I'd like to hear your personal opinions of Lady Catherine. Did she have any enemies that you are aware of? Anyone else who might benefit from her death other than Mr. Hugo Cartwright?"

"She was loved by everyone who knew her. Her only enemies were in the government and the police force," Florence said darkly.

"Perhaps not so surprising, Miss McCleland; she was imprisoned for spitting at one police officer and physically assaulting another, and while in prison engaged in a hunger strike. The police and prison authorities have better things to do with their time than force-feeding recalcitrant prisoners, I assure you. But of course you know this. You yourself were incarcerated for throwing rocks at the prime minister's motorcar." Florence stiffened in her chair, but said nothing. Dody realised that while Pike might have seen her side of the autopsy argument, he showed no sympathy to the plight of the suffragettes.

"And you, Dr. McCleland," Pike went on, fixing his eyes upon Dody. "Did you have an opinion of Lady Catherine?"

"I did not know her well enough to form an opinion."

Dody's opinion was that Lady Catherine was similar to the Pankhursts: domineering, controlling, and completely inflexible in her views, antagonising militants and nonmilitants alike. But this was hardly something she could say in front of her sister.

A little while later Dody and Florence stepped from the building into the swirling river mist. To hear Dody and that policeman talk so matter-of-factly about Catherine's death had been almost unbearable to Florence. The anguish and frustration that had been building up in her since they'd first entered the policeman's office finally burst its banks.

"He made it all sound like a childish game!" she sobbed. "I know you never cared much for Catherine and I appreciate that you said nothing negative about her to that unprepossessing little man. But Catherine was one of the best friends I had, devoted to the end. You might not remember this, but she put me up when I ran away from home, never telling Mother and Poppa where I was."

At seventeen she had fallen in love with a literary acquaintance of their mother's, taking it for granted that her liberal parents would agree to the marriage. But when they discovered the liberties the thirty-two-year-old poet had been taking with her, they refused to give their consent and banished him from their house. Florence had run away to London then, expecting her beloved to join her there. He never did. It was discovered later that he had a wife and two children secreted away in Blackpool. She still cringed with shame whenever she thought about it. Bloody men, she thought, shame they were necessary at all. With the exception of Poppa, the world would be a better place without them.

"And it was Catherine who convinced me to go back to Mother and Poppa," she went on, "telling me I needed to focus on other people more and less on myself; basically that I was a spoilt little brat. She encouraged me to help in the soup kitchen and with other charitable works, and it was through her that I joined the WSPU."

Dody pulled Florence to a stop under a lamplight, brushed a tear from her cheek, and put her arm around her shoulders. "There, there," she said.

Dear Dody. Florence did not know what she would do without her big sister. She kept on talking through her sobs. "But, Dody, how on earth are we to get justice for Catherine when no one on the police force will take us seriously? I had staked my hopes on that man Pike, but now I see he is as sarcastic and corrupt as the rest of them."

"I'm not of quite the same opinion, Florence," Dody said as they made their way arm in arm to their waiting carriage. "I think Pike would have been happy to let me reexamine Catherine if not for Shepherd. I'm thinking he might have doubts about the autopsy himself."

"Well, his doubts don't help us, do they? What are we going to do?"

Dody gazed around the foggy street as if making sure they were not being observed. "Don't worry; I have something up my sleeve. Literally."

Under the gaslight near their carriage, she revealed a police truncheon within the sleeve of her coat. "It was lying on the sergeant's desk in the waiting room. I took it when he was helping you on with your cape."

Florence felt her face break into a smile, marvelling at her sister's cleverness. "You've stolen it!"

"Borrowed. You see, Florence, even I will bend the law sometimes, if I think the cause is just."

"But what use is it to us?" Florence said, dashing away her remaining tears.

"I'll tell you as we go, but first we must find a chemist's shop that is still open."

Chapter Seven

Pike rarely turned down a request from the landlord at the Three Bells to entertain his guests, and tonight was a particularly special occasion—the wedding reception of the landlord's daughter. Pike's knee never seemed to pain him at the piano, and he manipulated the pedals with a jaunty spring that had long been missing from his walking gait. As his fingers melted into the piano keys, he left the unsettling scene in his office behind. How the superintendent was going to get away with a shoddy autopsy on a high-profile society figure wasn't his problem.

He had started the evening with a selection of traditional ballads and romances, joined by a quartet of young women from the Southwark workhouse. He'd first heard them sing in his local church, and whenever an appropriate opportunity arose, he asked them to join him when he played.

"But you're not staying for the whole night," he'd warned.

"Functions like this tend to get a bit out of hand, bawdy even. I don't want your innocent young minds corrupted." To which the girls had responded with a mixture of disappointment and mirth: "That's right, Captain—pure as the driven slush is what we are!"

The last song of the first bracket was a round, "Summer Is A-Comin' In," and his spirits soared with the melody as he accompanied the pure voices that cut clean through to the heart.

> *Summer is a-comin' in*
> *Loudly sing cuckoo*
> *Groweth seed and bloweth mead*
> *and springs the wood anew*
> *Sing cuckoo!*

The song ended to a roar of applause. The girls responded to the whistles and catcalls with mock curtsies, flinging lip back as good-naturedly as it was hurled at them. Pike decided the audience was ready for a change of pace. He would skip the Gilbert and Sullivan he'd planned and get straight into the rollicking music hall numbers everyone could sing along to.

But first, he escorted the girls to the pub door and handed each of them their sixpence, warning them not to dawdle lest they should find the workhouse door locked. Winnie Whistle threw her spindly arms around his neck and thanked him for the chance of escaping the workhouse for the evening.

"And I didn't cough once and spoil it, did I, Captain?"

"You did marvellously, Winnie."

Delighted with the praise, she offered her rouged cheek, pressing it to his lips before he could back away. "Better get that stuff off your face, Winnie," he said, holding her by the wrists at arm's length, "or they'll have you out the workhouse in a flash."

"Oh, give over, Captain." She laughed.

"She wouldn't be laughing like that if she knew you was the Old Bill," Brockman, the landlord, said as he joined Pike at the door. The clatter of the women's footsteps and a bout of coughing from Winnie continued for some moments after the mud-coloured fog swallowed them up.

Pike wiped the grease from his lips and tapped his nose. "Our secret, Mr. Brockman."

"Winnie's a lunger, is she?"

"I think she might be. Though the workhouse authorities assure me she's clear of TB." Pike would have liked to do more for her; the girl had a child and did her best for it. But he could hardly send her a hamper—the workhouse staff would surely keep it for themselves. He was glad he could slip her a sixpence every now and then.

He accepted a mug of ale from Brockman and took a long swallow, feeling more at ease in the dockland pub than he ever had in polite society or the stuffy confines of the officers' mess.

Brockman had been his regimental sergeant major and served with Pike in India, Afghanistan, and South Africa. He and his wife were the only people in the pub who knew Pike was a high-ranking Scotland Yard detective. To everyone else he was just the captain, an old army chum of the landlord—a gentleman who had fallen upon hard times and who kept to himself when not playing the piano.

"Are you sure I can't tempt you with a small stipend, Captain?" Brockman asked not for the first time.

"Against the law, I'm afraid. Police officers aren't supposed to take other forms of employment." Though with the appalling pay and working conditions of the lower ranks, they often did, and found themselves compromised because of it. For the first time since he'd started playing, his mind drifted back to Lady Catherine's autopsy. If accurate, the report ruled out bludgeoning by a uniformed officer's truncheon, but it did not eliminate plainclothes members of the force. Although better paid than the uniformed division, any member of the detective force might have been willing to stir up trouble for the sake of a few bob. So far he had not recognised any in the surveillance photographs behaving with impropriety, but he had yet to see the last batch of pictures. The death of Lady Catherine might have been unintentional; but in the heat of the moment boundaries are blurred, mistakes made, a brick or club impulsively grabbed.

If the autopsy report was accurate. His doubts over Mangini's competency took on more weight when combined with the woman doctor's concerns. Her reservations had made sense to him. The wisest course of action, he decided, would be to continue with his enquiries as if there had been no autopsy at all. He would begin by following up Mr. Hugo Cartwright's allegations and pay the gentleman a visit first thing in the morning.

"Have another on me, mate," Brockman broke into his thoughts. "And try one of the missus's fancy pies for your supper; she'd be mighty offended if you turned one down."

"Indeed I will, thank you, Mr. Brockman."

Brockman bellowed towards the bar for the servant girl to fetch over a pie, quick smart. Pike sank his teeth into the flaky pastry and savoured the succulent filling. He waved his appreciation to Mrs. Brockman, busy thumping slopping glasses onto a table in the far corner of the room.

He squinted through the smoky gloom. There was something familiar about one of the men she served: the rakish insouciance of the cap, the defiantly long hair tied back and snaking down his spine. The man raised his head. Dark brows knitted as he returned Pike's stare. Did he recognise Pike for what he was? Pike doubted it. Dressed in collarless shirtsleeves and with his cane out of sight, Pike doubted even Sergeant Fisher would recognise him from this distance.

He cocked his head towards the table and said to Brockman, "Those three men over there, are they wedding guests?"

Brockman squinted through the smoke. "Never seen them before, must be from off the street. This isn't a private function; I can't afford to turn people away. Maybe the missus knows—I'll call her over."

Mrs. Brockman joined them at the pub door. "Irish by the sound of their voices, and not regulars, neither," she said. "Say, Captain, what did you think of my pheasant pie?"

Pike tore his gaze from the strangers and dusted pastry crumbs from his shirtfront. "Best I've ever had."

"Then I'll get you another. You're looking a bit peaky, if it's not too presumptive of me to say so. I reckon you need fattening up. I'll put another by the pianner for you. That landlady of yours certainly ain't doing the job proper."

Pike sat down at the piano and began the next bracket, the bawdy drinking songs the dockland crowd could not get enough of. His mother would turn in her grave if she knew how he employed his talents now. From the far table, he could feel the black eyes of the Irishman burning into his back.

His subconscious took over. Against his bidding, his fingers picked out "Whiskey in the Jar." It was like a prompt. Now he knew the identity of the shadowy face. It belonged to a onetime Fenian, Derwent O'Neill. He'd seen it that very morning in a book of old mug shots he'd been flicking through on Shepherd's insistence—the superintendent remained adamant the Irish were behind the trouble at the women's march.

And he remembered the biography that went with the photograph. How could he not? Derwent O'Neill had been arrested on suspicion of being involved with a string of bombings in London—including that of the Queen Anne Hotel— ten years back. The cases against him had been thrown out of court owing to lack of evidence, though others had gone down. O'Neill had returned to Ireland and, as far as Pike knew, had not been seen on these shores since.

The crowd joined in with the lyrics. Pike felt the hair standing up on the back of his neck as the words took on a new meaning.

As I was a-goin' over Gilgarra Mountain
I spied Captain Farrell, and his money he was countin'.
First I drew my pistols and then I drew my rapier,
Sayin' "Stand and deliver, for I am your bold receiver."
Musha ringum duram da,
Whack for the daddy-o,
There's whiskey in the jar.

The song ended. Someone called out through the roars and stamping feet, requesting the popular music hall song "Brave Dublin Fusiliers!" In the present company, Pike knew the Loyalist song would cause nothing but trouble. The last thing he wanted was for the wedding celebrations to end in a donny-brook. He paid no heed to the request, ending the bracket with "Roll Out the Barrel," then took his drink and pressed his way through the crowd to where O'Neill and his friends sat. He pulled up a chair and joined them.

"Good evening, Chief Inspector Pike," O'Neill said. "Doing a bit of moonlighting, I see?"

"A favour for a friend. I've never met you, O'Neill. How do you know my name?"

"Perhaps for the same reason you know mine. You're famous, Mr. Pike, in my circle, that is." He waved his hand towards his three companions.

"Sinn Fein, you mean?—And famous for what?"

"Your luck, of course; maybe mine, too."

"You're talking in riddles."

"How lucky you were to have escaped the Queen Anne Hotel bomb. And how lucky I was to avoid Her Majesty's pleasure. But I'm sorry, this is terribly insensitive of me; please accept, Mr. Pike, my most sincere commiserations on the untimely death of your unlucky wife."

Pike raised his glass to his mouth to hide his flush at the scarcely veiled animosity. "It was a long time ago," he said, taking several swallows of ale. "The men responsible have paid for it on the gallows and I have other concerns now—such as your presence in London."

"Just wetting the head of me cousin's new bairn; a family reunion, you might say. This is me cousin and the new father, Sean." O'Neill pointed to a peach-faced lad no older than twenty-one. "He's the son of my Uncle Liam, hanged by the English. My father, Seamus, was killed—"

"Your family tree interests me vastly," Pike said.

O'Neill narrowed his eyes. "And this is me brother Patrick, who came over with me." Patrick was dark like his brother, but quieter and more serious, lacking Derwent's charismatic energy. "There's no law against a man visiting his family in England, is there, Mr. Pike?" Derwent added.

"None at all, but I think Special Branch will be interested to know you're in the area." Pike rose to leave, a visit to Special Branch added to his list of things to do in the morning. Since its recent formation, Sinn Fein had not been associated with any violent acts in London, but one could never be too complacent when it came to the Irish.

"Haven't yous got better things to do than spy on innocent family reunions?" Patrick O'Neill said. "I hear victimising the Irish is out of fashion in London anyway."

"Yeah," Sean O'Neill added. "The English police seem a lot more interested in stamping on their fellow workers on the docks and down the mines, men whose only crime is wanting to put more food in the bellies of their children."

"And punching women and putting their hands up their skirts, so we hear," Derwent O'Neill added with a sly glint to his eye.

Pike put his hands on the table and leaned towards O'Neill. "What do you know about that? Were you at the riot outside the House of Commons?" The notion was ridiculous, of course. Sinn Fein wouldn't bother with something as minor as stirring up a women's protest; the Fenians, from whom they had evolved, preferred ripping people apart with gunpowder and nail bombs. But the Lords were employing delaying tactics over the introduction of the third Home Rule Bill, and tensions were beginning to rise again. So Irish troublemaking couldn't be ruled out.

"Everybody knows." Derwent O'Neill laughed. "Maybe you don't need to go further than your own field to find the shit, eh, Mr. Pike?" He nodded to his companions. "We best be off, the air is too close in here." They rose as one from the table. "We'll be seeing you, Mr. Pike," Derwent said, doffing his cap in a mocking manner.

Chapter Eight

A chilly breeze had swept away much of the nighttime fog, and the flame in the oil lamp flickered as Dody held it up to the mortuary door. Florence shivered and took her sister's arm. "I don't know how you can bear to work in this kind of place."

"This mortuary is older and worse than most," Dody said. "Many are not much different to operating theatres these days. Now, are you sure you're going to be able to go ahead with this?"

"I can do anything provided I don't have to look at Catherine."

"Good girl, just leave that part to me."

Dody pulled the doorbell and within seconds Alfred was standing in the porch. When she held the lamp to her face, he recognised her immediately. "Dr. McCleland? Well, 'ow do you do, miss? What brings you 'ere, on such an 'orrible night?"

"I have something to ask you, may we come in? Oh, Alfred, this is my assistant, Nurse—"

"Nightingale," Florence said, holding up the lamp and giving the old man a sweet smile. Nightingale. Dody repressed the urge to smile. "No relation, I'm afraid," Florence added.

Alfred chuckled. "Come in, ladies, do. And what a pretty pair you are to be warming up such a cold foggy night, if you don't mind my saying."

They stepped with Alfred into the anteroom. The gaslights were on and sputtering, though the yawing mouth of the stairwell leading to the mortuary itself was dark as pitch. Dody was glad she'd had the foresight to take the lamp from the carriage. "How is your chest, Alfred?" she asked. "Did you manage to find a carbolic ball?"

"We've been so busy 'ere miss, can't say I've 'ad the chance to get 'old of one yet. That lotion you gave me is working a treat, though."

Dody reached into her bag. "I thought you might not have had the chance, so I picked one up from the chemist's for you this evening."

Alfred beamed. He took the ball from her and turned it over in his hands. "Bless you, Doctor, and may the good Lord reward you for your generosity."

"But now I'm going to have to ask a favour of you. I've just come from a visit to Chief Inspector Pike."

"A fine man that!" Alfred said between enthusiastic inhalations of the carbolic ball.

"A fine man indeed." Dody ignored the disdainful look on her sister's face and took a deep breath. "He asked me if I would have another look at Lady Catherine's head wounds before she's claimed in the morning by the funeral parlour."

She'd done it now, there was no going back. She could only hope that word would not get out, and that if it did, it would not cost her too dearly.

"This is most irregular, miss," Alfred said, placing the ball on the desk delicately as if it were a precious Fabergé egg. "Once the coroner has signed the release documents—"

"Quite right. The chief inspector said you were a noble upholder of the law and would not allow any interference with the body without written consent." At this, Alfred threw back his shoulders and puffed out his pigeon chest. "Consequently, he wrote me a note to pass on to you." Dody snapped her fingers at Florence, who patted herself down under her cape, searching for the note. Dody hoped the poor lighting would hide the quality of the garment, far too fine a cut for a mere nurse to be wearing.

"Well, where is it? Chop-chop, girl!" Aside, she said to Alfred, "She's new to the job, this is her first assignment with me."

"I can't find it, Doctor," Florence said with a wail worthy of Sarah Bernhardt. "I think I must have dropped it in the street. Shall I go back and retrace our steps?"

"Silly girl, we'll never find it in this fog." Dody exaggerated a sigh. "I fear we won't be able to get another note from the chief inspector at this hour. Alfred, is there anything you can do to help?" Her heart was beating wildly; she was asking more of Alfred than he could know—and she feared for his job, too.

Alfred rubbed his chin. "Well, I suppose I could let you down there, accompanied by me, that is, and then we can document your proceedings together—but you'll 'ave to sign the register."

"Thank you so much, I won't be long, I promise. Now if you'll just hand me the pen . . . "

At this Florence swayed, clutching the corner of the desk. "Doctor, the odour is getting to me . . . I think I'm going to be sick."

"Good heavens, girl—not in here!" Dody said, fanning Florence's face with her hand. Turning to Alfred, she said, "Would you be so kind as to take my nurse out for a moment? She needs some air. I can find my way to the cadaver keep without you, you need not worry. I only require a quick glance at the body and just enough time to take some measurements."

With a look of genuine concern, Alfred took Florence by the elbow and propelled her to the front door, clucking his tongue like a nursemaid. Dear old man. Dody would make it up to him somehow—keep him in carbolic balls for life perhaps.

"This is the last time you work with me, my girl," she called over her shoulder as she hurried to the stone staircase. Florence had once boasted that since her force-feeding experience, she could be sick on demand. Dody hoped she would put on a convincing performance.

Now time was of the essence. She needed to be out of the building before Alfred realised she had not signed the register; she could leave no official proof that she had been here. If she had read the conscientious Alfred correctly, he would not care to advertise his mistake. She was counting on that. Unless she could prove without a doubt that a policeman had bludgeoned Lady Catherine to death, she wanted no one else the wiser of her visit.

She descended the stairs, hurried through the mortuary, and entered the cadaver keep, which was even colder than the mortuary room itself. The beam of the lamp picked out six body-sized ice chests resting on a long wooden trestle running the length of one of the walls. Small shapes scurried from the sudden intrusion of light. The place dripped like a cave; melting ice trickled from holes in the chests to an open porcelain drain, which disappeared through a hole in the wall to God only knew where.

Dody placed the lamp on the floor, where a cold mist swirled and wreathed its glow. Her movements threw magnified, eerie shadows on the wall. She wasn't afraid of the dead; it was the living who frightened her. If the authorities discovered her deception, they might strike her from the medical register; she tried to reassure herself that medical men had done far worse than this for the sake of their science. Dr. Spilsbury himself might resort to similar measures in her situation; his fight against the incompetent system was legendary. If finding justice for Lady Catherine meant admitting to her clandestine activities, Spilsbury would come to her defence, she was sure of it. So might Pike, for that matter; there was an air of justice about the man which was rare in most policemen.

There were no names on the chests, only numbers. Hopefully Lady Catherine's body would not be the last. She heaved the lid off the farthest chest and met the face of a stubbly chinned, elderly gentleman. The next contained an alabaster girl. In the third she gazed upon the pugilistic face of a labouring man with the top portion of his scalp missing.

The lids of the ice chests were heavy and the exertion had turned her arms to rubber; a cool draft chilled the perspiration on her brow. With a loud creak, she prised open the fourth lid.

Catherine stared back from her pillow of ice.

Dody paused for a moment of respect, then reached out a hand to push a strand of bloodied hair from the icy face. "We didn't always see eye to eye, Catherine," she whispered, "but my sister loved you and that is what matters. This was not the end you deserved."

She lifted the lamp and positioned it on the trestle for maximum light. Ideally, an examination such as this would be undertaken in daylight, certainly not by lamplight in the cadaver keep. Even in daylight, the only natural illumination in the mortuary room came from a narrow row of small, ceiling-high windows. Mangini probably missed all manner of things during his cursory examination that she would have no chance of finding now. But hopefully those details would be irrelevant to what she was trying to prove. The shape, fragmentations, and depth of the wounds should tell her what she needed to know.

With a touch as gentle as if Lady Catherine were only sleeping, Dody lifted the head towards the light. With one hand supporting the neck, she began to probe the bloodied hair with the fingertips of her other hand, feeling for fragments of bone, trying to discover the exact locations of the wounds so she need only shave the hair where necessary. Once the wounds were exposed, she would take measurements of length, depth, and angles, using the ruler and recording her notes in a sketchpad she had brought.

The wind started up again, breaking the silence, and the lamp on the trestle flickered. The cold on her cheek grew in intensity and the wick flickered again, almost extinguishing itself. She let Lady Catherine's head fall back onto the ice and lunged for the lamp, only to knock it over in her haste.

Blackness closed in on her from all sides.

Alone in the dark, Dody was again a nervous medical student, horrified and repulsed by her first session in the dissecting room. Her teeth chattered. She groped along the stone floor for her Gladstone bag, determined not to let this setback deter her. Needled feet scampered across her hand. She choked down her scream. The rank smelly mist seeped into her lungs as icy fingers caressed her cheek.

Dody found her bag at last, up against the trestle leg. She fumbled with the catch and dived in, feeling for her smoking pouch and matchbox. Her first strike along the side of the damp ice chest failed to catch. Again she tried, this time upon the sole of her boot. It took several attempts before the match finally stuttered into a flame. With trembling fingers, she managed to set the lamp straight, remove the glass, and light the wick. "Thank you, thank you," she murmured, believing, despite scientific evidence to the contrary, that some form of God still existed. The glow of the lamp, so ineffective before, was at once as comforting as the light from her own fireplace.

Taking a steadying breath, she commenced her work.

Chapter Nine

Dody thanked Alfred for his offer to walk them to their carriage but insisted it wasn't necessary. So as not to draw attention to their presence in the mortuary, she had instructed Fletcher, their coachman, to park in a side street off Lambeth Palace Road. The breeze had dropped and patches of river mist had returned. Directly outside the hospital a team of labourers worked by lamplight, scraping up the straw spread on the road to muffle the sounds of the street and replacing it with a fresh layer. Other than these men, there were few people about and little traffic.

The sisters hurried through the dark from lamppost to lamppost, as one might scoot from one shady tree to another on a hot summer day. They paused to catch their breath under the last pool of yellow light before their carriage. If they needed to call for help now, Fletcher would be close enough to render assistance.

"Nightingale?" Dody said, raising her eyes to the lamplight.

"Sorry, it was the first name that sprang to mind."

"It was the last that sprang to mine."

"Did you manage to find out everything you needed?" Plumes of Florence's breath mingled with the fog.

"About as much as I could under the circumstances; the conditions were far from ideal. I won't be able to form any conclusions until I've completed my tests. Unfortunately I have a full day at the women's hospital tomorrow, so I doubt there will be time then."

"I hope it was worth it. I don't think I've ever vomited so much. All I had to do was think of that ghastly tube rammed down my nose and out it all came. Alfred was endeavouring to walk me to the hospital when you appeared—not a moment too soon, I might add."

"Good evening, ladies."

Dody froze.

Florence gasped as if she'd just caught sight of Jack the Ripper.

Chief Inspector Pike materialised through the mist as if from nowhere. "My apologies for startling you," he said, lifting his hat to them.

Dody was first to regain her composure. "I hope you are not following us, Chief Inspector?"

"On the contrary, I am making my way home from an engagement in Southwark. I caught the omnibus to the corner of Blackfriars Road and decided to walk home from there." He paused, using his cane to indicate their gloomy surroundings. "Seeing as the night is so pleasant and ideal for such a stroll."

"A stroll is good for the health regardless of the weather," Dody replied with affected haughtiness. "We called on Alfred at the mortuary to deliver him a carbolic ball."

"Yes, I saw you leave."

"Fletcher must be worried for us. I think we should be going now," Florence said, grabbing at Dody's arm. "Good evening, Mr. Pike." They turned towards the carriage without waiting for his reply.

He called after them, "Oh, ladies? Sergeant Fisher would very much appreciate the return of his truncheon—at your earliest convenience, of course. Thank you."

I t had been quite by chance that Pike had come across the women leaving the mortuary. There were easier ways to find out what they were up to without following them himself. His was a desk job; he was a gatherer of intelligence. He had an army of detectives and informers at his disposal, but he was glad, nevertheless, for the opportunity to see them in action with his own eyes. He was not surprised that Dr. McCleland was not content to let the matter of the slipshod autopsy rest. Nor was he perturbed that his orders had been disobeyed. He had hoped they would be.

He pondered just what she intended to do with any new findings. She would surely not make them public; that would be to betray herself. Would she trust him enough to confide in him? If the decision were left to Dr. McCleland's sister, Florence, the answer would surely be a definitive "No." The hatred of her kind for the police was no different from that of any common criminal, perhaps even more bitter. He sensed the older sister to be more flexible, however. There was a depth of understanding and maturity in those soft brown eyes that had drawn him to them. He could see that the doctor and he both worked for the same ends—the discovery of the truth, no matter how unsavoury it might be. He hoped he was not imagining this. He had no stomach for setting his spies upon Dr. Dorothy McCleland.

He continued to brood upon the problem as he crossed the Lambeth Bridge towards his lodgings off Millbank Road. No need to worry about being mown down by speeding motorcars here. The bridge had recently been deemed unsafe and vehicular traffic was barred, though there was still danger about. He banished thoughts about Dr. McCleland and the case to the back of his mind. He had seen too many bloated bodies pulled from the river to drop his guard even for a moment.

A group of men lounged in the shadows of one of the bridge's towers, and Pike tightened his grip upon his cane. He strained to hear the talk of the men above the slapping of water, and detected Cockney accents; not Irish, thank God. There was laughter, and he saw one snatch a bottle from another with an angry curse. So intent were they in draining every last drop from the bottle, they weren't even aware of his passing. He expelled a breath and commenced the steep descent from the bridge.

Though never quite as bustling as the docklands further downriver, it was hard to believe not long ago the Millbank district had been a crazy quilt of timber, cement, wine and coal wharves, crowded tenements, and dingy back alleys reminiscent of Dickens's London. The passing of the Thames Embankment Extension Scheme had brought the closure of most of the wharves and warehouses. Now only a few rusty cranes were left, elbowing their way across the river, waiting to unload the barges and lighters that would never come.

Pike picked his way through the bleak wasteland, still showing more sign of destruction than construction. Six thousand

people had been moved out of the surrounding slums and placed
in the blocks of red brick flats springing up all around the City
of Westminster. Like cats, many returned to the area they still
considered home, though there were few of the original land-
marks left for them—some boarded-up shops, a public house, a
crumbling warehouse or two. But it was cheap and meant that
on the rare occasion his daughter visited, he had money left
over for a few nights in a modest hotel on a safer side of town.

The streetlamps were spread further apart here. He stepped
in a pile of horse manure as he passed a group of ragamuffins
taking shelter against a stack of yet-to-be-laid sewerage pipes.
Out of habit he examined the thin faces flickering in the light
from the brazier, seeking a match to the wanted posters that
lined the passages of Scotland Yard. But the hollow look of
hunger was the only resemblance.

He was skirting a pile of rags blocking his way when the
rags moved. A skinny arm appeared and a woman's voice
begged him to buy a flower. He crossed to the other side of
the road, blocking his ears to her pleas. In years gone by he
might have succumbed, but the job had hardened him, his
compassion now tempered by practicality. He couldn't do right
by everyone, and he had more than enough charity cases for
the salary he drew.

The police pay was terrible and his decision to join the
force had been the last straw for his wife. The daughter of a
major, she'd felt betrayed when he resigned his commission in
South Africa. His joining the metropolitan police had driven
her into the arms of a guardsman, the same man who had
been killed with her when the hotel was bombed. Pike hadn't
needed the Irishman to remind him—a strange mixture of
grief, regret, and hurt pride still dogged him.

The wind was bitter. He rammed his free hand deep into his pocket and hunkered into his scarf. He made his way along Millbank Road. The putrid smell of the river mist dissipated, giving way to that of effluent and soot. There were few working streetlights in the vicinity of his boardinghouse. Like a blind man, he tapped the path with his cane, avoiding piles of refuse and potholes, until at last he caught the winking front lights of his clapboard lodgings.

Fated for eventual demolition, the boardinghouse had received little maintenance over the last few years, though it was quite comfortable. His rooms consisted of a small bedroom and sitting room and a bathroom on the landing, which he shared with two other gentleman boarders. When the time came for him to move, he would be hard-pressed to find similarly cheap lodgings so close to his work.

He prayed that his landlady, the widowed Mrs. Keating, had not waited up for him. He tried to ensure that he arrived home at the busiest time of her day, when she was serving the evening meal to her five gentlemen boarders—or so late that even she would not be awake.

His timing was wrong tonight. The flaking wooden door opened before he could put his key into the lock. Mrs. Keating stood there, swaying slightly, dressed in feathers and jewels as if she had just returned from an evening out.

"Mr. Pike, I was getting worried about you," she said. "You never told me nothing about missing supper tonight. But I've kept a lovely pig's trotter warm for you if you're hungry—my other gentlemen was most complimentary of the dish."

"I'm sure your supper was of your usual high standard, Mrs. Keating, but I'm afraid I've already eaten." Pike undid the buttons of his overcoat and removed his scarf, putting his hat and gloves on the hall table.

His landlady smiled and sidled towards him. "No collar tonight, Mr. Pike? And you who usually looks such the gentleman. Your blue cravat is back from the laundry, the one that brings out your eyes so well. I put it on your bed."

"Thank you, Mrs. Keating, you are most kind." The banister was pressing into his back as he attempted to increase the distance between himself and the invitation of the low-cut cleavage thrust towards his chest. This aging trollop was as lonely as he was, but she would have to look elsewhere for her comfort. He had his standards, and the womanising ways of his early youth were well and truly over. After the miserable years of his marriage to a woman he could never, apparently, satisfy, he had little taste for embarking on the whole catastrophe again.

"I'm very tired and will retire to my rooms," he muttered, turning his cowardly heel upon the foot of the stair. "I'm sorry, Mrs. Keating," he added softly.

Behind him he heard her huff of breath. "Well, you've got no letters. Not one from your daughter nor your sister, neither," she said with relish.

He turned and gave her a tight smile. "Then perhaps I shall hear from them tomorrow. Good night, Mrs. Keating."

Chapter Ten

By lunchtime the next day Pike had finished interviewing several more officers and detectives involved in the riot—without thankfully having to sack any of them. He picked up the photograph of his daughter from his desk. Despite his regrets about his catastrophic marriage, he could never look back and think of those years as wasted. His daughter's sunny smile cheered him up as it always did and encouraged him to keep going.

He asked Fisher to chase up the last batch of photographs to be developed and then set off along the endless corridors to the section of the building devoted to the offices of Special Branch.

Superintendent Thomas Callan listened intently as Pike reported his confrontation with the O'Neill brothers in the public house. Callan had been with the elite division of the Met since its formation when it was called the Special Irish Branch. Recently the "Irish" part of its title had been dropped and its responsibilities increased. Now it concerned itself with the gathering, collating, and exploiting of intelligence relating to any security threat, irrespective of origins. Britannia might still rule the waves, but at the dawn of the new century, her grip on the established order had become tenuous and she faced more threats than ever from both within and without.

Callan reassured Pike that the brothers' arrival in the country had been noted and their movements closely monitored. "So you can rest easy, Matthew," he said with a smile. "I'm sure they were just trying to provoke you. I think Shepherd is trying to divert you from the main issue—his own incompetence at handling the women's march. Ignore his suggestions, and proceed as you think best."

Not wishing to involve Callan in any breach of procedure he might be forced to make, Pike did not mention the inadequate autopsy or reveal his suspicions that there might be more than incompetency behind Shepherd's behaviour. It was gratifying to hear that his mentor was still counselling him to follow his own instincts. Pike relaxed into his seat. Superintendent Callan was one of the few senior police officers for whom Pike had a genuine regard.

"On the day of the riot, the brothers were with family in Kent," Callan continued. "Besides, they haven't been in the country long enough to organise trouble from behind the scenes."

"Have you any idea who issued the instructions for the police to act with such force?"

Callan shrugged. "What does Shepherd say?"

"He denies any such instructions were issued. He says the Whitechapel divisional sergeant briefed the men and suggests that orders had been misinterpreted."

"And the Whitechapel sergeant—has he been questioned?"

"Yes. According to Sergeant Fisher, he is saying the same thing: the men misinterpreted his instructions. Shepherd has forbidden us to interview him further. Apparently he is too valuable an officer to lose."

Callan paused and regarded Pike with concern. "I heard Shepherd at the club the other day talking to some of his cronies, complaining about you. Not your work," Callan responded promptly to Pike's look of indignation. "Even he couldn't find fault with that. He was implying you weren't physically fit enough for the job, that maybe it was time you were pensioned off. Do you think you might have been asking a few too many questions?"

Pike said nothing and turned his gaze to the window.

"How *is* the knee these days, Matthew?"

"It always plays up in winter, but come spring it'll loosen up again." He focused his attention on the snarled traffic in the street outside Callan's office, the muted sounds of jingling harnesses, clopping hooves, and motorcar engines.

"Then you've not taken up that offer at the Royal Victoria? Didn't the surgeon there say he could do something for you?"

Pike turned back from the window. "I don't want surgery." He would rather lose his job than find himself in the hands of army surgeons again. He ran his hand along the inside of his collar and found he was perspiring despite the chill of Callan's office. "I'm sorry, sir; I appreciate your concern, but the subject is closed." His mouth was dry. Reaching for his cane, he climbed to his feet.

"That's quite all right, old man, one can hardly blame you— I can only imagine what that South African field hospital must have been like. But if Shepherd does start on your case, don't forget there's a position waiting for you in my department."

"Thank you, sir."

"Where are you off to now?"

"Belgravia, to speak to a possible witness to Lady Catherine's death."

"I can organise a dispatch motor wagon for you if you like."

"Thank you, no. Shepherd might catch wind of it. As far as he's concerned, a brick-wielding Irish rough killed Lady Catherine. The less he knows about my continuing investigation, the better. I'll take my chances with the omnibus." He paused at the door. "Oh, one more thing, sir," he said, turning back. "What can you tell me of the McCleland family of Sussex? I know they have been considered troublemakers, but that's as far as my information goes."

"We had them under surveillance two or three years ago," Callan said after some thought. "It came to nothing, and we have since dropped it."

"Their politics put them under suspicion?"

"That, and the people they mixed with. They were patrons of the arts in Russia, mixed with the intelligentsia, personal friends of Tolstoy, et cetera, with socialist beliefs—you know the form." Callan gave a wry smile. "It's easy to be a socialist when you're rich, eh?"

"Left wing and upper crust—an interesting paradox," Pike mused.

"To which they are all probably blinkered."

Pike doubted this was the case of the elder daughter; she seemed to have her feet planted firmly on the ground. Then again, in her profession, she'd have to.

Callan continued. "And then one of Mr. McCleland's brothers was murdered."

"Political?"

"No, nothing of the kind; he was a university professor of English in Moscow, shot by a student who felt he deserved better exam marks."

"Good heavens."

"Quite. The McClelands presumably saw this as a sign that the country was going to the dogs—in any case, their socialist leanings were drawing the attention of the Russian authorities. They brought their daughter Florence—the older girl was already at school here—and their considerable fortune back to England, where they have lived the life of wealthy eccentrics ever since. Why the interest?"

"I've had recent dealings with both daughters."

"Miss Florence McCleland, I take it, the suffragette? You know, some of the higher-ups view the suffragettes as a greater threat to the British Empire than the Irish, the anarchists, the socialists, and the Germans all rolled into one."

"I find that hard to believe," Pike said. "The women were certainly troublesome, but hardly a serious threat. Why were those arrested on Friday released so quickly?"

"The government's afraid of more hunger strikes, I suspect. The torture of women doesn't exactly cast any of us in a good light. I'd say the Pankhursts' tactics appear to be working. You mentioned daughters, plural."

"The elder is an autopsy surgeon."

Now it was Callan's turn to look surprised. "Well, I suppose anything is possible when you consider how they were brought up. Good-looking women, though, so I hear, the younger one especially."

"Is she? I hadn't noticed." Pike smiled slightly, his second of the day.

* * *

The omnibus dropped Pike off a short walk from the Cartwright residence, one of a row of grand terrace houses fronted with trimmed box hedges in Lyall Street. He stepped back from the front door and looked up, counting five storeys including the servants' attic. The grey of the tall Georgian building seemed to blend in with the grey of the sky.

"Chief Inspector Pike, Scotland Yard," the butler announced as he opened the double doors of the opulent morning room. Lady Helen Cartwright remained seated at her writing desk, her back turned to the door. Pike used the same tactics himself on subordinates who needed reminding of their place. He took off his hat and scarf, thumbed open the buttons of his coat, and pointedly handed the damp items to the butler, whom he suspected had deliberately omitted to take them.

Hugo Cartwright acknowledged Pike's presence with a brief tip of his head, making no effort to move from where he stood warming himself by the fire, coattails lifted.

Despite his considerable height, Cartwright had about him an air of delicacy, enhanced by the fairness of his hair and skin, which would barely require a razor's scrape. His eyelashes were so blond they appeared tipped with snow. If he stood much closer to the fire, Pike feared he might melt.

Pike remained where he was, the butler hovering behind, as if waiting to eject him at the first sign of trouble.

Lady Helen Cartwright finally turned. She wore a gown of black tulle as befitted the mourning of her sister-in-law, Lady Catherine. "What is your business, Inspector?" she asked with a slight rise of her upper lip.

"I would like to speak to your son, please, my lady."

She gestured towards Hugo Cartwright. "Well, there he is."

"Alone, if you please, my lady."

She frowned, stood up from the desk, and glided over to the chesterfield. "That is up to my son—Hugo?" She had not lost her German accent, Pike noticed.

"I have no secrets from my mother, Pike." Cartwright's forthright manner sounded forced. "We both know why you are here. She knows I participated in the women's march, what I witnessed."

Pike looked at the dowager's stern face and glanced back at her son, trying and failing to establish eye contact. "I would prefer to speak to you alone, sir. Some of the matters we need to discuss are of a somewhat delicate nature."

"Very well," Cartwright said with a sigh, which might have been one of relief. "We can talk in the study. Please excuse us, Mother."

Cartwright led the way, showing no ill effects of his alleged trampling by the police horse. In the study, he offered Pike a chair, and pointed to a silver tray, where a set of decanters and glasses was arrayed. Each decanter was topped up to the same level; every glass sparkled. Pike politely refused the offer of Madeira. For himself, Cartwright filled a crystal glass and sat in a studded leather chair opposite, waiting for Pike to speak.

"Mr. Cartwright, it has been brought to my attention that you tried to make a statement to one of the police officers after the riot, but that he failed to file the report."

"That's correct. He didn't even take down my name."

"I am very sorry about that. Perhaps you could give me your statement now."

Pike wrote down Cartwright's story in his notebook; in most respects it confirmed Florence McCleland's account.

"Thank you, sir. Now I would like to show you some photographs." Pike reached into his briefcase. "I was hoping that you might be able to identify the man so that disciplinary action can be taken."

Cartwright stared for a moment at Pike, mouth slightly open. "Yes, yes, of course," he said.

He spent some time leafing through the photographs, pausing every now and then to sip from his glass. In their beehive helmets, even Pike would have had trouble recognising the policemen as individuals. Cartwright finally pointed to a man with a full beard. "That's him."

"Are you positive, sir?"

"Yes, quite sure. I recognise the beard."

"May I ask what you were wearing the day of the riot?" When Cartwright hesitated, Pike added, "If you are unable to remember, we could perhaps talk to your valet."

"That's not necessary. I had on my silk hat and heavy brown coat with fur trim."

Pike tapped the photograph. "That man is Constable First Class Morley, sir. I have found him to be most reliable. He has been in the force for a number of years."

"Then I would suggest he may be getting lazy."

"I happened to speak to him this morning. His version of events is somewhat different to yours."

"It is?"

"He claims he spoke to a man of your description, wearing clothes similar to those you have just described. He was part of the reinforcements sent early in the afternoon when the march first started getting out of hand. Just before he arrived at St. Stephen's entrance, he accosted and questioned a man running in the opposite direction from the trouble. Morley said the man was in a state of panic, begged him to go to the aid of the women, refused to give his name, and then took off at a run before he could be questioned further." Pike glanced down at his notes. " 'As if the very devil himself was after him,' were Morley's words. I would like to suggest that the man was you, and that for reasons known only to yourself, you chose to paint a different picture of events to your friends and your mother."

Hugo put his glass on the side table and stared into the fire. "For the record," Pike continued, "did you actually see Lady Catherine attacked by a policeman—or by anyone else, for that matter?"

Cartwright's reply was barely audible. "No, Chief Inspector, I did not."

Pike held back a sigh of relief. He no more wanted to find a policeman responsible for Lady Catherine's death than Shepherd did. He waited patiently for Cartwright to continue, taking in the large mahogany desk on which stern men and women stared out from silver frames. Cartwright's eyes darted towards them, too. Pike had seen that look more times than he cared to remember: it was the look of a guilty man before judge and jury.

"Something happened to me out there," Cartwright said finally. "Don't ask me what, I have trouble explaining it: the noise, the screams, the lack of control, people behaving like animals. I had to get away. I suppose I just panicked. I was trying to get help for my aunt, I really was . . ." He broke off and looked at Pike, as if inviting some kind of understanding comment. When none came, he left his seat and topped up his Madeira. "What will happen to me now?" he asked, his back still turned.

"Nothing's going to happen to you. This is not a military matter; you will not be shot for cowardice." *Though that is what you deserve*, Pike thought. "Nor will you be charged for making a false statement. You have not, in fact, lied to the police, only to your mother and your friends."

"Need they learn the truth?"

"That is between you and your conscience." Pike regarded the beaten creature before him, feeling no sympathy at all. "But you might wish to consider that the claims you made to your friends have stirred up considerable antipolice sentiment. Moreover, they could have resulted in a police officer being wrongly charged."

"I'm truly sorry, sir." Cartwright put down his glass and reached into the pocket of his morning coat for his wallet, extracting a number of crisp notes. "Look, if I can make up for this in any way, contribute to the police pension fund or whatever it is you call it . . ."

"Put your money away, sir." A man who would abandon a family member—a woman no less—to a riotous mob was beyond contempt, and a man who attempted to bribe a policeman was not much better. Both actions showed a singular lack of honour.

Tears were streaming down Cartwright's face. Pike turned his attention to the leaping flames in the grate, hoping to give the man time to compose himself. The whole situation was embarrassing. Men of Cartwright's cloth were supposed to have better control of their emotions. Hanged if he knew what Cartwright was doing at an hysterical cause like the women's march in the first place—his ghastly mother obviously didn't approve. The suffragettes were an impertinent, troublesome group of women, and much of what they did was just audacious spectacle. Their leaders tended towards too much money, too little common sense, and often more beauty than was good for them. In Pike's estimation, they were certainly not womanly.

He had always pictured the stately Emmeline Pankhurst as the face behind the women's movement. Now the face of a recent visitor to his office leapt into his mind: Florence Mc-Cleland. Just as wilful, but much younger and of even greater beauty.

He shook his head to clear the image and turned back to Cartwright. The young man seemed to be pulling himself together at last.

"Sir," Pike asked, "how well do you know Florence McCleland?"

"Quite well, she is a personal friend. Why do you ask?"

"It is my privilege to be asking the questions, sir. What do the letters *WSPU* stand for?"

A sweep of blond eyelashes. "Umm?"

"What do the colours white, green, and purple represent?"

"Really, Pike, how on earth is this relevant?"

"I put it to you that you do not know the answers because you are not a true supporter of the women's movement. That you joined the march only to ingratiate yourself with Florence McCleland, with whom you wish to become more than friends."

When Cartwright hung his head in defeat, Pike felt the first twinge of compassion for the wretched young man.

Chapter Eleven

No respectable restaurant or hotel would allow the breakfast meeting on their premises, so the WSPU was forced to gather in the draughty hall of an East End workingmen's club. Florence and some of her Bloomsbury members arrived before dawn, setting up the purple, green, and white bunting, the banners, tables, chairs, and abundant vases of flowers. By the time the hall was filled with women and she finally sat down at her own table close to the stage, Florence felt as if she had put in a full day's work.

Beside her, Olivia Barndon-Brown caught her eye and they exchanged smiles of satisfaction for a job well done. "How many have been released this month?" Olivia asked Florence as Miss Jane Lithgow pulled a chair up at the table.

"I've allowed for eight places at the table of honour, though I'm not sure if Lady Constance Lytton is well enough to attend. Her time in prison has left her quite ill," Miss Lithgow answered before Florence could form her reply.

"Olivia and me paid her a call yesterday," Daisy Atkins said, holding her cup up to a waiter pouring tea from a large metal pot. "She's right poorly still, isn't she, Olivia?"

"She is. Still, if she cannot be here, someone else will make the speech to our newly released sisters."

"She'll be here, I don't doubt it. I've never known such a brave woman." Florence nodded her thanks to the waiter as he placed a rack of toast on their table. She wished she could be as brave as Lady Constance. Florence could barely think about her ordeal, let alone talk about it to anyone other than Dody. She wondered if Constance had nightmares, too.

"Will you be joining us this afternoon for pistol practice at the Tottenham Court Road?" Olivia asked Florence, pulling her from her thoughts.

"I'm not sure yet. Dody will be home and I think she has made some plans."

Miss Lithgow raised an elegant, if sardonic, brow.

Florence frowned. Miss Lithgow turned her attention to breakfast. Florence had sworn not to tell a soul about her activities with Dody in the mortuary, but she had come close to it on several occasions, especially when people like Jane Lithgow all but accused her sister of being a traitor to the cause.

Molly Jenkins joined them with kisses all around. "Sorry I'm late, ladies. I wanted to come early to 'elp, but me old man stirred up one 'ell of a fuss, tried to stop me from coming. Look at what he did to me arm." Molly pushed up her sleeve and proudly exposed a mass of purple and red skin. There was a collective gasp from the ladies at the table: her bruises were deemed as much a symbol of heroism as the hunger strike medals many of them wore.

"Pig of a man," Daisy spat.

Olivia raised a cautionary hand. "Quiet, Daisy," she whispered. "Miss Christabel Pankhurst is making her way over here."

Daisy blushed, lowering her eyes, and Olivia gave her hand a reassuring pat.

Florence looked up with admiration as Christabel approached. Like her mother, Christabel was a beauty. They had the same shade of glossy dark hair and the same velvety bloom to their skin, though Christabel's rounder face showed no evidence yet of Emmeline's spectacular cheekbones.

"How are you, Daisy? Are the Bloomsbury ladies looking after you well?" Christabel put her arm around Daisy's child-like shoulders.

Daisy giggled. "Yes, thank you ever so much, miss, everyone is very kind to me."

Christabel greeted each woman at the table by name, taking a moment to add something touching or personal in each case. "Did you make the necessary telephone calls?" she asked when she reached Florence, a mischievous smile adding a cheeky lilt to her voice.

Florence smiled back. "Yes, and I think we'll get the response we're looking for. The secretary of the men's antisuffrage league was incensed that we should be using the premises of a working-men's club—I'm sure there will be a protest at the very least."

"Splendid."

"I just picked up Lord Curzon's latest pamphlet, 'Against Female Suffrage—The Unsexing of Women,'" Miss Lithgow said to the table at large. "He declares that those who join us will become thinner, dark-featured, lank, and dry." There was a burst of laughter and Florence's gaze strayed to the thin and dark-featured Miss Treylen, who was sitting next to Molly. She wasn't laughing, hadn't managed a smile for anyone except Christabel since her arrival. Working in an office would make anyone crusty and dry, Florence thought, then immediately felt ashamed. She was well aware of how Miss Treylen struggled to make ends meet, often forfeiting a day's wages to sell their newspaper. She had sold more copies of *Votes for Women* than the rest of them put together.

Florence's uncharitable thoughts transferred from Miss Treylen to Miss Lithgow. The woman always had to have her say, didn't she? She couldn't help feeling that Miss Lithgow deliberately set out to upstage her. Lord Curzon's pamphlet was old news; it had been discussed weeks ago when Catherine sent a brilliant retaliatory letter to *The Times*. Catherine. Florence allowed her gaze to stray to the place setting laid in honour of Catherine and felt a visceral wrench of grief. "I'll make it up to you, somehow," she whispered to herself.

Christabel and Florence resumed their conversation. "I telephoned several newspapers, too," Florence said. "I told them we would be starting an hour later than we actually are, so we can at least have our breakfast and attend to business before any trouble starts."

"You are a wonderful lieutenant, Florence. I don't know what the union would ever do without you. Perhaps you would like to say a few words outside the hall after breakfast?"

Florence felt the heat rise in her face and hoped her blush wasn't as obvious as Daisy's had been. While her respect for Christabel was boundless, she liked to think she wasn't quite as enslaved as Daisy Atkins. "Certainly, if you want me to,

Christabel." She crossed the fingers of one hand and hoped the trouble would start before the terrifying opportunity of speaking in public arose.

"Calling the newspapers was a splendid idea, Christabel," Olivia said. "There can never be enough martyrs for the cause." Then her eyes, too, fell on the empty place setting as a momentary hush settled on the table.

Christabel broke the silence and asked Florence, "How are your other plans progressing?"

"Perfectly, we have set a date for next week."

"Splendid." Christabel paused. "I don't want to throw cold water on you, dear Florence, but I hope you remember my instructions."

Florence glanced at the faces around the table and lowered her head. "Yes: I am not allowed to let myself be arrested."

"My lieutenants are far too important. I need every one of you on the outside of the bars for the time being."

At that moment a tremendous cry of welcome arose from the gathered suffragettes. Led by the visibly ailing Lady Constance Lytton, a group of seven women was being escorted to the stage. All seven wore dresses in the suffragette colours: white for purity in public and private life, purple for dignity, and green for hope. Christabel excused herself and rushed to take Constance's arm.

"Don't look so gloomy, Flo," Olivia said beside her. "You've been arrested enough; it's time the rest of us did our bit." Olivia must have taken her look of shameful relief at Christabel's instructions to be one of disappointment, and Florence did nothing to right her friend's misapprehension.

On the stage, Christabel introduced the women individually, giving a short account of their exploits and imprisonment, before they had their hunger strike medals presented by Mrs. Pankhurst. When the ceremony was completed and the medal recipients settled at their table of honour, Christabel lifted her hands for the members to stand and observe a minute's silence for Lady Catherine Cartwright and the two other women who had made the ultimate sacrifice for the cause. There followed eulogies to the three women, during which most of the audience audibly wept.

When the tears were dried, Mrs. Pankhurst began to speak. Her oratory gripped each woman like a fist, and her face shone with a radiance that seemed to light the stage. Everyone leaned towards the stage as if pulled by invisible strings, hoping to catch their share of her light.

"As the government is refusing to yield on female suffrage," Mrs. Pankhurst concluded her speech, "we have no choice but to adopt more aggressive forms of militancy!"

Florence's heart skipped a beat, and the women roared. Mrs. Pankhurst allowed the noise to continue for a full minute before raising her arms for silence. "But there must not be a cat or a canary killed. Our own lives and our own lives alone will be sacrificed for the cause!" More applause. *She plays the audience like a magician*, Florence thought. *We are all mesmerised by her.*

Now she introduced Lady Constance Lytton. Of aristocratic birth, Mrs. Pankhurst explained, Constance had joined the WSPU the previous year and been jailed for her part in a violent demonstration outside the House of Commons. Because of her high social status, she was classed as a Division One prisoner, which meant she was kept in comparative luxury, well fed, and allowed to wear her own clothes. The next time she was arrested, she had dressed herself as a working-class woman and gave a false name to the police. Sentenced this time as a Division Three prisoner, no more than a common criminal, she was kept in a cell resembling an animal's den and dressed in prison clothes. Upon refusing her ration of cabbage soup and stale bread, she was force-fed eight times. When her identity was finally discovered, she was released, but as a result of her brutal treatment on top of an existing heart condition, she had suffered ill health ever since.

Mrs. Pankhurst turned to the other women on the stage. "Lady Lytton has suffered what you have suffered. If she is feeling strong enough, I hope she will say a few words to our gathering."

Constance Lytton inclined her head in assent and the women roared their appreciation. "I commend your bravery, all of you," she said, not getting up from her chair. "It is a terrible thing you have been through."

Florence knew what was coming, what Lady Lytton was about to say next. She wanted to block her ears or leave the room, but that would draw attention to herself. She tried to focus on other things, the colourful spray of flowers on the table, the odour of freshly brewed tea, the exciting plans for next week.

"The reality surpassed all that I had anticipated." For all her efforts, Florence could not block out Lady Lytton's words. "It was a living nightmare of pain, horror, and revolting degradation. The sense of being strangled, suffocated by the thrust of the large rubber tube, which arouses great irritation in the throat and nausea in the stomach. The anguish and effort of retching whilst the tube is forcibly pressed back into the stomach, and the natural resistance of the body restrained, defy description . . ."

Florence could feel the tube in her own throat and in her

nose, the writhing of her body. The nausea began to rise. Her eardrums felt as if they were bursting. A sharp pain pierced her breast. Her eyes flickered around the room to her companions, knowing that several had endured similar experiences. But their expressions remained beatific, like the martyred saints of the Roman Catholic Church. *Does no one else feel it as I do?* she wondered.

O utside the workingmen's club, a small crowd was gathering. The sharp bite of the air, coupled with several cups of strong tea, had revived Florence's spirits. So far everything had gone to plan. The public meeting was about to begin, and the press would be arriving within minutes. They'd chosen this location—a common yard bordered on three sides by the hall, the boundaries of a pickle factory, and a brewery—deliberately, knowing that most of the workers in those establishments were against the cause.

Men and women congregated outside the factory gates ready for the change in shift, stamping their feet to keep warm, speaking wryly to one another as Florence's colleagues hoisted the banner. One man guffawed as he read the black-lettered legend: WE DEMAND VOTES FOR WOMEN.

Florence made her way through the chaffing, jostling horde, handing out pamphlets. "Leaflets! 'Citizenship of Women,' by Mr. Kier Hardie, 'The Prison Experience of Miss—'"

"Oi," a beery-looking artisan interrupted, pointing to Christabel as she mounted a vegetable crate next to the banner. "Is that the woman the papers are full of?"

Florence favoured the man with her most charming smile.

"Miss Christabel Pankhurst, yes indeed!" at which the man spat on the ground, barely missing her shoes.

Undeterred, Florence continued to hand out pamphlets while Christabel addressed the crowd amidst volleys of interruption and abuse.

"Friends," Christabel began. The crowd hooted. She went on as if she had received sincere applause, telling the crowd several things they would not have known, that, among other matters, the meeting had been called to pass a censure on the government.

The crowd laughed and booed.

"And to express our sympathy for the brave women . . ."

The staccato cries from the audience dissolved into a general hoot.

". . . sympathy for the brave women who are still in prison."

"Serves 'em right!"

Most of Christabel's speech was drowned out in the catcalling before it reached Florence's ears. And then Christabel was beckoning her to step upon the wobbling fruit crate. Florence hesitated, her heart pounding. *Courage, mon brave*, she said to herself. *You* can *do this*.

Someone nudged her in the back. It was Olivia. "Go on, Flo." She pushed a path for Florence through the crowd and then helped her onto the crate beside Christabel.

Florence clutched the bundle of leaflets to her chest and gazed upon the hostile mob. "What shall I say?" she whispered to Christabel. "I have nothing prepared."

"Say whatever you like." Christabel squeezed Florence's arm. "They're not listening anyway. Consider this practice."

"Oh, Lord. All right then." Florence frantically tried to gather her thoughts while Christabel introduced her.

"From a fine family of social campaigners, she has more than enough credentials to address you. I give you Miss Florence McCleland."

Above the noise of the crowd, Florence heard Olivia's distinctive whoop.

Florence took a breath and raised her voice. "Men and women of England—"

"Get a husband!" someone yelled.

Christabel nudged her in the ribs. "Louder."

"Men and women of England! We live in a man-made and a man-ruled world. Its laws are men's standards and formed by men. Since women, because of their sex, are barred from voting, we are denied all power in shaping or moulding our own environment, or that of our children. Men regard women as a servant class, and we are going to remain as such until we get the vote and lift ourselves out of it."

"The vote is the reward for defending the country," called a scathing voice.

Ah, good, she knew the answer to that. "No it's not," Florence said triumphantly. "Soldiers and sailors don't vote."

"Then it means fitness for military service."

"There is no law of nature that says women aren't fit for military service. Look at the Boer women—and the Russians. A woman can pull a trigger as well as a man, even though she is not so brutishly strong."

"Why, a woman can't never 'it nuffin!"

"Well, we jolly well throw our stones straight, don't we? When a women sees everything she loves threatened, you will be surprised how quickly she can learn the art of war."

The suffragettes in the crowd cheered louder than their antagonists. Florence had found her wings and was enjoying every minute of the flight. Moving her gaze around the crowd, she responded to their objections, addressing her words to particular individuals as she caught their eyes. She noticed two men in suits setting up a camera in a corner of the yard. Excellent. Then she glimpsed a woman pickle worker pass a crate of tomatoes over the factory railings. Good. The fruit would soon be flying, which meant the photographs would be even better than she had hoped.

Chapter Twelve

Duties at the New Women's Hospital and inclement weather both played their part in delaying Dody's tests. Two days had elapsed since her clandestine activities in the cadaver keep, and she was anxious to make up for lost time.

She had trouble keeping her patience as Fletcher, their coachman, stocky frame lumbering around their backyard, never quite got the gist of her instructions. He heaved the tool bench from the stick-house and placed it in front of the coal chute.

Dody suppressed a sigh. "Not there, Fletcher, you've hardly left room to swing a cat—closer to the servants' privy, please, towards the back wall." With much sweating and grunting, he dragged the bench across the mossy cobbles, until finally he had it placed in a suitable position. Here there would be plenty of room for him to swing each of the possible murder weapons: half a brick, a belaying pin, a piece of wood measuring four-by-two, and the policeman's "borrowed" truncheon.

"The first one, if you please, Fletcher," Dody said.

She sensed movement from the house next door. A sash window rattled open and a maid appeared, shaking out a floral bedspread. Pausing in her work, the maid watched as Fletcher removed a pig's head from a bulging sack resting against the stick-house wall. *Lord*, Dody thought, *don't let this be the start of more complaints from the neighbours.* Florence's steady stream of exuberant visitors had led to more protestations than she cared to remember. She prayed that this time they would not call the police.

Fletcher secured the pig's head firmly to the bench with a clamp, its snout to the back wall.

"All right, Fletcher, you know what you have to do."

"As 'ard as I can, miss?" Fletcher asked Dody with a some-what worrying gleam of excitement to his eye.

"Precisely—four sharp blows with the brick." Dody stepped back towards the scullery door and opened her umbrella. Fletcher picked up the brick. "On the count of three, if you please: one, two, three!"

The first blow hit the back of the skull with a hard, moist crack. Upon the second, bone and grey matter flew in all directions.

The sash window next door slammed shut.

By the third blow, the head was a pulverised mess with barely any flesh left upon the clamp for Fletcher to bludgeon.

"You can stop now," Dody said, shaking gristle and bone from her umbrella. "You're hitting much too hard, there's hardly anything left for me to examine."

"I did buy extra, miss."

"Good. Use the brick again, but not so hard this time."

Dody sensed movement from the scullery door behind her. She held up her hand for Fletcher to wait and stepped aside for Florence. Her sister appeared flushed and hatless, her hair dishevelled and her coat stained with what, on closer inspection, looked like tomato pulp. "Oh, Dody," she said between excited breaths, "you should have been there; we've had the most marvellous time! After our meeting there was a mob waiting for us—mostly men but some women, too—all behaving abominably. Christabel asked me to speak—can you believe it? I think I managed all right, too; really roused them up, and the newspapermen came and it was all photographed—we must pray the papers publish the pictures.

"And, oh, you should have seen Olivia! A particularly obnoxious brute attacked poor Daisy and stole her new straw bonnet. Olivia was marvellous, launched herself at the brute like a lioness defending her young and scratched him down the face with her nails."

"Sounds a little overzealous to me," Dody said with concern.

Florence did not seem to hear the comment, drew a quick breath. "Oh, and I called in on Hugo on my way home to see how he was and tell him all about the rally. That beastly chief inspector interviewed him, you know, and made him retract his statement about witnessing Catherine's beating—he was quite threatening apparently. Now more than ever we have to discover the truth . . ."

Florence stopped short, having finally noticed the carnage

in the yard before her. She took some brisk steps back and pressed herself against the scullery door. "Good God." She spotted a pig's ear at her feet and her hand rose to her mouth. "Now I can see why Annie didn't want me to come out here—Dody, you've turned the place into a slaughterhouse!"

"How else did you expect me to conduct my experiments? I need to compare the effect of blows to these pigs' heads with Catherine's head injuries, to see if I can match them to a specific weapon. Identifying the weapon might help us to identify the killer."

"Have you tried the truncheon yet?"

"Only the brick, and so far that was inconclusive."

"Well, I hope it's worth all this, this . . . mess."

Dody smiled. "Don't worry. When we're finished, Fletcher will clean up the scraps and give them to Cook to make into her delicious jellied pork brawn." She could not resist teasing her younger sister.

Florence paled. "Mr. Shaw is right, perhaps we should all become vegetarians."

"Fiddlesticks. Meat strengthens the blood. You have enough causes on your plate."

Florence swept her arm around the yard. "Can your experiments really tell us what we need to know?"

"I think so. Ideally, tests should be carried out on human skulls, but as I am not yet ready to add grave robbing to my résumé, pig skulls will have to do. A pig's skull is more robust than a human's, so what I have surmised so far is that the person delivering the fatal blows did not inflict anywhere near such damage as Fletcher, who pulverised the head with three blows alone."

"So the killer was not as strong as Fletcher?"

"Either that or he acted with more restraint. After all, it happened in the midst of a large crowd, and one must imagine a murderer would try to be as inconspicuous as possible. And of course, it may not have been intended as murder. Really, so much is supposition. At the most, this will eliminate some of the potential weapons and I am afraid that is all we can realistically hope for." She turned to Fletcher. "Clamp the next head, please. And this time I want four blows with the brick again, only not as hard."

Movement at the scullery door suggested they were to have more company. Not the neighbour's manservant in complaint, Dody prayed, but it was Annie. The maid covered her eyes and handed Dody a note then beat a hasty retreat. Ignoring Florence's raised eyebrows, Dody quickly glanced at the note and placed it in her coat pocket.

Fletcher flicked the remaining scraps of tissue and bone off the clamp. Before affixing the next head, he held it in his hands and stared into the pig's blue eyes with a smile.

"Oh my goodness," Florence exclaimed, turning her back upon the proceedings. "I'm not sure what is more disturbing, the blood and gore or Fletcher's obvious relish of it. I need a bath and a change of clothes. Let me know when you're finished."

Dody smiled at her sister. "Off you go then."

But Florence remained where she was. "That note," she said with a mischievous smile. "I couldn't help noticing the Home Office stationery. Another summons by your hero, perhaps?"

To tease was obviously not only an older sister's prerogative. Dody stalked across the slime-covered cobbles towards the clamped pig's head. Taking the brick from the coachman, she slammed it onto the cranium herself, barely pitting it. "Just a bit harder than that, please, Fletcher," she said, handing the brick back to him and dusting off her hands. She did not turn around until she heard the soft click of the scullery door.

Chapter Thirteen

The cabbie dropped Dody off at the Offord Road rank; already the crowd had gathered outside Pentonville Prison, where Dr. Crippen was due to be executed this morning. The sun's weak rays had yet to penetrate the bank of mist surrounding the prison, and while she could hear the crowd, she could see very little but blurred shapes and lanterns held high, blinking like animal eyes.

The mob was fractious; there was tension in the air. "It ain't right, is it, dear?" an old woman said to her in passing. "They've no right to keep us out, not tell us straightaway that it's 'appened—'angings should be public, they always was."

Dody gathered from the murmurings in the crowd that there would be no death knell to announce Crippen's passing. The crowd would have to make do with the lowered black flag and a printed announcement nailed to the prison door—a disappointing finale for such a sensational murder investigation.

No one stood aside as Dody approached the gateway, and she was forced to elbow her way through the crush. She tried to catch the eye of a policeman holding the crowd back from the prison entrance, but he paid her no heed, distracted by a conversation with two men standing before him.

"But did 'e really do it, that's what I want to know—what do you reckon, mate?" One of the men was asking.

"I'm not in a position to say what I think," the policeman replied stiffly.

"They say the Home Office has had letters from Cora Crippen from America. So, if she's livin' in America, 'ow the hell can they be 'er remains what they dug up in the cellar? It were only one fillet of flesh, after all."

"How can a dunderhead like you say he's innocent, when the best brains in the country say 'e's guilty?" the other man chimed in.

Innocent or guilty, it was a controversial topic and another reason feelings were running high. The policeman said no more to the men and cast a worried look over the crowd, as if at any minute he was expecting an outbreak of violence.

"Move along, you two." A second policeman joined the first and together the two officers elbowed the men towards the edge of the police line. Dody managed to squeeze herself into their vacated space only a few yards away from the prison door.

She called out to a poker-faced prison guard at the gate, waving her letter of authorisation until she finally attracted his attention. He took her note and began to read it aloud. She snatched the note back from the guard before he could broadcast her business further, though it appeared that the damage had already been done. A number of grey men wielding notebooks descended upon her, shoving and bumping one another in their haste.

"You are to assist with the Crippen autopsy, miss?"

"May we have your name?"

"Will you honour me with an exclusive? I guarantee my paper pays well."

"Sir, please let me in!" Dody pleaded with the guard; the crowd pressed against her and she was having difficulty getting air into her—she should never have given in and let Annie squeeze her into the corset this morning. The smell of damp wool from the dirty coats around her made her want to retch.

"Make way, police!" The voice carried an edge of authority lacking in the uniformed officers. Despite their boos and hisses, the crowd parted and Dody soon found herself on the other side of the prison gate, standing in a broad passage and gazing into the stern face of Chief Inspector Pike. She hastily let go of his arm.

"It would have been more prudent, Dr. McCleland, for you to have taken the back entrance," he said.

She waved the tattered note, hoping he did not notice how it trembled in her hand. "My instructions mentioned nothing of a back entrance."

His expression softened. "The press are no better than a school of feeding sharks—may I?" Before she had composed herself enough to answer, he had taken the note from her hand and read it. "You are to observe the autopsy conducted by the prison doctor," he said, "and take head measurements for the phrenological society?" He looked perplexed. Dody adjusted her hat. "Phrenology is the study of the relationship of a person's character to the shape of his skull."

"I am aware of that, Doctor, but I thought the science well and truly disproved."

"I think Dr. Spilsbury is humouring an acquaintance."

"With you as his instrument?"

"I am to observe the autopsy only, but while I am there, I may as well be of assistance if I can."

"You have arrived somewhat early. The execution is still an hour away, with the autopsy not performed for an hour after that at least."

"I thought it prudent to educate myself in the procedure." A crow, striding about at the end of the passageway, stopped and gave her a beady brown eye.

"You wish to witness the execution?"

"I have been granted no such permission, but I hope to inspect the scaffold and find out everything I can about it. Would you be so kind as to find me a prison guard willing to serve as escort and to tell me how it is done?"

"I doubt there is a guard to spare on execution day. But as I have also arrived early, I will be happy to oblige." A number of emotions might explain the look on his face, though none of them suggested happiness. Doubt, sadness, disgust, maybe. He offered his arm with the formality of an undertaker. "Allow me."

He must think me a ghoul, thought Dody.

They walked across the exercise yard towards B Wing, the ripe smell of the nearby cattle yard and slaughterhouse reaching them on the wind.

"Since the abolition of public hangings," Pike said, "the law requires executions to be performed in sheds like this." He pointed to a narrow, roofed structure. "Commonly called the 'topping shed.' It's built over a deep pit into which the body will drop. They store the prison motor wagon in the pit when it's not being used."

How practical, thought Dody. There was nothing sacred about life here.

Pike held open the door of the shed for her, and she entered the wood-panelled room with a trepidation she was determined not to show.

Her determination won through even when Pike spoke of long drops and short drops—all dependent on the prisoner's weight—and the fine line a hangman must walk between decapitation and slow strangulation. Then, before she knew it, he was asking her in a low voice, "How did your experiments go with regards to Lady Catherine's head wounds?"

Her heart missed a beat—he must have guessed the reason why she had borrowed the truncheon, and her presence outside the mortuary. Had Alfred spoken after all? Exactly what else did Pike know? She was relieved to see the arrival of two gentleman of the press, who stopped at the wooden rail a short distance away from her and Pike.

After nodding the men a solemn greeting, Pike repeated his question quietly but this time he added, "You have my word that your research will not be broadcast by me. While I cannot condone your actions, nor act upon any unsolicited findings, I might be able to use them as a discreet guide to aid me in my investigations." He broke off and nodded to another group of men positioning themselves next to the other spectators.

An elderly man caught Dody's eye and approached her, introducing himself as Wilson, the prison doctor. His eyes kept darting away towards the other men at the rail, and as soon as it was decorous to do so, he excused himself and left her.

Pulling out his watch, Pike said, "Not long now. The

execution party will be gathering. Soon they will be arriving at the condemned cell, where they will pinion the prisoner's arms to a leather belt and march him across the exercise yard to the topping shed. The procedure is performed speedily," Pike went on, "for the sake of humanitarian principles. The final stage can take less than a minute."

Less than a minute once the procedure was under way, but what of all the preceding long days and dark nights, Dody thought. They didn't bear contemplation.

She bit the inside of her cheek and firmed her resolve. "The man took a life. It is only right that he should pay for it with his own."

When Pike failed to reply, she opted for a return to their previous conversation; while uncomfortable, it was not as distressing. "I will tell you about my experiments on the pro-vision, as you say, that my findings are used with discretion and as a guide only." With a clunk of wood on wood, the assistant hangman tested the trap door. The sudden noise made them both start. Over the railing she glimpsed the edge of a brick-lined pit before the door was slammed shut once more.

"Indeed, in legal matters I believe that science should only ever be used as a guide, not a decree," Pike said. "Science is as fallible as anything else; mistakes can be made—how not?—a scientist is still a human being."

"Without a doubt, Chief Inspector"—Dody could not help the smug satisfaction that had crept into her voice—"but sci-ence is the proven victor in the Crippen case."

Pike turned to Dody. In a voice she had to strain to hear, he said, "Is it?"

Dody kept her gaze on the trap door. "Explain yourself, sir."

Pike paused to consider his answer before saying, "Excuse

me for a minute." He left her side and approached a gentleman wearing a shiny top hat with whom he spoke for a few
moments. Upon his return, he said, "I have secured permission
with the prison governor for you to remain in attendance for
the execution, should you wish it. This might present an even
better opportunity for you to, er, further your education."

Holding his gaze, she saw the spark of challenge in his
deep blue eyes. He was testing her; she couldn't leave now.
She couldn't afford to keep losing face with this man whose
path she would undoubtedly cross again. Just the memory of
meeting him outside the mortuary that night made her blanch.

Her hesitation must have led him to think she did not wish
to remain. "Allow me to escort you back to the main building then, Doctor. If we delay it much longer, we may pass the
execution party in the exercise yard."

Dody took a bolstering breath. "I wish to witness the
execution."

Pike's expression told her this was not the answer he had
expected. "As you wish, but I warn you, it is not a pleasant
experience, especially for a woman."

"I am sure it cannot be a pleasant experience for anyone to
witness, regardless of sex." Dody said no more, but continued
to look him levelly in the eye until he broke away to nod at the
prison governor. The manner in which the governor raised
his eyes to the ceiling made Dody wonder if she was the first
woman to be granted this dubious honour.

When the shed door opened a little while later, Dody shivered in the sudden icy draught. Within moments the execution
party had mounted the scaffold. What happened next was so
swift Dody barely had a chance to take it in. The chief execu-
tioner, a man with a squirrel-tail moustache, placed a white

hood over the condemned man's head and guided his feet to chalk markings on the platform. The noose was positioned, the simple slipknot snug against the left side of his neck. For a few seconds Crippen stood trembling in collarless street clothes next to a murmuring Roman Catholic priest. And then with a slam of the lever, he was gone. Dody gave an involuntary gasp, as if her own heart and breath had stopped also.

A sigh escaped all those present.

For a long aching moment the swinging rope was the only movement in the shed.

Dody stepped back from the rail. Pike remained rigid, as if standing to attention. And then she noticed that his eyes were closed—was he praying? Had he watched at all? A shiver rippled through his body and then he, too, stepped back from the rail. Taking out his handkerchief, he wiped a sheen of perspiration from his face. "There now, Doctor," he said, his northern accent more pronounced, she noticed. "Are you convinced that you have witnessed the satisfactory implementation of justice?"

The more she got to know this man, the more he perplexed her. Dody forced her weight into her legs to stop her knees from shaking. "For a policeman, you seem strangely averse to capital punishment," she said, working to keep her voice steady. The execution had affected her even more than she had imagined it would.

"Only when there is an element of doubt."

Dody let out a breath. "In this case there is no doubt. The lump of flesh under the cellar floor belonged to Cora Crippen. The hysterectomy scar was quite unmistakable. But this is not the time or the place for me to give you a lecture in forensic science, Chief Inspector."

"You do not need to patronise me, Doctor. I might not

understand the science, but I know about the investigation; indeed I was closely involved with it. One of the questions I raised was, how could a man who had so cunningly disposed of all but one of the body parts, be so careless with the hiding of the torso?"

"Criminals often become overconfident when they think they have got away with the crime," Dody replied. Then she flushed. Of course he knew that.

"Yes," Pike said sarcastically, "that was pointed out to me. But I also know a fair trial when I see one. The defence was quite incompetent, at the mercy of Dr. Spilsbury—he's quite the showman, you know, with his red carnation in his button-hole. He played the jury like a theatre crowd . . ." He stopped abruptly, seeing the heat flaming her cheeks. "Forgive me, he is your colleague, I shouldn't have said that."

Tempted as she was to fire back a long list of police bungles, she held back. When it came to the trial, she might be ignorant of the legal minutiae, but she was proudly intimate with all the forensic details. Crippen was guilty and justice had been met; there was no doubt in her mind about it at all.

She also knew professional jealousy when she saw it.

With tightened lips she turned her heel on Pike and joined the men filing towards the shed door.

"Wait," Pike held her back. "Where are you going now?"

"Into the pit to inspect the body," Dody said coolly.

He shook his head. "Protocol dictates the body hang alone unattended for an hour before it is cut down."

"Why?" As soon as the word was uttered, she realised it was a question she should not have voiced. Her hand went to her mouth as if she might snatch it back.

"To make sure he is dead, Doctor," Pike said softly.

Her knees buckled and suddenly there was no air in her lungs. She let Pike take her by the arm and escort her to the prison officers' canteen, where he revived her with a mug of sweet, milky tea. The room was large and draughty and they sat close to the potbellied stove.

"I shouldn't have expressed my views about the trial or Dr. Spilsbury so strongly to you, nor been so blunt about the body in the pit. I apologise if I was the cause of your distress," Pike said. "I'm Yorkshire born and bred and tend to speak my mind. This is not the first time I've got myself into trouble for it."

Dody accepted his apology with a faint smile and turned her face to warm the other cheek. "My sister often accuses me of possessing a sharp tongue; I, too, overreacted. I was very busy in Edinburgh, I missed much of the press coverage of the trial, so I know little of what went on in the court, although I do support Dr. Spilsbury's findings completely."

"No matter about the newspapers' accounts, they weren't always accurate." Dody heard Pike's boots scuffing against the floor under their table. Now they had made their awkward peace, the silence seemed to stretch interminably before them.

"But I did read about the ocean chase and that Crippen's lover had disguised herself as a boy. Oh, and the Marconigram sent by the ship's captain to Inspector Dew in London." Dody's calculated brevity had the desired effect. Pike stirred his tea with enthusiasm, tinkling the spoon on the side of the mug when he'd finished.

"The first criminal to be captured through wireless telegraphy," he said with a satisfaction that made her wonder if it was he who had initiated it.

"I can tell you hold much admiration for new technology,

but it puzzles me that you seem to have such an inherent suspicion of medicine—of forensic science anyway. Tell me, Chief Inspector, do you feel the same way about all medical scientists as you do about Dr. Spilsbury?"

He lifted his mug and spoke from behind it. Dody suspected that what he was about to say would not be the truth, or not the complete truth. "On the contrary, I have a lot of respect for the profession," he said.

"And female doctors?" she asked with the slightest of smiles.

"I have not known any until now." Pike paused and then said, "On the scaffold, you were about to tell me the results of your tests."

"How did you know about the tests?"

"Deductive reasoning, as Mr. Holmes would say." It was Pike's turn to smile. The even features of a handsome man shone briefly through his worn countenance. Dody relaxed, felt her strength returning. A policeman who could laugh at himself was not all bad, surely. If only she could loosen her corset—it was the constriction that had caused the near fainting spell, she didn't doubt it.

"The borrowed truncheon was the first indication that you were up to something," Pike said, "and then there was your night visit to the mortuary. Poor Alfred admitted to leaving you alone in the cadaver keep for at least thirty minutes."

"You bullied it out of him, I suppose?" Dody could not help herself. She wanted to trust this man, and she had to make the effort to trust the police in general if she wanted to work for the Home Office. But it was a challenge to undo a lifetime of conditioning in a matter of just days.

"And then there was a complaint about your man battering

pigs' heads at your address. It didn't need Sherlock Holmes to deduce what that was all about."

Dody adjusted her seat and smoothed her skirts. "I ruled out the brick and the wooden beam; there were no triangular indentations in the skull at all. As I suspected, Dr. Mangini's report was totally inaccurate. Lady Catherine's injuries were caused by a truncheon or a belaying pin."

"But you cannot tell which?"

"Unfortunately the weapons caused identical pitting to the skull."

Pike lowered his eyes. "So I might still be looking for a murdering policeman."

"I believe Hugo Cartwright retracted his statement."

"He did."

"Under threat of violence, I heard."

Pike looked up. "Violence? Who told you that?"

"Hugo told my sister."

Pike climbed to his feet in the manner of a man whose patience had finally run out. "Believe what you wish to believe, Dr. McCleland. I hope you find that today's experiences contribute satisfactorily to your *further education*." With that, he tipped her a small bow and left the room.

Chapter Fourteen

The body, not yet cold, lay on a table in the prison mortuary. Dody had been present when it was cut down in the pit, had witnessed Dr. Wilson putting his stethoscope to the chest and pronouncing the time of death. Even after a clean hanging, he explained, the heart could continue to beat for up to ten minutes.

In his professional capacity, Wilson was more willing to share his experiences than his earlier manner had boded. His tone remained pleasant and conversational. He even offered her a cigarette, which she refused in favour of her pipe. The odours in the prison mortuary weren't as bad as the hospital morgue, but the smooth smoke in her lungs was still preferable to the scratch of carbolic. Besides, the pipe had become an enjoyable habit and one she sometimes had trouble resisting.

Dody carried out her tasks as assistant, laying out an assortment of surgical instruments, sponges, enamel bowls, and specimen jars within easy reach of the mortuary table. With Wilson's permission, she took her tape measure from her bag—the same she had used to measure Lady Catherine's wounds—and recorded the head measurements for the phrenological society.

"Did Crippen make any last-minute confession, Doctor?" she asked as they began to remove the dead man's clothing.

"To my knowledge, no. I believe he maintained his innocence to the very end."

Dody felt something crackle in the top pocket of Crippen's suit jacket. She drew out a woman's photograph.

"His lover, Ethel Le Neve," Wilson explained. "Chief Inspector Pike had it delivered to him at the condemned cell a few days ago. Put it somewhere safe, will you? His last wish was for it to be buried with him."

Dody placed the photograph on top of the pile of clothing: suit, shirt, socks, undershirt, and drawers.

"The poor man was in quite a state last night," Wilson continued. "He tried to end it himself, you know, broke a lens from his spectacles and attempted to slit his wrists with it. Lucky the guard entered when he did. Make a note of these lacerations, please, Doctor." Wilson peeled back a dressing from Crippen's wrist to expose two bloodless incisions. "A fellow mustn't be allowed to cheat the hangman, eh, what?" he added in a jocular tone.

Dody said nothing; she would not be drawn into personal opinions. So far she had even managed to avoid looking squarely into the dead man's grey face. "Inspect the man's drawers, please, Doctor," Wilson said.

Knowing the reason for the task, she carried out her orders without distaste. Faeces and excess urine might indicate prolonged distress. Every minor detail must be recorded to provide evidence that the execution had been carried out as humanely as possible, so that any mistakes made might be prevented in the next. Semen would indicate ejaculation at the time of death, a common occurrence when the spinal cord is snapped.

Wilson pointed to the dead man's flaccid penis. "No priapism," he dictated to Dody.

His gaze travelled to the top of the body. "This isn't as clean as some, though. The hangman could have done a better job. No doubt we will find considerable damage to the bony as well as the soft structures of the neck—the drop was too long, in my opinion. I will have to note it in my report. The hangman, Mr. Ellis, will not be pleased; he takes considerable pride in his work. Help me turn him, please, Doctor."

Dody placed her hands upon the cooling skin and heaved. The body groaned as air was forced from the lungs. The buttocks and shoulders showed the beginning of lividity where the table had pressed.

Once more Wilson drew Dody's attention to the neck area, then asked her to pass him the scalpel. "Spilsbury would have liked a full autopsy, but time is against us," he said. "I'm afraid we won't be able to make use of those specimen jars. He should have done this himself, or pulled a few more strings. My budget does not extend to full autopsy when the cause of death is so obvious."

"Dr. Spilsbury is still on leave, sir."

"Ah, that explains his absence. In any other forensic pathologist, absence might betray a reluctance to perform a postmortem on a criminal his evidence had condemned—but not Spilsbury."

Wilson sliced through the skin and dissected the muscles of the neck, exposing the spine. The man knew his job, Dody did not doubt it, despite the awkward angle of the scalpel between his blunt fingers and the slight tremble of his coarse hand. She could not help comparing Wilson's style to Dr. Spilsbury's ambidextrous elegance with the knife. The difference was like that between a competent colliery band and the London Symphony Orchestra.

"Ah, observe, Doctor. It is as I suspected, fracture of third cervical vertebrae and dislocation."

When Dody failed to answer, Wilson waved the scalpel over the incision area. "I am expected to state my findings at the inquest within the hour, no time for much more. Any questions, Dr. McCleland?"

Dody shook her head. Wilson's comments about Spilsbury's lack of scruples had provoked an uncomfortable train of thought. She had been trained to save lives, not be responsible for taking them. But surely, the opposing voice in her head reasoned, the forensic pathologist was no more responsible for sending a man to his death than the arresting police officer, the judge, or the jury. If only she'd thought to remind Pike of this when he made his remarks about her *further education*.

"Are you feeling unwell, Doctor?" Wilson asked.

"I'm feeling quite well, thank you," she said, regaining her focus. "I hope that when you next perform a judicial postmortem, you might allow me to assist you again. I feel that it has helped very much with my continuing education."

"Splendid! You have been a most able assistant, I would be delighted!" Wilson said, smiling broadly beneath his bushy white moustache.

Chapter Fifteen

Pike shuffled the last batch of surveillance photographs aside. His concentration had begun to flag and he could not stop his thoughts from drifting to the slight, dark-haired autopsy surgeon; the delicate pucker of her brow when she was in thought, the curve of her mouth when she smiled, which seemed all the more valuable for the rarity of it.

What they had witnessed together in Pentonville, while not as horrific as some events he had seen on a battlefield, had still been confronting. Was it because of the persistent feeling he had that Crippen might be innocent? Yet he felt he could trust Dorothy McCleland's professional judgement; perhaps there was no mistake in the forensic conclusions that Spilsbury had drawn. Although she seemed as spellbound as everyone else by the man.

Whatever the reason for his own distress, the doctor, for the most part, had remained controlled and detached. Had

Pike not seen for himself her reaction to the possibility that the hanged man might have continued to writhe alone and unattended in the pit, he would have taken her to possess a heart of stone. They had formed a bond that even their acrimonious separation could not alter. He shuddered that their newfound intimacy should be founded on something so terrible.

His thoughts were thankfully interrupted when Sergeant Fisher entered his office.

Pike leaned back in his desk chair. "How are your investigations going, Sergeant?" he asked Fisher. "Have you found anyone who might have hated Lady Catherine enough to want her dead?" Other than a blood-frenzied bobby, he prayed.

Fisher shrugged. "She certainly stepped on a few toes, sir; she was quite outspoken in her views."

"The WSPU women have many different viewpoints, all of them extreme. How was Lady Catherine different? Did she anger any of her WSPU group? What does your informant say about that?"

"Nothing, sir, 'sept she doesn't think that was the case. But when the Bloomsbury group started to become more militant, Lady Catherine didn't like that too much either."

"The Bloomsbury group has recently had an influx of working-class women—perhaps that was the root of the problem? They do tend to be more violently demonstrative," Pike said.

"Yes, sir. Apparently she was hostile to the working-class members, didn't want to allow them into the group. Apparently it was Florence McCleland who persuaded her to moderate her views."

"A more persuasive young lady I can hardly imagine."

"My informer tells me Lady Catherine was devoted to Miss McCleland—saw herself as the young woman's guardian, I believe." Fisher took a breath and fixed his eyes on the wall above Pike's head, and Pike prepared himself for something he might not wish to hear.

"Sir, remember how there was talk about them planning to assassinate the prime minister?"

"Yes, that was ruled out as a jest; you told me so yourself."

The sergeant cleared his throat. "Yes, well, some of the ladies have now taken up pistol shooting."

Pike slammed his hand onto his desk. "Dash it all, man—this puts a very different complexion on things. How long has this been going on?"

"It's a recent development, sir. That's all I know."

"We'll have to inform Special Branch about it all the same." Pike uncapped his pen and began to scribble Callan a note. "Anything else?"

"There's probably nothing to fear. Mrs. Pankhurst has ordered, quote, that not a cat or a canary is to be harmed."

"There's rogues in every group, Fisher." Pike was thinking of the police officers he'd been forced to sack—they'd hardly followed orders. "It may be time to pull the informer out, I don't want her to be put in any kind of danger." Pike took a cigarette from his case and lit it.

"Not just yet, if you don't mind, sir. She says they're planning something for next week."

"Can you guarantee her safety?"

"She told me she wants to stay—she knows the risks, sir."

"Desperate for the money, is she?" Pike gave in with a sigh. "Very well, then." He opened the cashbox in his desk drawer and handed Fisher two gold sovereigns.

"Thank you, sir." Fisher put the coins in his waistcoat pocket. "Besides," he said after he signed the account book, "they wouldn't hurt a woman, would they? It's against their creed."

"I would have thought you'd been in the job long enough to avoid such generalisations, Fisher." Pike's eyes strayed to one of the photographs on his desk. It showed a modishly dressed young woman swiping at a policeman with a rolled umbrella. He looked at it again and placed it on top of the pile of those he had already examined. "When women behave like men and upset the natural order, who can say what they may do."

Pike put the scribbled note to Callan aside and placed a clean piece of paper over the blotter. He began to list their suppositions. "She might have been killed by someone in the group who had opposing views to her own—who else?"

"We've ruled out Cartwright, haven't we, sir?"

"I think so."

"What about the men's antisuffrage league? There was a few of them at the riot. Lady Catherine's letter in *The Times* a few weeks ago might have humiliated some of those gentlemen. She wrote, quote, the men's antisuffrage league was no better than muscle-bound bulldogs. And then she added some insulting things about their manhood. The editor was forced to remove some words, but you could tell what they was—no words a lady should know about, if you ask me, sir."

Pike grunted and ground his cigarette butt into the ashtray. "Find out how seriously her letter was taken, how much anger it provoked. Go through the photographs again and look for familiar faces—I've nearly finished with this lot." Pike removed another photograph from the envelope, looked at it, and placed it on the pile.

"Have we eliminated a bobby from our enquiries then, sir?"

Pike sighed. "No, I'm afraid not. Nor a rough, nor anyone

disguised as one, whether he be police detective or Irish. Leave that side of the investigation to me; there's no point both of us treading on the superintendent's toes."

He added "bobby," then "rough" to their suspect list, realising it was not much bigger than when he had started. After replacing the cap of his pen, he slid the photographs towards Fisher and climbed to his feet. A walk along the Embankment might clear his head and loosen his knee.

There were a few photographs left in the envelope. He glanced at the last one as he moved it towards Fisher's pile. In the background was a scuffle between a bobby and a suffragette, but in the foreground . . . he looked at it again, closer, and froze.

He sank back heavily into his chair, his cane clattering to the floor beside him.

"Sir, are you all right? Can I get you anything?" Fisher moved to Pike's side.

"I'm fine, thank you. Take the photographs and go."

"And that one, sir?"

Pike glanced down at the photograph still in his hand. "No, not this one," he said. What the devil was he going to do about this? He reached for the telephone as Fisher closed the door behind him.

Chapter Sixteen

Dody watched from the sidelines as the battle in the top paddock raged on. Opposing teams in their red or blue sashes wielded tree branches and fought violently for possession of the hockey ball, hitting, trampling, and lunging at anyone who tried to stop them. Family member, friend, young or old, male or female, no one was spared. Even Rupert had been persuaded to play. His captain had positioned him near the goalposts and told him not to move. A clever strategy, Dody decided. Rupert was far more effective as an obstacle than he was in any form of active defence.

Without leaving his position, he made a halfhearted attempt at blocking Florence's dribble towards the goal. She hit him in the shins with her prickly branch and sent him tumbling to the ground with cries of agony. Florence let out a warlike whoop and, with skirts tucked into her knickerbockers and ponytail flying like a schoolgirl's, she dashed towards the goal to enthusiastic cries from her team.

"Go, Flo, go!" Dody pulled her fingers from the arnica salve and clapped her sister on, much to the consternation of the ten-year-old cousin she was treating at her first-aid post.

"Please don't stop, Aunt Dody, my knee's killing me," young Oscar whined.

Florence scored, narrowly missing three geese that had sauntered onto the playing field from the frozen pond. The geese honked with indignation and Florence's team cheered. Only when the applause had died did Dody's attention return to her patient. "Come now, my brave soldier, it's only a bruised knee, it doesn't need amputation." She finished applying the ointment, patted him on the back, and returned him to the fray.

They had grown up playing Fabian hockey, their father maintaining it promoted kindliness, resilience, teamwork, and a healthy circulation. Her parents would not play host to anyone who would not participate in a hockey match at least once, even if it was just a question of ducking at the oncoming ball, as was the case with Rupert Sotherby.

The Irish brothers showed no such timidity. It seemed even Florence might have met her match in the older brother, Derwent O'Neill. After the next bully-off, with Florence in possession of the ball once more, he ran abreast of her across the lumpy paddock, left hand lunging with spectacular ferocity. But Florence was nimble and lithe and outmanoeuvred him with her skilful ball play, back-sticks, and feints. And then, as she lifted her stick for another victorious goal, the Irishman hooked her around the ankle with his crook-shaped branch and sent her facedown into the frozen sod. His brother Patrick immediately helped her to her feet while Derwent, less the gentleman, took possession of the ball and cracked a goal for the opposition. Despite his dirty play, when the final whistle blew, Florence's team was the victor.

Players congregated around the lemonade table, steam rising from them through the chilly air. The maid could not pour the drinks fast enough. Dody busied herself daubing the wounded with arnica and applying sticking plasters to cuts, grateful when she could finally join in with the merriment.

Derwent pushed a damp curl from his eyes and said to Florence, "I'm sorry, Miss McCleland; I hope I didn't hurt you. For a moment I was back hurling again."

"That's quite all right, Derwent. My father always says the rules of the game are that there are no rules." Florence pulled her skirts from her knickerbockers and brushed the grass and mud from her thick stockings, her cheeks rosy with exertion.

Dody handed the panting Irishman a tall glass of lemonade. "One of the few rules that we do have here at Tretawn, Derwent," she said, "is that we call one another by our Christian names—even the servants call us such. I am Dody and my sister is Florence."

"Charmed, I'm sure," Derwent said, looking appreciatively at Florence.

"Where's Poppa now?" Florence said, pretending ignorance of the Irishman's gaze.

"Cutting wood with George, he won't be long. Mother wants us to be ready at the luncheon table as soon as he comes in. You hockey players have just enough time for a wash and change of clothes."

"Come on, you two." Florence took the Irish brothers by

the hand. "I'll show you where you can sluice off." The ragtag band of hockey players followed Florence's lead and headed towards the house.

Dody was crouched on the ground, packing up her Gladstone, when a hand gripped the back of her coat sleeve. She turned and found herself looking into the miserable, mud-smeared face of Rupert.

"Dody, I can hardly walk. Did you not see me lying out there in the paddock? Did you not notice that I had not come in with the others?" he asked.

"Oh Lord, Rupert, I'm so sorry. Are you badly hurt?"

Rupert sank to the ground at her feet. "I don't think I'll ever get the hang of this damned game; give me hockey any day. I'm sorry if I let you down, Dodes."

Dody pushed up the leg of his grass-stained flannels to examine the line of welts down his shin. She dabbed his cuts with antiseptic and helped him to his feet.

"I hoped we might have gone for a walk after luncheon, but now I fear I won't be able to. My body aches all over," he said.

Tempted as she was to put off the occasion, Dody knew she had to get the conversation over and done with as soon as possible and strengthened her resolve. She had changed a lot in the last year, mixed with men of eminence such as Dr. Bernard Spilsbury. This shedding of her blinkers had not come a moment too soon. What, she wondered, had she ever seen in someone like Rupert?

"I'm sure you will be able to make it to the rose garden if the weather holds. If not, we can sit in the library." Dody pulled his arm over her shoulder. "Come on, let's get you into the house and cleaned up for luncheon."

* * *

The dining table, a split Russian redwood shipped from Moscow, could seat up to forty. Today, twenty-five family members, guests, and servants sat upon its bench seats, chatting amongst themselves and nibbling on salted herrings as they waited for the arrival of their host. Dody found herself flanked by the Irish brothers, with Florence sitting opposite. Rupert was seated next to her mother towards the end of the table.

Dody glimpsed her father outside the French windows, washing himself at the horse trough with George, the yard-man. No one was surprised when Nial McCleland appeared moments later in his Russian peasant clothes: embroidered tunic and baggy trousers tucked into soft boots, which he prised off and left at the door. He greeted his guests, enquiring in his cultured baritone how they had fared at hockey, then kissed the top of his wife's head, his untrimmed beard and hair still dripping from his wash. Dody's mother, Louise, put her hand to her wreath of grey plaits, felt the moisture there, and shook an admonishing finger at him. She met Dody's eye with a smile before her fond gaze returned to her husband, who was making his way to the head of the table, clapping family members and friends across the shoulders as he passed.

When George had finished tending to the fire, he took his seat at the servants' end of the table. Any servant not involved in the serving of the food was obliged to dine with the family and join in the conversation. There were two additions to the servants' end, raw-boned country girls who came in on a daily basis to see to the heavy cleaning and laundry. Dody's heart went out to them. How uncomfortable they looked sitting with their "betters" at a table like this, and eating such strange, foreign food. One of the girls, seated on the other side of Derwent, had not touched her borscht and looked longingly at the untidy loaf of black bread just out of reach. Derwent did not think to pass it, and it was clear the girl did not dare to ask.

Dody passed the bread and whispered to the girl, "Don't worry, you'll get used to things here at Trctawn."

Derwent O'Neill was listening. "Marvellous," he said with relish. "I love everything about this place—the simple way of life and all." He pointed to the ornate silver tureen with his dripping soupspoon, daubing the table with blobs of pink.

Dody sensed he was making fun of her family. "My parents might aspire to the simple way of life, but they are not as fanatical as some," she said. Derwent was now shovelling soup into his mouth as if he were a starving man. Surely he was playing the fool, aping the lowest manners. She had never seen a workingman eat in such a way.

"A wealthy aunt of ours has four boys," Dody said. "She forces them to attend the village school, where they are beaten and bullied continuously. While I believe that all men are equal, I cannot see how the world will be made a better place for that."

"And anarchy, militancy, extremism—what do you think about these delicate subjects?" Derwent asked.

Her father's beliefs had tempered with time. The Fabians, whom he had joined since his return to England, believed in social change without revolution. As Dody considered her reply, she could not help but notice the resemblance of the Irishman—with his goatlike beard, unshaven cheeks, and curly black hair tied back with a leather thong—to the wild-eyed revolutionaries who had sat around the dining table in years gone by.

Florence put down her soupspoon. Both she and Derwent watched Dody intently as they waited for her reply.

"I do not condone violence of any kind," Dody said, "but I think nonviolent extremism is sometimes necessary if only to open the way for some form of moderation. By *moderation*, I mean a society that has justice and order and that cares. One where both men and women can coexist as equal partners."

"Equal partners, Dody?" Florence's eyes twinkled. "You mean as between the forensic scientist and the policeman?" Dody had related to Florence the circumstances under which she had witnessed the hanging, and how she had felt torn between opposing sides. Perhaps, Dody thought with a sigh, that was always to be the fate of her and her family.

She frowned at her sister across the table. It was all very well to tease Dody about her predicament in private, but not in the presence of strangers. Derwent O'Neill would hardly see her role with the police in an unprejudiced light.

Thankfully, Florence realised her faux pas. "And you, Derwent," she asked quickly. "How do you view the women's movement?"

"We don't care for it much," Derwent said, wiping the soup from his lips with the back of his hand. "We see it as of marginal importance and it detracts Westminster from our own cause."

A spark flared in Florence's eyes. She glared back at the Irishman for a moment. "Well, I appreciate your honesty," she paused. "On *this* subject, in any case."

Derwent ignored both her icy tone and its implications. "You're welcome, I'm sure," he said with a disarming smile.

"By your cause, you mean Home Rule, I suppose," Dody said. "I would be interested to hear what it is you are hoping to achieve from the government. Patrick," she said, turning to the younger brother, who had said nothing at all yet, "perhaps you could tell me."

Patrick cleared his throat and considered his words. "It is imperative that we become a self-governing nation. The English have never understood the Irish, and it is ridiculous that they should attempt to rule over us, oppress us with the pretence that they do it for the good of all men. The English have taken everything that is good about my country and given nothing back in return. Your average Irishman's wages are worse than those of the Englishman, as are his living conditions. Even our food is exported to England. There is famine in our countryside—"

"But what about the oppression of Irish womanhood?" Florence interrupted. "Surely you do not seek freedom from oppression for men alone?"

Derwent cocked his head and affected an almost unintelligible brogue. "Don't you be worrying your head about Irish womanhood around us, my girl. They can have all the freedom with me they want."

Dody attempted to catch her sister's eye. *Stop now, Florence, please stop now,*" she willed. Florence paid the unspoken message no heed. "You know, Dody, one thing I cannot abide," she said, loud enough for everyone at their end of the table to hear, "is people who try to ingratiate themselves in this house by adopting manners and attitudes other than those into which they are born. Like those who affect an uncouth manner when they certainly know better." At this she turned to Derwent O'Neill and shot him with a triumphant smile.

"And your father?" Derwent asked casually.

Florence lifted her chin. "My father might dress like a

peasant but he never adopts the manners of one. He is as much at home in Buckingham Palace as he is the local public house. Class means nothing to him; education and social justice are his driving ideals."

"You think my brother and I are not what we seem?" Derwent asked with a hint of amusement on his lips. He finished his soup, this time spooning it towards the outer rim then dabbing his mouth with a starched table napkin.

"I hope you are not what you seem," Florence said. "Your cause has no chance if you are."

"I think you've met your match in that one, Derwent." Patrick laughed.

Derwent raised his wineglass to Florence, the glint of desire in his eyes unmistakable, the curl at the edge of his mouth dangerous. "Touché, Florence McCleland."

Dody noticed the wolfhound asking to be let out at the French doors. As she passed Derwent to reach the dog, she whispered, "My sister is also not as she seems. Tread carefully, Derwent O'Neill, or be accountable. To me."

She did not linger to gauge his response. Two servants, a man and woman dressed in ordinary street clothes, cleared the remnants of the first course from the table. When one of the new girls rose to assist, the manservant clicked his tongue and ordered her to remain seated. Dishes of steaming Russian dumplings filled with potato and minced meat as well as shish kebabs, cabbage, and mashed potatoes appeared on the table along with decanters of fine French wines. The rest of the meal passed in relative equanimity.

After the meal, Louise McCleland called the brothers aside. "Now, Derwent, Patrick, I believe we have something to discuss in the library."

She rejoined her daughters in the kitchen moments later. "They need more help with their writing than I expected. I'll have to get back to them this evening."

Writers? Dody thought. Derwent and Patrick were writers? Who would have imagined that?

Dody and Florence helped their mother pack up the leftovers. The kitchen was the heart of the house; her parents ate there with the servants whenever they had no visitors. Bunches of herbs and knotted onions dangled from wires stretched wall to wall. A massive Victorian range dominated one wall, a huge vat of water bubbling upon it ready for the washing up. The plumbing was basic, and a single cold-water tap in the scullery was the only source of water downstairs. The servants still bathed in a tin tub by the range, while family and guests had their hot water hauled upstairs to their bedrooms. Dody's father viewed electricity with suspicion. Little wonder their mother had fought so passionately for the townhouse, Dody thought. Not only did it serve as a London base for her daughters, but it was a handy bolthole for Louise McCleland when the deprivations of country life became too much to bear.

With George's help, they carried the baskets of food outside, where the pony and trap waited for them at the hitching rail. Louise gave the pony a sugar cube, scratched it between the ears, and announced that she would drive it to the vicarage herself.

George untied the stamping pony, keeping a firm hold of it. Dody noticed the stiffness with which her mother mounted the trap. "Your hip looks to be bothering you, Mother. Why don't you allow George to deliver the food?" She looked to the lowering sky. "There's a feeling of snow in the air."

No one spoke for a moment. The expectant hush of pending

snow was broken only by the occasional caw of the rooks from their haphazard nests high in the leafless trees.

"Mother is making a point, Dody," Florence said. "If she comes back with frostbite, she thinks she might be able to persuade Father to purchase a motorcar." Florence leaned into the trap and tucked a fur rug around her mother's legs, which were already encased in a skirt of rich tweed. While tolerant of her husband's eccentric dress, Louise McCleland had never been in favour of Russian peasant clothes for herself.

"Nonsense, my dear, I need to talk to the vicar in person. There is a new widow; her husband was killed last week, run over by a feed wagon. They had a hard enough time making ends meet when he was alive. Now I don't know what's to become of them. The children are half starved as it is."

"Mother, the people need rights, not charity," Florence said.

And I hope they soon develop a palate for Russian food, Dody thought.

"One can't fight for rights on an empty stomach, Florence dear," their mother said. "Tell the young Irishmen to meet me in the library at four o'clock. We can discuss our business when your father comes in for his tea."

"What exactly is their business here, Mother?" Dody asked. "I have an unpleasant feeling about them."

"Oh, Dody, they are harmless fellows, you mustn't worry." Louise picked up the long switch and was about to tickle the pony's back with it. "Oh, one more thing, can you make sure your Rupert is around also, Dody? There is something I need to discuss with him, too."

"*My* Rupert?"

Her mother lowered the whip and pulled back on the reins.

The pony pawed at the ground and shook its untidy mane. "If you think otherwise, you really should let him know, my dear."

"Yes, Dody, you are being cruel, keeping him hanging on like this," Florence said with a twinkle.

Dody shot Florence a cool look before returning to her mother. "What do you think of his play? Are you really going to show it to Mr. Shaw?"

Her mother appeared to be searching for something diplomatic to say. "I really gave him no encouragement, you know. All I said was that I thought it . . . ah . . . interesting."

"In other words, you think it rubbish—Mother, you are no better than me!"

Louise gave her daughters a smile, clicked her tongue, and spun the trap towards the village at a rapid trot, pea gravel pinging out from under the wheels. The sisters watched in silence until the trap rounded the bend of the long driveway and was swallowed by rhododendrons.

"You weren't so dismissive of Rupert last year," Florence said. "Don't tell me you are now as against marriage as I am. When I spoke at the rally, a man in the crowd yelled for me to get a husband. It was hard not to laugh—but then again, I am married to the cause and you are not."

Perhaps it was easier for Florence to reject the idea of marriage because of her unpleasant experience with the poet. Dody had yet to have any intimate experience with a man, unpleasant or otherwise. Her studies had left little time for that. But she was curious, and it was not as if certain feelings had never been stirred.

"I suppose my year in Edinburgh changed me. Before that, I had little hope of a specialist career," she said. "Now I am a specialist doctor—even if it is in one of the less popular branches. I could not give up my career now for a man like Rupert. Perhaps someone more suitable will come along, but I am in no hurry. And if I become too old to find a husband, well, so be it. There are surely worse fates that could befall a woman."

Florence turned a full circle on her toes. "Well, Dody," she said with a satisfied sigh. "I can't see either of us settling down with a young man, suitable or otherwise, for a long time to come." She swept her arm to take in the old Tudor manor and the fine gardens surrounding it. "How could either of us settle for less than this?"

Dody knew it was not just the bricks and mortar to which she referred.

Chapter Seventeen

The pier pointed into the churning sea like a dead finger. Bad weather meant the gates were locked, the slot machines silent, and the bandstand empty. Pike took his daughter's hand and they dashed from the pier gates, down the deserted promenade to a tram shelter. He sat down immediately on the hard bench. Violet remained standing and gazed through the glass at the angry grey sea.

The cold air stung at their cheeks. Pike undid his scarf and tied it around his bowler.

She giggled. "Daddy, you look like you have toothache." She had given up trying to keep her own hat on her head and stuffed it under the straps of her school cape.

They watched the curling waves crash against the sea wall. The pebble beach was deserted; further down, fishing boats waited patiently on the beach for the storm to pass and ragged seagulls clung to their naked masts. Pike had still not broached the subject of the photograph, and Violet's boarding school's visiting afternoon was rapidly drawing to a close.

"Tea?" he shouted.

They held hands as they splashed around the traffic and headed to the tearooms on the other side of the road.

At a sweets stall next to the tearoom he bought two sticks of rock candy with HASTINGS written all the way through them.

"One for Marjorie," he said as he handed them to her.

At the mention of her friend's name, Violet's mouth turned down.

"What's the matter?" Pike asked.

"Marjorie's no longer at my school. Her mother has sent her to Switzerland to improve her French and German," she said.

Pike waited, sensing there was more to come. When Violet failed to elaborate, all he could think to say was, "Oh," missing his chance to probe. The two girls were inseparable. Whatever Violet had been involved in, Marjorie would have been, too.

In the crowded tearoom they took off their outer garments, draped them over the backs of their chairs, and ordered tea for two and knickerbocker glories.

Violet lifted her cup in a toast. "To Mummy," she said.

Pike guessed she was hoping he might say something nice about her mother. She did not remember her mother at all, and loved to hear stories about her. He clicked his cup against hers, remained silent, and cursed his own inadequacy at conversing with females.

Violet took it upon herself to fill the vacuum. Barely pausing to draw breath, she launched into an account of how Gloria Bradshaw had got stuck in a tree and been rescued by a teacher with a ladder; how much better this jelly was compared to what they got at school, which in summer was riddled with tiny red spiders; how she was dreading next term when swimming started again—didn't he think it cruel that they were forced to bathe in the sea when there was still frost upon the playing fields?

He responded with the occasional nod and a wan smile. He was running out of time, damn it. Eventually she gave up and concentrated on the concoction of fruit, jelly, cream, and ice cream. He had no appetite and hardly touched his. When she began to scrape the ice cream at the bottom of her glass with the long spoon, he pushed his dessert over for her to finish.

"Violet, there's something I need to discuss with you," he said just as she said,

"I've been selected for the lacrosse team, Daddy."

The sudden shock of both of them speaking at once plunged them into silence once more. Outside the wind howled, waves crashed against the sea wall.

"The lacrosse team, that's very good," he said absently. Then he reached inside his suit jacket and removed an envelope. He passed it to her across the table and knocked over one of the empty parfait glasses, and everyone in the tearoom fell silent and turned their heads to look at them.

Violet flushed with embarrassment. *Good start*, Pike thought glumly.

She delayed removing the contents of the envelope until she was certain everyone had returned to their own murmurings. Pike watched her closely.

She looked at the photograph and paled. God only knew what memories it was stirring. The photograph shook in her hand; she tried to slide it back into the envelope, and failed. Pike took it and cleared a space for it on the table between them.

"Look at it again, please, Violet."

Her hand went to her mouth. She shook her head; he could see her fighting back tears. And suddenly he saw in her face what he had not seen on the photographic paper—the terror she must have gone through in the middle of that violent scrimmage. Good God, what had she been through?

Pike remembered the first moment he'd seen the photograph in his office—her hat awry and face pinched and anxious—he had telephoned the school immediately. The headmistress had assured him she was absolutely fine, had suffered no ill effects from "the unfortunate incident outside the tube station" other than the loss of her purse. He had only half listened: the headmistress's words had nothing at all to do with the protest outside the House of Commons. He had made arrangements with the school to take Violet out at the weekend and hastily rung off.

The look on her face told him he must be looking stern. "Violet, you have to tell me all about it, tell me right from the beginning," he said. "You have nothing to fear. What is done is done."

Violet bit at her bottom lip. "I'll be expelled . . ."

"The school does not appear to know. I won't tell them and I will not be angry. You have my word."

Violet would not meet his eye. When she finally spoke, her voice was barely above a whisper. "We heard about the demonstration from one of our teachers—many of us at school agree with the idea of women's emancipation."

Pike almost choked on his tea. "Women's emancipation? You are fourteen years old!"

"Daddy, you gave your word!" Her voice rose.

He wiped his mouth with a serviette. "Carry on."

Violet took a deep breath and spoke with more courage. "I

am nearly fifteen. I was spending my weekend break at Marjorie's house in Hampstead Heath. We caught the tube into London, telling Marjorie's mother we were going shopping, and we met with the protesters outside Caxton Hall. We saw the Pankhursts, they were marvellous—if only you could have heard them—and all the ladies were terribly kind."

"I'm sure," Pike said without enthusiasm. But he was glad they had been kind to his little girl.

"But things started to go wrong as we neared the Houses of Parliament. Other people joined in the march and started to heckle us and fight. Then the police came and they were absolutely horrid, the worst of all." Violet dropped her eyes again. "They made me feel ashamed."

Of me? Pike thought. She looked up at him and he saw a look in her face he had never seen before, strained and defiant.

"Were you hurt?" he asked.

"A little. I was knocked to the ground and banged the side of my head." Violet touched her cheek. "The bruise has only just gone. It was a policeman who did it, you know. My dress was torn, and for a while I lost Marjorie, and that was awful."

"It's all right, my dear, I am relieved you came to no worse harm." Pike kept his voice calm but inside he seethed. He had put his daughter in one of the finest girls' boarding schools in England, partly to protect her from the brutish behaviour of men. But instead she had been exposed to suffragette ideology and nearly killed. By a policemen, no less. He felt sick.

"When I found Marjorie, she had received similar treatment to me," Violet continued. "She had a cut on her head and was terribly frightened. We tried to keep out of the fighting, but it was all around us. Then suddenly a young lady came to our aid and led us down a back alleyway to safety. If not for her,

I think we would have been killed. She took us to the railway station, where we caught the tube back to Marjorie's house."

"Did this lady have a name?"

"Yes, Miss McCleland."

Florence McCleland. Of all the confounded things! Pike could feel the rise of colour in his face.

Violet frowned. "Daddy, what's wrong?"

"Nothing, nothing at all," he said, exercising all his restraint. "Though it seems that I owe a debt of gratitude to this young lady." He lit a cigarette and tried to calm himself. "And then I suppose you had to explain your condition to Marjorie's mother?"

"We said we were attacked by youths in the street outside the station and had our purses stolen. She took us to the police station and we had to make a statement to the police."

"You told a lie to the police?"

"Yes." Violet lowered her eyes.

God in heaven, Pike ran his fingers through his hair. If this were to get out, his career, already tenuous, would be in ruins. And so would her schooling—and then what?

He picked up the photograph and pointed to the bobby in the background, struggling with a woman. "Is this the policeman that hurt you?"

"No, that wasn't him."

Pike reached into his pocket for another envelope of photographs. He had retrieved them from Fisher and brought them with him, thinking that Violet might have seen something that the cameras had failed to pick up. Now he felt ashamed that he had planned to quiz his daughter in this way. But if she could point out the bobby who had knocked her down, that would be one positive outcome of this sorry day.

He was hardly surprised when she stopped at the photograph of Dykins. Her pale face blanched even further.

"Is that the one?" Pike asked her gently. She didn't answer, but nodded faintly. Then he saw her eyes fill with tears before she buried her face in her napkin.

"My dear." Pike reached out and touched her arm.

"Just a moment, I'm sorry . . . I need to go to the powder room."

"Of course."

To Pike, the ten minutes it took for Violet to return seemed like an eternity. She'd washed her face; he could tell by the diamonds of moisture clinging to her hairline. And her hair, previously dishevelled from the wild weather, had been brushed smooth and retied, her school hat once more planted firmly on her head.

"Violet, is there anything else you want to tell me about that policeman?"

"No, there's nothing else, just what I already told you."

While Pike hoped to God that was the worst of it, something told him she was holding back, protecting him. He knew damned well about the bestial behaviour of the men at the riot, knew his daughter would have been an irresistible target. She straightened in her chair—yes, that was it. Perhaps it was best for them both that she did not give all the details. Suddenly she appeared very grown up.

"Well, I can tell you something," he said, hoping to make her smile. "I had the pleasure of sacking that policeman myself, the day after the riot. His unprofessional behaviour was well documented."

"I'm glad. He could be hanged for all I care."

Pike winced.

"Violet, there is one more thing. I am trying to discover what happened to this lady." He put in front of her a picture of Lady Catherine Cartwright while she was still alive. "Did you see what happened to her?"

"Yes, I did, Father." This time Violet answered with an accusatory coolness that chilled him. "She was lovely and wore a beautiful hat with purple feathers on it. She talked to Marjorie and me before everything turned horrible. I saw her being brutally beaten about the head by a uniformed policeman."

"You are completely sure that this is the woman you saw?"

"Yes, it was her. Is she all right?"

When he didn't answer immediately, she slowly nodded. "She's not all right, is she? If she were, she could tell you what happened herself."

Still he couldn't speak, but she must have seen the answer in his eyes.

"She's dead, isn't she? She was so nice to us. I didn't realise she had been killed."

Pike felt his heartbeat quicken. "Killed by this policeman?" He pointed to Dykins.

"No, not that one. Another."

They searched for his face among the other photographs, but were unable to find it.

Chapter Eighteen

Dody was reading by the fire when her sister entered the morning room.

Florence looked taken aback. "I thought you were studying in your rooms."

"The fires upstairs have only just been lit. I'll stay down here while my rooms warm up." Dody returned to the report in her hand. The visit to her parents had been a pleasant break, marred only by Rupert's behaviour. She wasn't sure what he had been more upset about when he stormed from her parents' house—the ending of their fictitious engagement or her mother's rejection of his play. She suspected it was the latter.

Now that they were back home, she had a lot to catch up on before morning. "I'm studying a proposal written by Dr. Garrett," she said to Florence, "on the feasibility of setting up a new women's clinic in the East End. The idea has merit. We could use one of the vacant warehouses dotting the area. It would need private funding, of course."

Florence's mind appeared to be on other things. She'd had several mysterious telegrams from her suffragette colleagues whilst she and Dody were still in Sussex—there was no telephone at their parents' house—and each one seemed to have left her that bit more agitated. On the train home she'd been edgy and unable to keep still and unwilling to confide. Now, she fidgeted with her silken belt, twisting it askew. "Dody, I will soon be receiving visitors. If you plan to remain here, I will have to ask Annie to open up the drawing room for us and I don't think she will be too pleased about that."

"Visitors?" Dody said. "Not the Irish brothers, I hope?"

With brisk steps, Florence moved to the mantelpiece mirror, unpinned her hat, and tossed it on the settee. "Since when have you been so against the Irish? We still have family in Cork. Theirs is as worthy a cause as any."

"Of course it's a worthy cause. But you yourself pointed out that Derwent O'Neill is not what he seems."

"Yes, he is obviously more educated than he pretends; that is clear."

"I fear there is more to him than that," Dody said, searching her sister's face.

Florence ignored her concern and stood in front of the mirror, needlessly patting at her pompadour. "I would not object to getting to know him better. He might be useful. The Fenians certainly knew how to make themselves heard."

Dody placed her papers on the wine table. "With bombs, Florence—surely you don't mean that?"

"No, of course not. But I wouldn't mind discussing strategy

with him someday. Who knows, we might form a united front." Florence moved towards the tray of decanters. "A quick sherry before you leave?"

"Derwent O'Neill made it perfectly obvious he doesn't give tuppence for the WSPU. And no, thank you, to sherry."

"Well, in any case," Florence said, pouring herself a generous measure, "it's not the Irishmen coming to call, but some of my committee ladies. And if you don't mind, Dody, we would like to have the morning room to ourselves."

Dody pursed her lips. "Secret business, Florence?"

"Something I would prefer you not to hear."

"Dangerous?" Dody rose from her chair.

"You said yourself one needed extremism to promote moderation. Didn't Mr. Shaw say the suffragettes should shoot, kill, maim, and destroy until given the vote?"

Dody looked to the ceiling. Her sister drew Shaw like some would draw a pistol. "I said extremism can lead to moderation—*can* being the operative word. Florence, have you not done enough? You could have been killed at the march. It might very well have been your body and not Catherine's I was called to look at. And what about the force-feeding? Could you go through that again if you were arrested?"

Florence gulped her sherry in a single swallow. "I won't be arrested. Please, Dody, don't make me explain. I don't want you compromised in any way."

"We share a house. You are my sister."

Florence paused. "I can always find myself new lodgings. While you were in Edinburgh, I came and went as I pleased. I managed to survive quite well without an older sister looking out for me, telling me whom I may see, how I may conduct myself—"

"Don't be ridiculous. I simply want to make sure you're safe."

"Ridiculous? That's how you've always seen me, isn't it? Well, Dody, I am sick of hearing it."

Dody gripped her sister's arm. "Florence! I am sorry. I had not realised I was doing that, I was just concerned. But you are quite right, truly, and I am sorry. Now please, have your meeting in privacy; I will go upstairs right away."

Florence would not be mollified. "No. We shall take our meeting elsewhere, and I shall stay at Olivia's. Perhaps for a few days."

The doorbell rang, followed by movement in the hall and women's voices. Florence straightened her belt once more as Annie showed the group into the morning room. Dody wished them good evening, gathered her papers, and mounted the stairs with a heavy tread. How stubborn, how impetuous her sister was. Hopefully, come morning, she would see reason. Ridiculous. In a few moments she heard the door open and close again. Then all was silent.

Chapter Nineteen

Pike turned down Brockman's request for a few tunes and took a seat in a discreet corner of the pub beneath a mournful stag's head. He glanced around the half-filled room. No surprise that Brockman wanted some music to liven the place up—Pike had read casualty lists to men less gloomy than this lot. Whether they were unemployed or on strike pay, their beer was taking a long time to drop.

Not so Pike's. He downed his tankard, then signalled to Brockman for another, promising himself that this would be his last. The third, which he justified by his need for a good night's sleep, he drank with only slightly more restraint. This much beer on an empty stomach? He was a fool. He couldn't think straight with alcohol, but tonight it seemed the only alternative.

Upon his return from Hasting's to London, he'd walked from the station to his office and switched his bowler and overcoat for a cloth cap and donkey jacket, his collar and tie for a homespun muffler. After examining the photograph of Violet once more—that small, strained, white face—he had locked it in the bottom drawer of his desk. This was one picture he would not be handing to Fisher for further examination— the others he had replaced in the pile for Fisher, to be used as evidence. Then he had caught an omnibus to Brockman's.

He took another swallow of beer. He was withholding evidence. In a few seconds he had cast aside his values and lowered himself to protect his personal interests. He'd heard other men justify similar behaviour with petty excuses more often than he cared to remember, and he'd always viewed them with contempt. Now it was he who had turned his back on his principles.

He took some comfort in the knowledge that his deceit would never stretch to covering up the truth itself. He would find a way of proving that Lady Catherine had been killed by a uniformed police officer, without involving Violet.

But how? His mind turned to a recent article about advances in blood identification in *The Police Review*. Apparently, certain substances had been discovered that could identify the owner as belonging to one of several blood groups. The results were not as specific as fingerprinting, but since that was not possible in this case, such a blood test might be a useful alternative. If Lady Catherine's blood group was found on a particular officer's truncheon—the article suggested that no more than a single drop or stain was required—his suspect list could be narrowed considerably.

He pushed back his cap and scratched his head. He would need a valid reason to test the men's truncheons without arousing suspicion. An equipment inspection might do, he decided.

But was this kind of forensic test possible, and, if so, how long would it take?

There was one person who might be able to tell him. He stood and tipped down the last of his pint. It was too late to call on Dr. McCleland now, but he would make an appointment to see her in the morning. He had kept her secret; perhaps now she could be trusted with his.

Initially, it did not occur to Pike that the man walking some distance behind him on the bridge might be tailing him. Although it was late when he'd boarded the last omnibus to Lambeth, there had still been activity in the street outside the pub: a hawker braving the damp chill to sell the last of his pies, a group of men standing around a glowing brazier of roasting chestnuts. In retrospect, Pike remembered, it was from this group that the man had stepped and joined him on the omnibus.

And then followed him off.

The sobering realisation cleared Pike's head quicker than a dunk in the icy river. He tuned his ears to the sharp ring of his follower's boots. The man was making no effort now to disguise himself. Whenever Pike increased his pace, the footsteps quickened, too. Along the bridge he slowed to skirt puddles of brittle ice. If he slipped now, he had no doubt the man would be on to him in no time.

Not even a rat stirred amongst the festering piles of refuse waiting for the barges which, come dawn, would be jostling and shoving like ducks for bread along the riverbank. The space between the towers at the end of the bridge was empty of vagrants tonight. If there had been anyone in the vicinity of the unburied sewerage pipes, they had crawled deep inside, seeking out what little warmth they offered.

Thirty yards from the end of the bridge, instead of taking the wider street to Millbank Road and his lodgings, Pike veered into the shadows of a narrow alley and ducked into a recessed doorway. Sure enough, the echo of footsteps grew louder and the man from the omnibus passed him by. Pike expelled his breath and waited several minutes before stepping from the doorway.

"Oi, where do you think you're going, Pike?"

Pike spun in the direction of the familiar voice. He should have guessed there would be two of them; damn his drinking. That they should have chosen tonight of all nights.

"Dykins?" Pike narrowed his eyes and peered at the figure looming through the mist.

For an answer, Dykins put his fingers to his mouth and blew a shrill whistle. Within seconds there were footsteps advancing quickly from the other end of the alleyway. Pike had no intention of waiting to see what the men wanted. He feinted to the left of Dykins and, as the big man lunged, ducked to his right and dashed as fast as he could down an offshoot of the main alley. He couldn't outrun his pursuers for long, but with luck, he might make it to Millbank Road and flag a cab before they caught up to him.

But luck was not on Pike's side. With fear hammering at his heart and his eyes focused on the distant streetlamp, he failed to notice the sheet of frozen gutter spill stretching like a black mirror before him. He lost his footing and skidded the length of the ice on his stomach, cane skittering off into the darkness. On hands and knees he scrabbled desperately, groping for his cane along the alley wall, ice cutting into the skin of his hands and through the fabric of his trousers. Then he heard their pounding feet, the rasping of their breath, and their cursing as they, too, hit the ice.

Dykins fell upon Pike, pinning him down with his weight. Pike caught the blurred features of his companion; it was Joe Excel, another of the sacked officers, skidding like a hockey ball towards them.

Was this it, Pike wondered as he struggled against Dykins's grip, or were there more men in the shadows, waiting for their turn at him? One he might manage, two possibly, if he could find his cane. Three or more and he was a pig's breakfast.

"You're going to pay for what you done, Pike," Dykins snarled as he pulled Pike to his feet and shoved him against the alley wall. "Families to feed and no 'int of a job in sight—give 'im one, Joe."

Brass knuckles gleamed on Excel's hand. Pike felt the blow to his stomach clean through to his spine. He dropped to the ground, drawing up his knees and fighting for breath. A kick from Dykins to his kidneys forced his body into a painful arch. His arms flailed and his hands smacked against the ground. A loose cobble shifted under his palm and he curled his fingers around it; it would have to do.

Dykins grabbed him by his jacket and hauled him to his feet once more. Pike went limp, making it impossible for Dykins to hold back his arms and keep him on his feet at the same time. His head sagged, the hand holding the cobble hanging loose by his side. He knew he would have to let Excel get dangerously close to use the stone with any effect.

Dykins struggled to keep Pike vertical. "Save some for me, Joe." He spat on the ground. "Nancy pen-pusher's soft as butter, just about gorn already."

Excel drew back his fist and aimed once more at Pike's stomach.

Pike was unable to block the blow completely, but slamming the cobble into Excel's face softened the follow-through. Excel crumpled without a sound and Dykins's grip loosened. Pike spotted his cane and dived for it. His fingertips were brushing the smooth wood when Dykins grabbed him by the ankles and yanked.

"Gotcha!" Dykins roared, and his boot caught Pike in the side with an audible crack. Then Dykins slammed his boot down on Pike's leg. Rockets of pain exploded in Pike's knee. He felt every nail in the big man's boot and he cried out, clutching at his knee as waves of pain coursed through it. His screams made even Dykins hesitate. Stepping back, he nudged Excel with his boot. "Get up, you lazy git, 'e's 'ad enough. Time we left before someone 'ears the racket."

Although his knee felt shattered, Pike managed to reach his cane. He flicked the clasp, unsheathed the slender sword secreted within the handle, and lashed out at Dykins.

"Me legs, me legs, you bastard!" Dykins screamed as he fell to the cobbles.

Pike heaved himself up against the alley wall, fighting off waves of nausea and pain. A wide moon peeped from behind a scudding cloud and gave him a clearer view of the two men lying on the ground before him. Excel was out cold on his back, his face a glistening mask of bloodied flesh, his breath hanging in white wreaths above his head. Dykins lay on his side, moaning, legs clasped to his chest.

Pike put the tip of his sword to Dykins's throat. "Ever heard of death by a thousand cuts?"

"We wasn't going to kill you, Chief Inspector, just pay you back for what you done, that's all."

Pike believed him. If they'd wanted to kill him, they would have brought more than a set of brass knuckles. "The Chinese know just where to make the cuts for a man to bleed slowly to death. The last cut is to the throat, here." Pike pressed harder. He sensed the outer layer of skin yield under his blade.

Dykins yelped. "You've paid us back, me legs is shredded, Excel's dead—what else do you want?"

Pike released the pressure. "Excel's not dead, he's breathing. I want to know who put you up to the violence at the women's march. I can't believe so many of you would have risked your jobs for no reward."

"The sergeant took aside those of us 'e could trust," Dykins said hastily. "Told us to put the women in their place. He said a bunch of roughs from the wharf 'ad been organised to cause trouble, too, and told us to turn a blind eye to 'em."

"Irish?"

"No, I don't think so."

"Organised by whom?"

"Superintendent Shepherd, sir, acting on orders from the top, they say."

No surprises there, Pike thought. He had suspected Shepherd had conjured up the Irish to divert him from the truth, thinking that was Pike's Achilles' heel.

"From the Home Office?" he asked. Since a militant suffragette had attacked Churchill, there had been no love lost between the Home Secretary and the "troublesome" women.

Dykins shrugged. "We was given six pounds each, sir, told to keep schtum. The superintendent said 'ed make sure we didn't lose our jobs, and if things got dodgy, 'ed arrange transfers for us."

"He didn't count on the photographic evidence," Pike said with contempt. "Even Shepherd can't get you out of that, you fool."

"Then 'es going to find us something else, security work, or the railways!"

"Don't count on it. And what about the death of Lady Catherine? Who was responsible for that?"

"It's what I told you in the office, sir, none of us done it, honest to God, I'd slit me own throat if I lied!"

"Not if I get to it first." Pike again tickled the man's throat with the tip of his sword. Then he moved it down Dykins's front, slicing the buttons off his coat. "You can swear to that, can you, Dykins? The surveillance photographs show you following your own agenda for most of the time."

"I ain't got eyes at the back of me 'ead, 'ave I?"

Pike sliced through the seam of the man's coat sleeve for his impudence.

"But if it was one of us what done it, I would have 'eard something about it after, I'm sure," Dykins yelled.

Pike cut through the thick belt at his waist and then his braces.

"Oi, what you on about? I told you what I know!" With a loud sob, Dykins rolled onto his stomach and attempted to slither away, his trousers bunching around his knees.

Pike's blade returned to Dykins's throat, prodding him to roll once more onto his back. "Your legs aren't cut too badly," he said, "and I can't have you following me. Your choice: I cut further into your legs or I cut your clothes off."

"I'll fuckin' freeze!"

"Head back towards the bridge and someone will find you." Pike attempted to sever the man's bootlaces, but he had trouble seeing in the dim light and sliced through boot leather as if it were tomato skin, nicking the side of Dykins's foot in the process. "That one was for the girls and women you manhandled outside the House of Commons," he said when Dykins screamed. He wanted to remove the man's boots, but didn't see how he could do so without falling down and staying down. Glancing at the unconscious Excel as he slipped the sword back into his cane, he said, "And don't forget Sleeping Beauty here."

He was unable to put any weight on the leg Dykins had smashed, so he leaned into his cane and hopped away, hugging the shadowy course of the alley wall until he was out of Dykins's sight. Then he stopped, leaned against the wall, closed his eyes against the pain and dizziness, and pondered his options.

He could not stop himself from shaking. His knee felt as bad as the original injury all over again, but then at least his batman had been available to boost him onto his horse and lead him to safety. He was not far from home, but Mrs. Keating would doubtless send him to the hospital. And if Shepherd discovered the extent of his injury, it would be all the excuse he needed to pension him off. As a penniless civilian, there was little he could do about the corruption, incompetence, and callousness that had resulted in the deaths of three women and the emotional scarring of his daughter and her young friend. His only hope of ridding the force of scum like Shepherd was by remaining in it.

He might be unable to change the past, but by bringing to

justice those responsible for Lady Catherine's death, he might help Violet come to terms with it—and perhaps restore some of her lost faith in him, too.

There was only one thing for it. He took an agonising breath and began to hop towards the lights and cabs of Millbank Road.

Chapter Twenty

Dody lay in her bed, not quite awake, nor fully asleep. Disconnected images merged into one another in her mind: a swinging rope, a hockey match, a warm corpse with the face of her sister. Then it was she herself lying on the mortuary slab, manhandled by attendants, the powerful light blazing in her face . . .

She gasped.

"It's all right, miss, it's only me." Annie stopped shaking her and stepped back from the bed.

Dody pushed the hair from her eyes and squinted through the bright light at the parlour maid. "Annie! What is it?" It must be urgent for Annie to be waking her in the middle of the night. Then the memory of her dream caused her to sit bolt upright. "Florence, has something happened to Florence?"

"No, miss. As far as I know, Miss Florence is safe at Miss

Barndon-Brown's flat. It's a gentleman at the door, says he's with the police."

Dody swung her legs over the side of the bed and pushed her feet into her slippers. "It has to be about Florence," she said, unable to shift the grip of panic.

"No, miss, that's the first thing I asked. He said he needed to speak to you about something else."

"Did you ask him in?"

Annie handed Dody her dressing gown. "No, I kept the chain on the door while I spoke to him and left him out on the doorstep. He's dirty and dishevelled, and more than a smell of beer on his breath. More like a beggar than a policeman if you ask me—shall I wake Mr. Fletcher and have him seen off?"

"Did he give you a name?"

"He did, but I couldn't tell you, miss, he was mumbling something chronic . . . Bike maybe."

Dody moved quickly to the door.

"Shall I go get Fletcher?" Annie repeated.

"No, first I want to see if it is who I think it is."

They approached the front door together. Dody drew the bolt with Annie twitching at the sleeve of her dressing gown. At first Dody saw no one. Then, illuminated by the porch light, she spotted a bent figure half-sitting half-lying on the lower step. "Chief Inspector, is that you?"

"Dr. McCleland?"

It was Pike, undoubtedly.

Releasing the door chain and flinging the door wide, Dody rushed to his side and crouched on the step. "You are hurt?"

"Sorry to disturb you at this time of night," he said between the violent chattering of his teeth, "but I have much to report and nowhere else to go. I'm afraid I can't stand. I'll need some help, I have hurt my knee."

"Help me get him inside, Annie. I know him and he is a policeman."

They reached under Pike's arms and heaved him into the hall, where they sat him down in a flimsy chair. He was hatless and muddy and his trousers were torn.

Dody glanced up the long staircase leading from the hall. "He needs to be put to bed, but we'll never get him up the stairs. The chaise in the morning room will have to do."

Dody couldn't tell if Annie's look of disgust was due to Pike's filthy condition, his occupation, or both. "But the chaise has only just been cleaned," the maid said. Then she added eagerly, "I could call a cab and have him taken to the hospital."

Pike straightened as best he could. He was shaking violently. "No, please, Doctor, we must talk."

It must have something to do with Catherine's case, Dody thought. His knowledge of her clandestine activities in the cadaver keep had made them allies of a sort, albeit cautious ones. Dody looked at his face, pale and taut with pain and desperation.

"No, Annie, no hospital yet. I might be able to see to him here. Cover the chaise with a sheet. Then fetch me some towels and blankets, a bowl of hot water, and my medical bag."

While Annie set up an improvised hospital bed, Dody poured a glass of brandy and put it in Pike's hand. The fiery liquor made him cough and he doubled over, clutching his side.

Dody urged him to straighten, placed her hand inside his jacket, and felt along his ribs, provoking a gasp of pain. "I'm not yet sure what has happened to your knee, but you have at least one fractured rib," she said. "Were you attacked?"

Pike nodded, hugged himself, and rocked forward on the chair. "Cold," he muttered.

"We'll soon warm you up." She looked into the morning room. Annie had finished setting up and was stoking the fire.

Dody observed Pike's knee as they helped him from the hall. It showed little stability; he could hardly bear weight upon it, the slightest shift of angle causing it to twist unnaturally to the side. Not a ruptured cruciate ligament, she prayed, an irreparable condition that would leave him more crippled than before.

They slipped off his sodden jacket, stretched him out on the chaise, and removed his boots. Using scissors from her bag, Dody cut through the seams of his torn trousers and long underwear, peeling back the layers of fabric to expose his leg from ankle to thigh. His knee was twice the size it should have been, a bluish ball of fluid streaked with blood from multiple grazes.

"Get me some ice, Annie."

"There's none, miss. Cook don't stock it in winter." Annie's face was set in sullen disapproval.

"Then scrape it from the street!" Dody snapped. Florence's prejudice against the police had spread to the girl like a disease. "Find me some ice, and then go to bed," Dody said more gently. Whatever Pike had to say, she decided, it would be safer heard alone.

Returning her attention to Pike's knee, she probed as gently as she could. Under the swelling, she could just make out the oval shape of the patella, lateral to where it should have been and moving like a living thing under her touch. He flinched and sucked in his breath.

"Your kneecap is dislocated," she said.

"I thought as much," he gasped. "It has happened before."

"What was the original injury?"

"Shrapnel."

"It was removed?"

Pike swallowed. "No, I . . . the hospital tent . . ." He broke off.

Dody could see no point in questioning him further; her observations told her all she needed to know: the rapid beat of the pulse at his neck, the sweat popping on his brow despite the coolness of his skin, the dry lips. The prospect of surgery clearly terrified him.

"I'm going to give you something to ease the pain, and then I will bind your ribs and reduce the dislocation of your knee. I will ice it, stabilise the joint as much as possible with strapping, and then splint it. You will not need surgery now, although I would advise it at a later date when the soft tissue damage has healed. The wear and tear of the shrapnel in the joint will only lead to more complications like this."

As she spoke, she checked the pulses in his leg. "Wriggle your toes, please. Good. I can see no evidence of nerve or vascular damage."

Dody pulled a bottle of laudanum from her bag. Pouring water into a sherry glass, she added the powerful analgesic with a pipette, carefully counting the drops. "Here, drink this," she said when she had mixed the concoction.

He hesitated, glass in hand, and inspected the contents with suspicion. "There are things we need to discuss. This will put me to sleep."

"It probably will, but there will be time to talk before it does. You do not want to be fully awake when I manipulate your knee, believe me." Troubled eyes looked back into hers. She instinctively placed her hand upon his and gave it a squeeze. "You have to trust me. I will do nothing more than what I just explained." She paused, wanted to ease some of his tension. "And who knows, sometime in the future, after surgery, you might even be able to ride that boneshaker bicycle of yours."

He looked at her for some seconds, then gave in with a sigh and raised the sherry glass.

"Good health, Chief Inspector," Dody said, allowing herself a small, self-congratulatory smile.

She woke in the chair to the swishing of curtains and the turning of the room from black to grey. Annie switched on the standard lamp. "I think you'll need the light, miss, it's a grim old morning."

Dody yawned and turned her gaze up to the window. A brisk wind whipped the trees in the front garden and rattled at the windowpanes. A motorcar chugged past, headlights still blazing. She had kept the fire going for most of the night, but had slept soundly for the last two hours. Now only a few valiant embers still glowed. Annie prodded and poked at them, added kindling and fresh coal from the scuttle, and after a few puffs of the bellows, the fire was roaring again.

Annie sank back on her haunches, wiped dirty hands on her apron, and glanced at the sleeping man. "How is he, miss?" she asked through pinched lips.

"Really, Annie, one would think that you had hoped him to die in the night."

"No, of course not, Miss Dody, but I was worried Miss Florence might return and find him here. Then sparks would fly." She rammed the poker into the coals to illustrate her point.

"Well, Miss Florence didn't return, did she?" Then, attempting to curb her impatience, Dody said in a more even tone, "He was quite restless earlier on, but sleeping soundly now by the look of things."

She got up from the chair and stretched. Moving over to where her patient lay, she took his pulse, finding it slow and steady. Although his skin appeared pale against the shadow of his stubble, the careworn look she associated with him had vanished, and he looked younger than she had originally thought, perhaps no more than forty. She marvelled at the restorative nature of sleep and wished she'd had more of it herself.

"I'll take my bath now before he wakes," she told Annie. "Tell Cook to prepare a light breakfast for two to have in here in about half an hour."

"Half an hour, miss?" Annie said with incredulity. She had not yet come to terms with the fact that Dody was quite capable of getting dressed unaided in less than an hour.

Pike was awake when she returned to the morning room, and she was just in time to stop him from climbing to his feet.

"No, Chief Inspector, no," she said gently, easing him back down.

He rubbed his face and attempted to smooth his tousled hair. "Thank you, Doctor, but you've done enough." He looked down and discovered he was dressed only in undershirt and drawers and hastily pulled the blanket up to his neck. "If you could just hand me my clothes, I will be off." Now there was too much colour in the pale face.

"I'm afraid it won't be that simple. I had to cut your trousers to pieces to get at your leg last night. As for the rest of your things, Annie has taken them away for laundering, all but your jacket, and that is drying in the kitchen."

"Launder them? But I need—"

"I will send my coachman to your lodgings for more clothes later. I can't let you bear weight on that leg just yet, and when you do, it will have to be with a pair of crutches." She poured him coffee from the breakfast tray Annie had brought in.

"Crutches?" Pike said. "I can't be seen with crutches. Didn't I tell you last night that I could lose my job if Shepherd discovers my knee has worsened?"

"Then you must stay out of sight for a few days. If you think someone from the force might visit you at your lodgings, you are welcome to stay here until you can use your cane again."

Pike shook his head. "I appreciate your offer, but no. Not only does it show a singular lack of propriety"—at this Dody could not help smiling—"but it would be most unwise, politically speaking. Neither of us can afford to advertise our new, er, alliance."

For a moment she thought he had been going to say friendship. How would she feel if he had? Annoyed? Would she have thought him overly familiar or would she have been flattered? Whatever the case, she was glad he had not said it.

"Only until this evening then, when we will devise a plan. Here, you must eat." She handed him toast and marmalade and took some for herself. "Surely you would like to be close at hand to hear what I find out about the possibility of testing the truncheons for Lady Catherine's blood group?"

Pike placed his untouched toast on the table next to his coffee. With a sigh of defeat, he sank back against his pillow.

Dody gulped down the last of her coffee, glancing at the mantelpiece clock as she did so. "It's almost nine o'clock. If I don't go now, I will be late for ward rounds. I'll bring you back some crutches from the hospital, but it won't be until late this afternoon. On no account are you to put weight on that leg, or remove the strapping from your ribs, or tamper with the splint—it must be firm to keep the patella in place. Annie will bring in your meals—and a chamber pot for your convenience."

He turned his head away. His hand went to his leg under the blanket. For the first time he seemed aware of the improvised contraption. "The splint . . . ?"

"I'll show you." Dody pulled back the blanket and revealed the cardboard splint put together from one of Florence's newspaper boxes.

His eyes widened in horror as he read the black print down the front of the device—VOTES FOR WOMEN!

Dody smiled. *That ought to keep him in his place.*

Chapter Twenty-One

The cab made swift progress along the macadam road to the New Women's Hospital, and Dody had plenty to occupy her mind during the short journey. Pike had not been exaggerating when on the doorstep last night he'd said he had important things to report. He knew the truth now—that the police had attacked women at the riot, that Lady Catherine had been bludgeoned by a policeman, and that this had been suppressed. Surely it would have been in Pike's best interest to bury his head in the sand, but he had given her his assurance that he would do everything in his power to get to the heart of the corruption, and expose it's rotten core. But at what cost? He had already come close to losing his life at the hands of ruffians he had sacked, but what of the others, the men who had even more to lose? What steps might they take to silence him?

And then there was the astonishing fact that his daughter had actually witnessed the murder—if murder it was. Dody had only found that out when Pike had woken in the night muttering Violet's name. She had assumed he was referring to a wife, but after she had soothed him with more laudanum, he told her that his wife was dead and that Violet was his daughter. He made her swear, for both their sakes, that she would not make his daughter's involvement in the riot public knowledge.

For a fleeting moment Dody forgot her cares and smiled as she watched the drizzly streetscape speed by. So, the staid, straightlaced chief inspector had a suffragette-in-the-making for a daughter! The irony was quite delicious; how she wished she could tell Florence.

Florence.

The smile faded from her face. Florence's abrupt departure from the house had been worrying and hurtful, though in hindsight it was just as well, given Pike's arrival. But Florence was sure to hear the news from Annie, and then what? A policeman was a policeman to Florence, no matter how hurt and helpless he was, and no matter how convinced Dody was that they could trust him. This would surely drive yet another wedge between them.

She forced herself to concentrate on the day ahead and put a stop to this useless fretting. How illogical, how unlike her it was to worry about something that might never happen. If only she'd had the time for a soothing morning pipe before she'd left home.

Stepping out of the cab, she paused outside the front of the hospital, one of the first built expressly for women. She gazed up at the building's unusual façade, a sight that always invigorated her spirit. The windows were of all shapes and sizes: arched and circular and some were leadlight, with a quaint little wooden portico presiding over them. The unique features seemed to join voices and cry out, *Look at me, look at me, I have dared to be different, I have defied all odds and I have succeeded!* Medicine for women had progressed a long way in thirty years, and Dody felt proud of her own small part in it. Without waiting for the hospital porter, she pushed open the heavy front door.

The ward rounds took up the better part of the day, and it was past teatime when she finally made her way to the pathology department of St. Mary's Hospital. A tall white-coated figure was alone in the laboratory, stooped over a microscope at one of the benches. For a moment she thought it might have been Spilsbury himself. The door banged behind her and the man turned to look up. He pushed an untidy fringe of greying hair from his forehead and squinted across the laboratory through a pair of thick-lensed glasses.

"Dr. McCleland, isn't it?" he asked. "Well, I'll be—thought you were still in Edinburgh."

Dody hurried over to where he sat and shook his hand, hiding her disappointment. Dr. Eccles was a fair man. He was one of the few who not did not discriminate between male and female doctors. "I've been back for just over a week, Dr. Eccles—though it feels far longer than that. Edinburgh seems a long way in the past now."

"Fully qualified and raring to go, eh? I believe we'll be seeing a bit more of you now you're with the Home Office. Spilsbury spoke very highly of you when he returned from Scotland. I think you might even have changed his opinion about lady doctors—and that's no mean feat, believe me."

Did Spilsbury really say that? Dody felt her colour rise. She consoled herself that, even with his glasses on, Dr. Eccles would probably not notice. "I'm glad to hear it, sir."

"I believe he will be seeking a personal assistant when he comes back from leave." Eccles's thick lenses glinted. "Perhaps you will apply."

"Oh . . . perhaps." There was nothing Dody would like more than to be Dr. Spilsbury's assistant. But she would not want to reveal her interest now, had no wish to betray herself to Eccles. Hers was a silly girlish crush—she knew that and would never take it further, even if Spilsbury were to show more than professional interest in her. Still, there was no harm in dreaming—was there?

She made a play at examining the rows of specimen jars above Dr. Eccles's head. "And how are things at St. Mary's?"

"Can't complain. The surgeons are at last taking our work seriously; sending pathological specimens to us is quite *de rigueur* these days." He pointed to a box of slides before him. "Tumours mainly, for identification. The old sawbones are finally becoming aware that not everything can be infallibly identified with the naked eye alone."

"But no talk yet of an exclusive police crime laboratory here as they are planning for Lyon?"

Eccles became wistful. "Ah, if only. We'll just have to leave that to the French for the time being. At least we can learn from their mistakes." He indicated a lab stool. "Sit down and tell me what I can do for you. If it's purely my company you are after, may I suggest dinner at the Savoy Grill? The whitebait comes highly recommended." His lips moved into a smile; he was a shameless flirt—and happily married with half a dozen children. Dody knew very well that if she were to accept the invitation, he would probably fall off his stool in shock.

"One day I might take you up on your invitation," she replied graciously, arranging her skirts over the stool, "but tonight I'm afraid I'm otherwise engaged." He looked relieved. "I was hoping you might shed some light on the latest blood analysis techniques for me."

Eccles removed his glasses and leaned back against the bench. "What is it you wish to know?"

"A simple test that can be done quickly on a bloodstain to determine the owner's blood group."

"I believe research is being carried out, but the development of a simple test is some years away. The Frogs will probably get there first; they always do."

"So there is no way I could test a weapon for a human blood group?"

"None, other than the presumptive test, which will only show you if the stain is, in fact, blood at all."

Dody saw herself seated on a stool like this in the draughty Edinburgh laboratory as she performed the basic test for haemoglobin. Again she felt her elation when she saw the reactive fizz of the reagent when it reached the red blood cells. She had not even contemplated the possibility of working out the identity of the owner back then. Chief Inspector Pike seemed impressively ahead of the game.

"Blood alone won't help you much," Eccles said, "and it would be a rare truncheon indeed that would have no human bloodstains on it at all."

Dody agreed, although she would not dream of saying such a thing to Pike. She was sorry, too, that the blood testing had turned out to be a dead end, for he would be disappointed. How strange, she thought, a week ago she would not have given tuppence for his feelings.

Olivia Barndon-Brown lived in a comfortable flat at the top of a dazzling white terraced house about a mile's walk from the McClelands' Bloomsbury residence. Dody instructed the driver of the motor taxi to wait in the street for her until she had finished her business. She would have walked home from here, but for the borrowed crutches.

In the hall Dody waited for the doorman to climb the stairs and announce her arrival to Olivia. She pondered how she might make peace with her sister without actually encouraging her home immediately. Olivia, who appeared to be the peacemaker of the group, might help, though everyone's nerves had been frayed since Lady Catherine's death and even the affable Olivia had seemed unduly agitated, her smile not so ready of late.

She looked over her shoulder and up the stairs. They were taking a long time. It occurred to her that if Florence were to suggest that Dody was a threat to their pending operation, Olivia might very well instruct the doorman to say there was no one at home.

At last she heard someone descend the stairs. She turned, expecting to see the doorman, but it was the Irishman, Derwent O'Neill, a grin stretched across his unshaven cheeks.

"What are you doing here?" Dody asked, the shock of seeing him overriding any semblance of good manners.

O'Neill stopped on the last step and loomed over her. His eyes slid down her body and rested for a moment on her breasts. "I'm the advance party, sent to flag a cab for the ladies." Lifting his gaze, he glimpsed her cab through the parlour window. His smile broadened. "Talk about the luck of the Irish—and motorised, too."

"That is my taxicab," Dody said stiffly. "You will have to find another."

There was a flurry of footsteps down the stairs and Derwent stepped aside for Florence, Daisy Atkins, Olivia Barndon-Brown, and Jane Lithgow and her glassy-eyed fox to pass.

"I'm escorting the ladies to the Rose and Crown. Would you care to join us, Dr. McCleland?" O'Neill asked.

Florence fussed with her gloves and would not meet Dody's gaze.

"Really, Mr. O'Neill," Florence said, "my sister wouldn't be seen dead in a public house."

Derwent gripped Dody's elbow and spoke in her ear, so only she could hear him. "Come on now, it does a woman good to loosen her stays every now and then."

Dody shook him off and said loudly, "Florence, when can I expect you home?"

"I'm not sure yet. I need some more clothes. I'll telephone Annie to bring some over."

"Tell me what you need and I'll organise it."

"Why can't we 'ave that taxi—we'd all fit into that," Daisy said.

"Because it's Dr. McCleland's," O'Neill said, mimicking Dody with an arch haughtiness.

"But what are them things jammed against the window?"

"Crutches for a patient, Daisy," Dody said quickly. Florence lifted a sceptical eyebrow, which Dody's conscience took to mean: *Since when has the delivering of medical supplies been one of your duties?* "And now I should go," she added. "The patient has just been discharged from hospital and is quite immobile without them. Please telephone me, Florence, we need to talk."

She hurried out of the front door, feeling several pairs of eyes on her back. Derwent O'Neill's mocking laughter accompanied her in the taxi all the way home.

Chapter Twenty-Two

Nellie Melba's liquid soprano seeped through the closed door of the morning room and into the hall, where Dody stood removing her coat. "Si Mi Chiamano Mimi"—she had not listened to the aria since leaving for Scotland. She stood still for a moment and closed her eyes, letting the melody soothe her jangled nerves. But it was not to be for long.

She heard the swing door from the kitchen and opened her eyes to see Annie wringing her hands.

"I'm so sorry, miss," the maid said, reaching for Dody's hat and coat. "This were all I could think to do to keep him where he was—I must have put this particular disc on for him half a dozen times." She turned towards the morning room and took a deep breath as if about to enter a lion's den. "Now you're home, maybe he'll let me turn it off."

Dody put up her hand. "It's all right, Annie. Leave it."

Annie looked relieved and started backing towards the downstairs door.

"He hasn't got a contagious disease, you know, Annie."

"Yeah, well, he's a copper, isn't he?" Annie briefly cast her eyes to the ceiling. "Is there anything I can get you before dinner, a sherry perhaps?"

"I know it's a bit late for tea, but I'd love some all the same. Bring in a tray for two. Has he eaten anything today?"

"Cook made him sandwiches for lunch and he ate the lot."

"Good, he must be feeling better." Dody leant the crutches against the hall chair.

The girl stood where she was, clutching Dody's hat and coat and scrutinising her face. "The tea, Annie," Dody reminded.

Annie made twirling motions with her fingers. "Um, perhaps, miss, you'd like to go upstairs first, brush your hair and have a little wash?"

Dody glanced at her reflection in the hall mirror. "Oh, what a mess, I see what you mean." It wasn't the flying tendrils of hair—they were fairly normal after a busy day at the hospital—it was the red-rimmed eyes betraying her tearful journey home from Olivia's flat.

Annie softened her tone. "Will Miss Florence be home soon, miss?"

"Next week, I think," Dody said vaguely, mounting the stairs to her rooms. "The tea, please, Annie."

Nellie Melba was still singing when Dody entered the morning room ten minutes later. Pike must have persuaded Annie to replay the aria when she had delivered the tea tray. Lost in the music, he lay on the chaise, eyes closed, one hand waving rhythmically as if he were conducting Miss Melba himself.

Dody cleared her throat. His eyes flew open and he started to get to his feet. "No, please, stay where you are," she said as she went to his side.

"I'm sorry," he murmured. "Habit. I hope you didn't mind me listening to your gramophone. I have never had the chance to hear one play before—it's quite wonderful."

Dody smiled. "But not as good as Miss Melba in person, or so I have been told."

"True. No machine could possibly capture the essence of that lyrical soprano—it must surely be heard in its natural form to be believed." He settled back against the pillows and Dody placed the back of her hand against his forehead.

"Good. No fever. How is the knee feeling?"

"A little throbbing, but not as much as last night. May I take it that you enjoy music, Dr. McCleland?"

"I enjoy music very much, though it's years since I managed time for a concert—hence the gramophone. Did you see my disc collection? I also have some marvellous Caruso recordings."

"I would have liked to hear more, but it seemed easier for your maid to keep playing the same one."

Dody settled herself in the chair opposite him. "Machines frighten her. I'll give her another lesson so you can listen to whatever you like tomorrow."

He shook his head. "I plan on taking the eight-ten to Hastings tonight. Annie telephoned my sergeant and had him bring over my things." He pulled back the blanket to reveal a pair of flannel trousers. "Not the best for winter weather, but they are the widest cut I have and I managed to fit them over the splint. I am taking up your suggestion; a few days away and I can return to work right as rain."

"I'm sorry, I will not hear of you leaving tonight." *Good-ness*, Dody thought as she heard herself speak, *I'm sounding like a bossy matron.*

"I am your prisoner?"

"The earliest you can leave is tomorrow," Dody continued in the same tone, "but only after a thorough examination. You also need to practise walking with the crutches."

"I have used crutches before."

Idiot, she chastised herself. Of course he had. The crutches were not really at the heart of the matter anyway. After the disastrous meeting with Florence, her only consolation was that she would not be coming home to an empty house. She realised then, as she looked sternly at him on the chaise, that she liked him, desired his company even. Lord, Florence would be mortified. But, of course, there were also valid medical reasons for him staying where he was.

"The swelling must diminish before I can allow you to leave," she said. "I'm afraid you are destined for another night on the chaise. My coachman will take you to the station tomorrow morning, provided I think you are fit enough for the journey to Hastings." She reached for the teapot and poured them both a cup. "If you continue to argue with me now, I will not give you the crutches at all."

Pike held up his hands in defeat, a hint of amusement in his expression. "Very well then, but I think your long-suffering maid probably deserves a bonus for having put up with me all day."

Dody allowed a slight smile back. If Pike knew the extent of poor Annie's suffering because of his presence, he'd recommend more than a bonus. Dody cut Pike some cake, which he ravenously devoured. She found she had no appetite and left her plate untouched. "Where do you plan to stay in Hastings?" she asked.

"A guesthouse where I've stayed before," Pike replied. "They're sure to have vacancies at this time of year."

"And what of Superintendent Shepherd?"

"I had my sergeant tell him that I am struck down with influenza and the doctor's orders are for a seaside cure. I'll use the time to visit my daughter again, think about the case, and study the surveillance photographs once more." He nodded to his briefcase on the floor. "Sergeant Fisher brought them here for me. There may be something in them I've missed."

"You can trust this sergeant of yours?"

"He is one of the few men in the force I would trust with my life."

When Annie appeared to clear the tea tray and draw the curtains, the conversation returned to music. Pike told Dody that an ex-corporal he knew worked at the Covent Garden box office and sometimes provided him with discounted tickets to musical productions. Then he surprised her. If he could obtain tickets, would she care to join him and his daughter to see Miss Melba perform in *La Bohème*?

Dody surprised herself even more by accepting the invitation.

By dinner, she found her appetite had markedly increased. Annie brought them fish pie with potato mash and broad beans cooked in bacon, which they ate at the card table, Pike's splinted leg propped on a chair. Dessert was chocolate tart.

"My sister's favourite pudding," Dody remarked over a second glass of hock. "Cook always made it to cheer her up on the last day of the school holidays."

"I take it the young lady is away at present?"

"She is staying with friends."

"Ah." Pike searched her face with uncomfortable intensity. Dody regretted bringing up the topic of Florence. She wondered if the inspector knew something about her sister that she did not. It was time to change the subject. "I nearly forgot to tell you, I made enquiries at the hospital today, and discovered it is not yet possible to conduct blood testing for group type."

"Ah well, then I shall have to find other means," Pike said. "It is no matter, thank you for trying." He was still looking intently at her.

"What is it?" she asked. "Why do you look at me like that?"

"Pardon me for saying this, but I thought you looked somewhat distraught when you first came home."

Dody touched her cheek—was he capable of detecting invisible tear tracks, too?

She composed herself. "Have you siblings, Chief Inspector?" There, she'd brought up the Florence topic again, albeit indirectly. It was hard not to when there had been little else on her mind.

"Please call me Pike; it's less of a mouthful. And yes, I do, a sister, quite a bit older than myself. She still treats me like a small boy and seems to disapprove of most everything I do."

"I think Florence must feel the same about me," Dody said ruefully.

Pike looked at her intently again. "You disapprove of your sister's activities?"

"Sometimes. Some of them." Dody scanned the table and latched on to the wine bottle. "More wine?"

It would be safer to switch the conversation to him, Dody decided as she filled his glass; men always enjoyed talking about themselves. "I can't imagine what a sister would find to disapprove of in you," she said.

"Are you mocking me?"

"A war hero, I am told, and now a high-ranking policeman—what is there to disapprove of or mock?"

"Unless one has something against the police, I agree. But I assure you, my sister is a passionate upholder of the system—any system," he added wryly. "But, you see, I didn't follow the path for which I was supposedly destined. I defied my parents and joined the army to avoid auditioning for the Royal Academy. I had a certain talent for the piano, but it was little more than mediocre. I decided it best to let my family down sooner, rather than later."

"So you became an officer in the army?"

"Not initially, I had neither money nor connections."

"Parents?"

"My father was the son of a vicar and a natural philanthropist—I never quite understood why he never went into the church himself. Perhaps he felt he could do more good moulding young minds as a schoolteacher."

Dody smiled, encouraged him to continue with a nod of her head.

"Mother came from a reasonably prosperous ironmongering family, had the benefit of quite a good education for her day. I think she married Father hoping to change him, hoping he would obtain a teaching position in a public school." Pike shrugged. "But he never budged, quite content in the village school even if it meant an insubstantial salary and no prospects. Mother used the money she earned teaching piano to buy my sister and I decent clothes, private tuition, and elocution lessons." Pike smiled at the memory. "It was only when she discovered that in the army I had risen through the ranks to captain that I was finally forgiven."

And rising through the ranks was no mean feat, Dody thought as she regarded him across the table. He straightened in his chair. She could see he did not expect praise for his achievements; he was simply revealing a part of himself that few would have guessed.

An outsider in the army because of his class, and probably an outsider in the police force because of his military status. They had more in common than she might have imagined.

"And your parents, are they still alive?"

"Alas, no."

Annie cleared the table and brought in coffee. They moved to their seats by the fireplace, and the conversation drifted into a comfortable silence. Pike swirled his brandy, apparently deep in thought. The fire crackled in the grate; the mantel clock chimed ten. Dody excused Annie and was about to leave for bed herself, when Pike stared into the fire and said, "When you see your sister next, you might attempt to persuade her to modify her activities, be wary of her associates."

"You mean the women of the WSPU?"

"Not only them." He looked away from the fire to meet her eye. "I believe she has been seeing an Irishman by the name of Derwent O'Neill, a former Fenian who has a history of making bombs." He paused briefly, and then said, "I am aware that he and his brother recently spent time with your family in Kent."

The remark snapped Dody out of her comfortable fog of sleepiness. "You have been spying on my family?" She could hardly speak she was so angry. She should have taken Annie's advice and never let him into the house. He had lulled her into a false sense of security with his vulnerability and his cultured behaviour, and now, typical of his kind, he had revealed his baser self.

Pike maintained a level gaze. "The O'Neills, like all political extremists, have been watched since their arrival in the country. Special Branch left a report on my desk, which Sergeant Fisher brought along with my things this afternoon. I feel I owe it to you to let you know that the Irishman was seen with your sister this morning."

Dody pursed her lips. "They met at my parents' house and have obviously become friends."

He seemed undaunted by her coldness and confirmed this with an impertinent question. "May I ask the reason for his visit to Sussex?"

"You may not, but as you already have, I feel obliged to answer."

"You have kindly taken me into your house and given me medical attention; I am in your debt. You are not obliged to answer me at all."

"I will tell you then, but only for the sake of my family's reputation. Derwent's brother Patrick has written a play about the Irish struggle and was hoping my mother would use her literary connections to have it produced. Derwent was simply accompanying his brother. My mother had to turn it down, however, though not because it lacked artistic merit. She said the play would be so heavily censored the message would be lost entirely."

"I see—like Mr. Shaw's satire of the government and the suffragettes?"

This new evidence of the range of his knowledge startled her for a moment. "Yes, like *Press Cuttings*. If a play written by someone as influential as Mr. Shaw could so easily be squashed, Mother knew Patrick O'Neill's wouldn't have a chance, even though it was in her opinion very good. As for Mr. Derwent O'Neill, I think I can assure you his bomb-making days are over. He uses a different weapon against the British government now, the power of argument and persuasion." When Pike failed to respond, Dody stood up from her chair and gripped the mantelpiece. "There now, are you satisfied? Is the interrogation complete?"

The lines on either side of Pike's mouth deepened and he suddenly looked very weary. "I'm sorry, but I felt I had to ask, to warn you." He was silent for a moment, and then said, "I know your sister means a great deal to you and that you would not like to think of her mixing with dangerous people. Your family does have a reputation . . . "

The man was impossible, all the more because secretly she agreed with him. Pike's fears for Florence were her own. Derwent O'Neill was a dangerous man; she was sure of it. But Pike had no right to speak of her family's reputation.

"My family, Chief Inspector, has passions. Passions that you could probably not begin to understand."

Pike did not flinch. He continued on his intended course. "There's more. There is a weighty intelligence file on Derwent O'Neill, and among the many items sent over by the Dublin police, there are several reports of his taking uninvited liberties with young ladies—he has never been prosecuted on this count, mind. His victims have not been willing to face public attention in the courts."

Victims? So her instincts about O'Neill had been more than correct. She sat back down and covered her eyes with her hands. Despite the warmth of the fire, she felt herself shudder.

She looked up to see Pike hobbling towards her. "Stay where you are—your knee," she ordered, though her voice had lost its command.

"Damn and blast it, do you never cease playing the doctor?" Pike leaned over and clutched the arm of her chair. "Well then, let me play the policeman. Let me put it to you that you know your sister has been keeping company with O'Neill, and that the two of you fought over this, and that is the reason she is currently staying with friends and why your eyes showed signs of weeping when you arrived home this evening."

She closed her eyes, fearing what else he might read in them. Tears caught in her throat but she would not allow them to spill. "You notice too much, Pike," she said.

He remained where he was for a moment, looking down at her. Then he reached out and touched her arm. His hand lingered for a moment. The warmth of his touch brought unexpected comfort, and then something more. Deep blue eyes studied her face with concern and she found she could not meet them. "There now, I'm sorry for upsetting you," he said. "I'm sure your sister is perfectly safe; she is, after all, a formidable young woman."

Dody nodded, her energy for an altercation gone, like sparks up the chimney. "No, you were right to tell me. And it is true, you have merely confirmed my own suspicions about the man, and for that I am grateful," she said, glad that her voice did not betray the internal tremor his touch had triggered. She patted his hand. "Now please, return to the chaise, I am quite all right now."

Once he was settled again and her thoughts restored, she said, "The trouble is, Florence is not amenable to advice from me at the best of times, and right now we are barely talking. I don't know what I can do."

"Then perhaps she will work him out for herself."

Dody shook her head. "For all her brashness, she is quite the innocent. She has had little experience with that type of man. She's also impulsive and blinkered. All she seems capable of thinking about these days is her wretched cause."

Pike took a small silver case from his briefcase and offered Dody a cigarette, which she leaned over to take. She would have preferred her pipe but didn't have the will to get up and fetch it from her bag in the hall.

He held up his matchbox. "I'd light it for you only . . ." Dody shook her head and indicated for him to throw the box, which she deftly caught with one hand. Pike looked impressed.

"Can you have O'Neill arrested?" she asked after lighting up and inhaling deeply.

"On what charge?"

"Oh, come now, since when have the police needed a reason to arrest someone?"

Pike furrowed his brows as if to say, *Please, not this jousting session again.* She knew she had overstepped the mark and immediately regretted it. "I'm sorry. I shouldn't have said that; not all policemen are tarred with the same brush." She wanted to tell him that she feared the suffragettes and O'Neill were planning something dangerous together, but stopped herself. She had no proof as to what they were up to, and more important, she knew where her loyalties lay—not with the militants, but with her sister.

He made a good show of forgetting her flippant remark. "O'Neill is already being watched," he said. "I can alert

Special Branch to be more vigilant, but other than that, there is little I can do."

"I will send Florence a note warning her about O'Neill. I won't say how I found out about him, just that it has come to my attention." Dody left her cigarette in the ashtray and moved to the writing desk by the window. "I imagine she will take little notice of it, but it might at least open her mind to the possible dangers of the association." *Not to mention the dangers of the bombs*, she added silently to herself.

Chapter Twenty-Three

"Do you wish to reply to the note I delivered earlier, Miss Florence? Miss Dody was most particular I ask." Fletcher carried a bulging sack of tools from the porch of Olivia's flat and deposited it on the floor of the carriage.

Florence caught Olivia's eye and looked briefly to the inky sky. "What, right now?" Eight o'clock at night outside Olivia's flat was hardly the time or place to be entering into a correspondence with her sister. "I'll see her tomorrow when this is all over," she said. "Does she know you've brought me the carriage?"

"I've said nothing about it to Miss Dody or to Annie, miss. They think I'm just running errands. And anyhow, I really did need to see the coach maker about the new upholstery—"

"Good man," Florence cut him off, no keener to enter a discussion about upholstery than she was to write a note to her sister. "And that policeman has gone?"

"Left this morning, took him to the station myself."

"And good riddance," Olivia said. "I'm afraid your sister has sunk considerably in my estimation, Flo. Never in my wildest dreams could I have imagined that she would go harbour the enemy."

Florence sighed. The news had upset her, too, though she was damned if she would let it distract her from the mission ahead.

"What was in the note anyway?" Olivia asked.

"Just Dody being a worrywart. Derwent O'Neill apparently has a reputation with the ladies. Probably some tosh told to her by that policeman."

Olivia snorted. "I'd like to see O'Neill try something with me."

Florence rubbed her arms to warm them, her eyes on the doorway of Olivia's building. "Daisy and Jane. What's keeping them?"

"Calm down, old girl, they'll be moving as fast as they can."

"I know, I know. I just can't bear all this horrid waiting. Fletcher, go and fetch the trunk, please. They must have finished packing it by now."

"Are you sure you can trust your man?" Olivia said as they watched him lumber towards the door.

"Fletcher's a good egg; he told us about the policeman, didn't he? Still, the less he knows about this operation, the better. He'll go straight home after he's dropped us off. We'll make our own way back, even if it means walking—it'll be easier without the equipment anyway."

"I'm not piggybacking Jane."

Florence laughed. Olivia always managed to lift her mood. "It's a shame Molly Jenkins can't make it; we could have used her muscle."

"Probably locked in the house by her brute of a husband."

Fletcher came out of the building, his back stooped under a large trunk. Jane and Daisy followed, Daisy giggling in high spirits. Olivia moved towards her and put an arm around her thin shoulder. "Try to keep calm now, Daisy dear."

"But it's all such a lark, ain't it?"

Olivia did up the buttons on Daisy's coat. "Now, you must tie your scarf around your face when we get there. That way, even if we are seen, no one will recognise you."

Daisy responded with an angelic smile. "Yes, you, too, Olivia."

Florence had been reluctant to allow Daisy along. She felt it was unfair to endanger the girl. Devoted to the cause though she was, Daisy was inclined not to think and she could easily, albeit unintentionally, betray them. But Daisy had begged and pleaded, and Florence had been outvoted. She turned to Jane Lithgow. "You packed the wires and the blasting caps?"

Jane Lithgow lifted her chin and said, "Of course. And the acid and the dynamite—they're all in the trunk."

Florence had her doubts about Jane, too. The regal Jane had never so much as pulled a weed from a window box, let alone survived a Fabian hockey match. How on earth, she wondered, did she think she could destroy a golf course?

The night was clear and cold. As the sound of clopping hooves faded into the distance, Florence and Jane carried the trunk to the grassy velvet of the eighteenth hole, where Daisy and Olivia, each illuminated by a shrouded lantern, had begun their work. Daisy was slicing through the turf next to the sandbunker with her shovel as if she were digging a vegetable patch. Olivia stood at the pole that marked the hole, struggling to undo the strings of the club flag.

Florence blew into the scarf covering her nose and mouth, her breath unnaturally loud to her muffled ears. Every now and then the silence was broken by a whisper, the clank of metal, the hoot of an owl from the nearby copse. Daisy giggled. Florence hissed her silent, then saw what had set her off. Olivia had replaced the club flag with their suffragette pennant of purple, green, and white and was standing to attention before it. She made a caricature of a military salute, prompting another fit of giggles from Daisy. Florence hissed for silence again. The golf course had no watchman, but the police occasionally patrolled the neighbouring common and it was important that they remain as quiet as possible.

From the trunk Florence took a bucket and a small drum of water while Jane unwound the last of the padding around a wicker-covered bottle. She stood up, carefully holding it reverently in her arms as if it were a newborn babe. "Acid to water, acid to water . . ." Jane chanted.

"I can't see what difference it makes," Daisy said. "Take the kettle to the pot, or the pot to the kettle, it's all the same tea."

"If we do it wrong," Jane said with relish, "we will blow ourselves up."

Daisy took a hasty step back. "Really?" Olivia shot Jane a poisonous look before putting her arm around the terrified girl.

"That is what Mr. O'Neill said."

"Oh, do try to get on, please," Florence snapped, exasperated that Olivia, whom she could usually rely on, should choose this moment to become belligerent.

Florence poured the water from the small drum into the

bucket. Daisy gulped a breath as Jane removed the glass stopper from the bottle and slowly added the acid.

Florence looked at the rolling topography about her. "Where shall we put it?"

Olivia pointed to a gentle dip of smooth grass above the sandbunker. *As good a spot as any*, Florence thought as she carried the bucket over with the others following. Jane insisted that because she had such a fine copperplate, she should do the honours. She reached into her pocket and brandished a stiff bristle paintbrush.

"Hurry up then," Florence said. "Before the bristles dissolve."

They held the lanterns close as Jane etched out the letters with a steady hand onto the green. The air around them became filled with the sharp tang of smouldering grass.

Even Florence had to admit that Jane's dedication to detail was worth the frustration—the words VOTES FOR WOMEN! were so meticulous, they could have been printed in *The Times*. Perhaps, she thought, one day those words really would make the headlines. She hoped she would be alive to see it.

Daisy clapped her hands. "Do you think the PM's really going to see this?"

"Do you never listen? He's playing golf here tomorrow morning, girl. He won't be able to miss it," Jane said.

Florence waved her hand for silence again. "All right, girls, well done—to the clubhouse now. Jane and Daisy, I want you to scout around the building to make sure there are no signs of life, within or without. Check the storage sheds around the back, too, if you can."

The two women lifted their skirts and walked briskly towards the gravel parking area and clubhouse beyond.

"We'll leave everything we don't need behind," Florence said to Olivia as they bent to lift the trunk, much lighter now without the bottle of acid, the water drum, and the bucket.

The clubhouse loomed magnificently out of the darkness, its Grecian-style front entrance glowing in the moonlight like a temple. How fitting, Florence thought, that one group of oppressors should pay homage in this way to another. She smiled to herself—this lot of oppressors were in for a surprise.

They placed the trunk carefully at the top of the steps and began to assemble the explosives according to Derwent O'Neill's instructions. With purple, green, and white ribbons, they tied bundles of dynamite to each of the front pillars and embedded the blasting caps. Then came the tricky part of twisting the blasting caps to the detonator wires. Derwent had made them practise this at Olivia's flat wearing gloves. At the time, it had gone quite smoothly, but the real thing proved far more of a challenge with nerves and the cold making their hands shake.

"I wish I could take my gloves off," Olivia complained.

"Well, you can't. Remember what Derwent said about fingerprints?"

"Sounds like a load of codswallop to me," Olivia said, soldiering on.

At last the caps were connected and Olivia began to unravel the spools, trailing the wire first across the parking area, then the defiled eighteenth hole, and finally over the rough towards a small copse. Florence followed behind with the oak detonation box, the last of the objects from the discarded trunk. When studying the plans of the golf course earlier, she had estimated the distance from the front entrance to the copse to be about eighty yards. To her disappointment, she discovered it was closer to a hundred.

"Blast," she said. "I'd hoped to use the copse for cover when we detonated the explosives. I should have come during the day and measured it for myself instead of relying on those silly plans."

"In this bastion of male supremacy, that would have been harder than what we're doing now," Olivia said. "One whiff of woman on the wind and they'd probably have set the hounds on you."

"I'm jolly glad they don't have any hounds. Ah well, no harm done, the place seems deserted enough."

They felt more confident now they were away from the clubhouse. With steadier hands, it took only a few seconds to wind the wires under the butterfly screws of the detonator box.

The moment had almost arrived. Florence's heart leapt with excitement. All they needed was for Jane and Daisy to return with the all clear. She crouched next to the box, eyed the T-bar, and smiled at Olivia through the shimmering light of the lantern. "Who's going to do the honours?"

Olivia reached into her pocket. "I have a penny, we'll toss for it when the others join us."

"What can they be up to? They're taking an age."

"Maybe they found a cat?"

"Or a canary."

A sudden commotion from behind the clubhouse cut short their nervous laughter. Raised men's voices—shouts and shrill whistles—and then the terrible sound of a woman screaming.

"Oh my God, they've been caught—Daisy! That's Daisy screaming! What are they doing to her?" Olivia gasped.

Florence extinguished the lantern and pulled Olivia down to a crouch at her side, holding tightly on to her arm as she struggled to get away. "You won't do any good," she said urgently. "You'll only get arrested, too—remember what Christabel said, we cannot let ourselves get arrested! We are needed on the outside of the bars, where we can do some good."

"Hang Christabel, Daisy needs me!" Olivia shook her off and ran from the edge of the copse.

"Stop, Olivia, please stop!" Florence whispered after her, but in moments the sound of Olivia's screams joined those of the others. *What were they doing to them?* She felt terrible holding back, but there was nothing she could do to help them; it was pointless to even try. And the idea of disobeying Christabel's orders was almost as abhorrent to her as the thought of being arrested again. A Black Maria crackled over the gravel and pulled into the parking area. It must have been waiting close by. Then she realised: *It had been waiting for them.* Someone had given the game away. She watched with horror as her three friends were bundled into the back of the police vehicle like sacks of coal.

There was a shout from the portico; the dynamite had been discovered. Silhouettes of uniformed policemen scurried about, lamps casting flickering shadows up the Grecian pillars. Florence watched as a man reached out to grasp one of the bundles of dynamite; saw another pull him roughly back. She swung her gaze to the detonator box. The raised plunger seemed to call out to her. In her head she heard Derwent's soft lilt: "It's just a matter of pushing it down, simple as that." As if pulled by a magnetic force, her hand moved to the box and rested lightly on the T-bar. The mission could still be a success, just a little pressure . . .

She pulled her hand back. She couldn't do it. The men were too close. Their plan had been to blow up an empty building. She could not wilfully injure a fellow creature, even if they were the damned police.

There were more shouts; they had found the detonator wires, and several police were running towards the copse.

"Oh, bloody hell!" Florence yanked the wires from the detonator, kicked the box onto its side, and set off at a crashing run through the tangled undergrowth.

Chapter Twenty-Four

"This might sting a little," Dody said as she applied the antiseptic to the angry scratches on Florence's cheek.

"Ouch—Dody, you did that on purpose!"

No more tears, dear Florence, please, Dody silently pleaded as she leaned over her sister on the bed. Florence had had far worse injuries than this on the hockey field and not so much as uttered a squeak. "Why should I hurt you on purpose, silly goose?" she said.

"Because of what I've done."

"I think you've suffered enough from the consequences of your actions, don't you?"

"I suppose you're going to tell your new friend all about this now."

"New friend?"

"That man Pike, the policeman you kept in our house for

two nights, the one Annie did all the running about for, and the one, I suspect, that you sneaked to about our operation."

Dody clenched her jaw. It was all she could do to restrain herself from increasing the pressure on Florence's cuts. "Don't be ridiculous; I knew nothing about this operation of yours other than a suspicion you were all up to something with Derwent O'Neill." She threw the damp swab into the bowl and began to pack up her equipment, clattering and clanking the enamel bowls together. "If word reached the police, I assure you, it was not from my lips. You never told me what you were planning, or where or when it was to be, which is just as well, because with the benefit of hindsight, perhaps it would have been a good idea if I had told the chief inspector."

Florence leaned back into her pillows and stared at the ceiling in silence.

This was unusual; her sister always liked to have the last word. As Dody finished putting away her equipment, she thought back to her conversation with Pike by the fire. He had probably known about the operation then; his sergeant would have brought him the information along with his things. Pike's words of warning had been calculated to sound generalised, but he must have been hoping she would read more into them. Perhaps she would have if she'd known exactly what was going on.

Florence creased her brows and said in a small voice, "No, you're right, of course you wouldn't sneak. I'm sorry to have said such a thing. My head's in such a muddle, but I do believe you, honestly. And Dody, I'm sorry I was such a pig the other night."

"That's all right, Flo. We were both a bit distraught."

"Someone betrayed us, though; the police were tipped off,

ready and waiting." She turned to the clock on the bedside table. "The girls will be in front of the magistrate soon. I must be there to give them moral support."

She attempted to swing her legs over the bed, but Dody grabbed them and pushed them back.

"No, Florence, please don't go, I beg you," she cried. It seemed as though she were forever having to restrain people from rushing about before they were ready.

"If you go, all you will do is betray yourself. Have you looked in the mirror? There are cuts and bruises all over your face, and your foot almost torn to ribbons."

Florence made no more attempts to leave the bed. "I lost my shoe crossing a stream," she said miserably, "and then had to walk half the night to get home."

"You forgot your hat, too, by all accounts. No wonder no self-respecting cabbie would pick you up."

"A tree branch whisked it off and I didn't dare stop to retrieve it."

"The police probably have it by now, and might even manage to trace it back to you. You can't risk an appearance at that court."

Florence pressed her palms to her eyes. "I feel so awful. I've run away and left them to a fate worse than death itself."

"You were following orders." Dody softened her voice. "Sensible orders, too. Besides, darling, you've done your bit."

"So have they. Oh, Dody, I'm such a miserable, cowardly creature."

"Now stop that, you are just working yourself up into a state. The others may have been arrested before, but you are the only one of the group who has endured force-feeding. How could anyone expect you to go through that again—Christabel

Pankhurst certainly doesn't. She needs you working for the cause outside jail, not inside. And I certainly couldn't bear the thought of you enduring that again."

"And I will feel each suffocating shove of the tube with them, I know I will." Florence began to sob, great gasping sounds that seemed to shake her from the inside out. Dody took her sister in her arms and stroked her rich dark hair until the sobbing ceased and she fell into a fitful sleep.

Dody heard the telephone bell as she was on her way downstairs and reached it before Annie. The voice was familiar, but so full of fuss and bluster that Dody missed the caller's name.

"A woman's body, Doctor, found swinging from a roof beam; can't say if it's suspicious or not. I'd like you to have a look at it before we take it to the morgue."

"Is that you, Superintendent Shepherd?"

"Indeed. I need you now . . . most inconvenient, the police surgeon and Pike both away with influenza."

"Where shall I meet you, sir?" The line crackled, either with interference or Shepherd's impatience, Dody could not tell which.

"I've dispatched a motor wagon to fetch you."

The new housing reforms had yet to reach this East End neighbourhood, Dody observed as she gazed through the window of the motor wagon. The street was dirty and bleak and full of carts and barrows; the police motor wagon was the only motorcar on the road. She sensed that the Royal London Hospital was close by but failed to catch a glimpse of its distinct iron railings owing to the sweep of tenements on each side of the road. She sank back into the squeaking upholstery. She viewed the Royal London with the same yearning a pauper might have outside an inviting upmarket restaurant. Famous for its services to the East End poor, the hospital still barred its doors to female medical students and doctors.

As they drew up, scattering a group of listless children, a young policeman opened the motor wagon door for her and introduced himself as Constable Blunt. "This way, Doctor," he said, indicating a doorway behind him. He seemed anxious to get off the street, no doubt because the area was notorious. Nevertheless, Dody remained where she was, looking about her. Blunt cleared his throat. "The lady was found in this one." He pointed again to the open door.

"In a moment," Dody told him. "I need to get a feeling of the environs first." Even after death, she thought to herself, a place like this would surely cling to the skin like soot.

Blunt plunged his hands into his coat pockets and stamped his feet. Dody gazed at the old-style tenement block before her. Other than the numbers on the pitted door, nothing could distinguish this set of flats from its neighbours on either side. The rank odour suggested a midden close by, one that took more than just household waste. Victorian tenements such as these lacked the internal conveniences of the new flats that were being constructed elsewhere in London.

Wooden poles for washing jutted out over the street from balconies on the upper storeys. It was hard to imagine the sun's weak rays ever reaching this dingy part of the city, where shirts and trousers hung stiff and twisted, as if in a perpetual state of rigor.

Blunt glanced warily up and down the street. Children chased a hoop down the footpath, while others squatted in doorways and stared vacantly at their more energetic companions. Women passed by carrying pails and jugs to collect water from a standpipe in a nearby alley. The water was only switched on intermittently and they had to take advantage of it while they could, storing it in their rooms for later. Dody had discovered this when she treated the mother of a small child who had drowned in a tub of water stored in their flat. The mother had been admitted to hospital suffering from hysteria, and there was little Dody could do other than offer her sedation.

The constable broke into Dody's thoughts. "Please, Doctor, we needs to be upstairs and off the street. If the villains don't get us, the superintendent will." He picked up her medical bag, giving her no choice but to follow. "Watch your step, the body's upstairs, top floor." She stepped over a pile of rotting vegetable matter, passed through the doorway, and was immediately confronted with a long narrow stairway. Although it was cold, the gloom and fug of the apartment block felt stifling, the skylight at the top of the stairs letting in only a feeble light.

They came to a landing fronted with multiple doors exuding an unpleasant mixture of the odours of urine and boiled cabbage. Sounds of a bitter domestic argument reached them from behind a door on the next landing, but the constable marched on, seemingly oblivious to the cursing and crashing.

The last landing was perhaps a little cleaner than those below it. One door was ajar and from it wafted the scent of lavender water.

"In 'ere, Doctor." The constable knocked and pushed the door fully open, whereupon Dody was forced to renew her acquaintance with the cigar-chomping, loose-jowled Superintendent Shepherd.

She tried to take in the scene in the room, but found her

view obstructed by his bulk. She suspected this was his way of asserting control; only when he was well and truly ready would he permit her to examine the body. Shepherd was telling her about life in the tenements, speaking to her as if she had only just left school. Dody found herself wishing she were dealing with Pike. While he could be formal and stiff, he would not address her with such condescension.

"Oh, please," she said, losing her patience at last, "tell me what you must and then let me examine the body."

Shepherd took a step back and rubbed his strawberry nose. "Yes, very well." He cleared his throat. "A female colleague of the deceased raised the alarm first thing this morning." The pomposity of his vocabulary clashed with the rhythms of his London accent. "It was the custom of this lady and the deceased to accompany one another to their place of employment every morning. When the deceased failed to meet her outside, the lady climbed the stairs to the deceased's room, fearing her friend had taken ill. Upon reaching the landing, she discovered the door unlocked and the deceased woman hanged."

"The name of the dead woman, please, Superintendent."

"Miss Agatha Treylen. A shipping clerk at St. Katharine docks."

Dody kept her face expressionless. She was not going to admit that this was another of her sister's colleagues—the poor, drab Miss Treylen, whom she had met only once at that WSPU meeting when she'd first returned from Edinburgh. "We've not found a note yet." Shepherd nodded towards Constable Blunt, riffling his way through the drawers of a handsome Chippendale tallboy. An inlaid writing desk near the window looked also to have been recently ransacked, its drawers hanging open. These two fine pieces looked incongruous among the other furnishings: a rag mat, a simple washstand, and a cheap plywood wardrobe. The ashes in the grate had long since died, though somehow the lavender seemed to soften the edge of the bone-aching chill and the scent of death. What circumstances, Dody wondered, could have reduced a woman like Miss Treylen to a place like this?

Shepherd finally stepped aside. "It looks like suicide, but I need to rule out murder. Hope you can oblige, Doctor."

The body had been cut down, and lay stretched out on a narrow iron-framed bed. Next to the bed was an overturned chair, and above this, a cord, possibly from a dressing gown, dangled from a ceiling beam. The cord had been cut through, leaving the noose embedded in the soft flesh of the woman's throat.

Suicide seemed to be the most likely explanation; regardless, Dody pushed away the pen and paper Shepherd thrust under her nose. "I am not ready to sign the death certificate yet, Superintendent. I must cover all possibilities first."

Shepherd heaved a sigh and stepped back towards the small window.

Dody had learned much from Dr. Wilson at the Crippen autopsy and was keen to practise some of her newly acquired skills. Despite her eagerness, first she gazed respectfully at the body for a full minute, as was the custom she had developed in Edinburgh. Shepherd probably thought she was praying, and indeed it could be argued that this ritual was the closest she ever got to prayer these days.

She made a mental note of the blackened face and the bulging, bloodshot eyes. She tried to read their silent story—terror and despair, almost certainly. This had been a slow death through strangulation, nothing like the quick snap of the neck of a legal execution. Dody removed her gloves and gently pressed down the eyelids, holding the pressure until she could be sure they would not spring back open.

Miss Treylen wore day clothes: a black pleated skirt, shiny with wear; a woollen shawl pinned with a cheap brooch; and a plain white blouse with its stiff collar removed. Dody took a scalpel blade from her bag and sliced through the noose, careful not to inflict any more damage to the disfigured neck. The knot had been positioned at the back, she noticed. In a judicial hanging it was on the left side. With the constable's help, she turned the body onto its side, pulled back the neck of the blouse, and pointed out the inverted V-shaped bruise to him.

"But couldn't someone have knocked her out or strangled her with his hands before stringing her up?" Blunt asked.

Shepherd gave an exasperated sigh as if to say, *Let her get on with it, man*. But it was a reasonable question and one Dody felt deserved a reply. "If she was manually strangled," she told him, "there would be more bruising around the neck, possibly even a handprint visible." She allowed the body to fall back, unpinned the dull brown hair, and ran her fingers over the scalp. "I can feel no lumps, and there appear to be no other injuries to the head. Unfortunately I can't at this time rule out the possibility that someone may have put the noose around her neck and strung her up while she was alive. The scene might easily have been manufactured to imitate suicide."

Shepherd turned from the small window. "At what time did the lady expire?"

Dody spent a moment manipulating the corpse's lower jaw, examining the fingernails and limbs. "Rigor mortis has not yet started to wane. I estimate that this lady met her death in the early hours of the morning."

"Well, at least she did it properly. Unlike some."

"Yes, I suppose she has saved you some extra paperwork, Superintendent. Failed suicides must be extremely tiresome for you."

Agatha Treylen's limbs showed no signs of bruising. Dody undid the woman's blouse and continued to look for evidence of a struggle.

"Not just paperwork, there's court proceedings and jail expenses, too," Shepherd said.

"Shall I start questioning the neighbours, sir, see if she had any visitors last night?" Blunt asked. The lad must have felt the mounting tension and wanted to distance himself from it.

Shepherd held up his hand to silence the constable. He kept his eyes fixed on Dody as she went about undoing the dead woman's corset. At the last of the fastenings, Dody felt the crinkle of paper beneath her fingertips. Reaching between the layers of clothing, she removed a folded square of paper. Barely had she read it before Shepherd snatched the note from her hand and waved it at the constable.

"Don't bother with the neighbours," he said with an air of satisfaction. "This note will tell us what we need to know."

Chapter Twenty-Five

Florence declined Annie's offer of soup and fell silent. She had not touched a morsel since her arrival home at daybreak. She waited until Dody had been served and the maid dismissed from the dining room before continuing to talk.

"I telephoned Jane's and Olivia's solicitors while you were out," she said. "All three have been charged with criminal damage and sentenced to three months' hard labour at Holloway Prison."

"Are they all in the same division?"

"Jane and Olivia have been classified as first-division prisoners—political prisoners—while poor Daisy has been put in the third division."

"Because of her class?"

"The magistrate maintained it was due to the nature of her crime, which he saw as manual labour. He must have considered the other crimes to be more genteel, I suppose.

Goodness only knows what would have become of me if I had been caught—the gallows, probably."

Dody suppressed a shudder. If Florence had witnessed what she had at Pentonville Prison, she might not be so flippant. "Which means Jane and Olivia will be spared the indignity of broad-arrow uniforms, receive better quality food and less arduous labour, while Daisy will suffer treatment of the worst kind. I thought Lady Lytton had put an end to that kind of discrimination."

"Obviously not." Florence lowered her gaze to her empty table setting.

"Did you manage to get some sleep this morning?" Dody asked.

"My body was tired but my mind wouldn't stop. I awoke not long after you left and started making telephone en-quiries." She paused. "You do know what this means, don't you, Dody?" Her sister's earnest look made Dody reluctant to ask for fear of hearing the worst. She lowered her eyes to her soup.

"Olivia will go on hunger strike," Florence said. "Her solicitor said she announced from the dock that while incar-cerated she would refuse all form of food and drink until all imprisoned suffragettes, regardless of social status, are treated as political prisoners."

"Are the others striking, too?"

"I don't know, not sure if the others have the same kind of pluck."

Annie and the scullery maid slipped into the dining room with their dinner of gammon steaks and parsley sauce. Dody insisted that Florence eat something. "It's not you on the hun-ger strike," she said.

Florence shivered, but took a small mouthful. "I do wish Cook would not serve such heavy meals when there are only the two of us at home."

Dody waited for Florence to push her half-finished meal away, then asked Annie to leave them. "I have some distressing news, Florence. I was called to a suicide this morning, a young woman from Whitechapel."

"Oh, poor you, how terrible," Florence said absently.

"I'm afraid it's someone you know. Agatha Treylen."

Florence straightened, giving Dody her instant attention. "Whom did you say? Miss Treylen?"

Dody outlined the circumstances of the woman's death, but did not reveal the contents of the note. She wanted to make sure Florence could cope with the news before adding the twist at the end of the tale. "But what I don't understand," she said as she concluded her narrative, "is how a reasonably educated, apparently respectable woman like Miss Treylen could end up living in a place like that."

"I'll tell you why," Florence said with a flush to her cheek. "It's what this whole fight is about—that men and women should be treated as equals. It was Miss Treylen's circumstances that prompted her to join us in the first place. Miss Treylen is"—she took a sip of wine to calm herself—"*was* a married woman unable to obtain a divorce from her husband."

"I thought divorce was easier for women now."

"The laws are better than they were, but still men can obtain a divorce if their wives commit adultery; women if their husbands commit incest, or adultery coupled with desertion, cruelty, or unnatural practices. Agatha's husband frequently beat her. She thought that was a good reason to leave him, but the law did not. Not only has she been unable to divorce him, but she has not received a penny from him either. And to add insult to injury, when he discovered she'd found an office job at the docks—employment which pays only half that of her male counterparts, I might add—he demanded she contribute towards the welfare of their child, whom he took from her."

"But surely no law would expect her to do that?"

"He claimed she owed it to him because she deserted him. And she believed him, because—you may not believe this, Dody—he's a lawyer. A lawyer who earns one hundred times as much as she does."

That a professional man should beat his wife did not surprise Dody. From her work at the hospital she knew that, contrary to popular belief, it was not only the working-class man who used physical force against women.

"Christabel Pankhurst, who has studied law, but is not allowed to practice—"

"Because she is a woman," Dody finished for her.

"Don't mock me, Dody."

"I'm sorry. Please continue."

"Christabel was going to see what she could do to help, but the pressure for Miss Treylen was obviously too much to bear." Florence dabbed her eyes with her napkin.

"Poor Miss Treylen," Dody said and meant it.

"I'm glad you feel sympathy, Dody, but can't you see, the system has to change!" Florence banged her fist upon the table to emphasise these last words.

That's more like it, Dody thought, surprised that the table banging had not come any earlier. "Of course I see," she said. "My dear, you are preaching to the converted."

Florence turned her head away. "Sometimes I wonder about you, after everything you went through to study medicine . . ."

"Florence, that is enough, we are slipping from the point. Please let us not get into our methodology argument again. There is something else I need to tell you. Miss Treylen left a note addressed to the Bloomsbury Division, which I'm sure you will be given when the police are finished with it. In the note she confessed to telling the police about the golf course sabotage in return for payment. She begged you all to forgive her."

The angry flush left Florence's cheeks, and she became deathly pale. Dody left her seat and put an arm around her sister's shoulders.

"That explains everything, doesn't it?" Florence said. "I don't blame Miss Treylen at all, and of course I forgive her. It's the police I cannot forgive, those scavengers who prey upon the weak and the helpless. I could so easily have pressed that plunger when they were gathered about the clubhouse entrance. Derwent wanted us to kill police, I'm sure of it. Even though he never said anything outright, he hinted—he hates them even more than we do . . ." Her voice trailed off as if she could not face the direction her mind was taking her.

"I cannot tell you how glad I am that you didn't," Dody said, closing her eyes to try to hide the horror she felt. Had her sister acted on the impulse, she would have crossed the line from the obsessively passionate to the deranged fanatic. Once that line had been crossed, no psychiatrist on earth could pull her back.

Not wishing to upset Florence further, Dody said no more on the subject. Agatha Treylen's suicide had caused her to miss her morning duties at the hospital, and she told Florence she would be out for the rest of the afternoon.

"I have to go out also," Florence said, leaving her chair and hobbling over to the bell to summon Annie to clear the table.

"I would much rather you didn't. You should stay at home and rest with your foot up. You have had quite an ordeal."

"My mind will not let me rest. And anyway, I promised I'd call on Lady Lytton to discuss the golf course disaster."

Chapter Twenty-Six

Dody put down her pen and paused for thought. She was in the habit of updating her diary every evening, but had returned from the hospital late the previous night too exhausted to do anything. Her watch had been even grimmer than usual. Upon her arrival she had been required to sign two death certificates, septicaemia cases brought in during the night, both the result of criminal abortion. Next she'd assisted the house surgeon in repairing the prolapsed uterus of a woman who had recently given birth to her tenth living child. After that she'd seen to the admission of a malnourished fifteen-year-old, pregnant to her father. Between then and the night locking of the hospital doors, she had treated two babies with diphtheria and organised a young girl into isolation with a suspected case of poliomyelitis.

Her watch had at least ended on a high note, with the successful delivery of abnormally presented twins. It was the euphoric look on the father's face she'd carried into her dreams that night, and not the misery of those unfortunate others.

She yawned, put a full stop at the end of her diary entry, and was about to pull the bell for some morning coffee when the door flew open and her sister blew in amongst a whirlwind of rustling pink silk.

"Oh thank goodness, you are still here," Florence said, one hand over her breast as if to calm a fluttering heart. "I wasn't sure if you were at the hospital today or not."

"I only work three days a week at the hospital. Today I plan on studying at home."

"Of course, you can choose your own hours, can't you? Considering the amount of time you've spent there, one would think you were getting paid for it."

With so few hospitals willing to employ female physicians, the only alternative to being labelled an incompetent "shilling" doctor was to give one's services for free in order to gain experience. In this respect Dody was lucky; she was of independent means and could afford to give her time gratis, though there were still plenty of other obstacles to overcome that no amount of money could smooth.

"What is it, Florence? Do you really care whether I am paid or not?" She pointed to the jumble of textbooks on her desk. "I have much to get done here."

Florence was pacing the room, her dress rustling with every step. "They have started force-feeding Olivia. Dody, I beg you. Please do something!"

Dody sighed. "There's nothing I can do to stop it. These measures are ordered by the court and enacted by the prison physician."

"Well, you could supervise, couldn't you? Make sure the

procedure is carried out safely? The doctor who fed me was a brute. Not only did he force me to swallow his wretched tube, he slapped my face when I protested. And when I refused to lie still, four wardresses were called in to hold me down. It was tantamount to, well—"

Rape. Dody said the unmentionable word in her head, the act that was implied but never said aloud by any of the victims of force-feeding. The procedure was brutal and cruel and if, in her capacity as a doctor, she were ever asked to perform it, in all but the most extenuating of circumstances, she would surely refuse. But still, Florence was right—there should be something she could do to try to ensure the procedure was carried out in a safe and humane manner.

"Dody, are you listening to me?"

"Be quiet for a moment, I'm thinking." She tapped her nails on the leather surface of her textbook. "At Pentonville," she mused aloud, "I met an agreeable doctor called Wilson. He is sure to know the Holloway physician. I will telephone him and see if something can be arranged."

Dody put the telephone down, wishing that every door could be opened this easily for her. She looked towards the grandfather clock in the hall. She had just enough time to search her new textbook for poliomyelitis before she was due at the prison. A ring of the doorbell stopped her halfway up the stairs. As Annie was nowhere to be seen, Dody made her way back down and answered the door herself.

Pike lifted a shiny silk hat. "Good morning, Dr. McCleland."

He appeared much improved. The sea air had put colour

into his cheeks, and he was dressed as smartly as any city gentleman.

"Well, this is an unexpected surprise." She could not hold back the delight she felt at seeing him looking so well. "How is the knee?"

"Much better, thank you." He took hold of the crutches propped on the front pillar. "I thought it was time I returned these—may I bring them inside?"

"Please." She stepped aside to let him pass. He leaned the crutches against a stack of Florence's boxes and turned to face her, his weight propped on his cane.

"You are back at work now?"

"I start officially tomorrow morning—with a meeting in the superintendent's office."

"Something you are no doubt greatly looking forward to."

He responded with a smile. "And in the meantime I am out taking the air."

"I would like to examine your knee."

"Another time, perhaps. I'm sure you have better things to do."

"Nothing that can't wait a minute or two, and besides, you are as much my patient as anyone." She put her hand out for his hat and gloves and placed them on the hall table as Annie pushed through the downstairs door. The maid's face fell. After a curt nod from Dody, she helped Pike off with his outdoor things. Under his coat he wore a dark frock coat with silk lapels, a grey waistcoat, and matching cravat.

"She seems as pleased to see me as ever," Pike remarked as he watched Annie drag her feet off to the cloakroom.

Dody indicated the door of the morning room. She wanted him ahead of her so she could assess his gait. He leaned more heavily on his cane than he had before the beating, she noticed, but he certainly didn't require the crutches. He sat on the chaise and began to roll up his trouser leg, but stopped with a sudden intake of breath, his hand reaching for his side.

"Your rib is still troubling you?" Dody asked.

He straightened with care. "Sometimes, yes."

"Here, let me." She knelt before him and finished rolling up the trouser leg for him. "When did you remove the splint?" she asked, finger and thumb exerting gentle pressure on his knee.

"About two days ago." He breathed out. "My daughter found the writing most amusing. I believe she has cut it out and kept it to show her school friends."

"Are you getting used to the idea that you and your daughter have different views upon the matter?"

"I am not made of stone, Doctor; I am capable of seeing the humorous side of some situations. But this will not prevent me from doing everything in my power to stop her from getting involved with the hysterical activities of the unwomanly suffragettes." She hit a tender spot and he drew another sharp breath. "Fortunately there is not much of this term left for her to make mischief in. Her maternal grandparents will be keeping a close eye on her during the Christmas holidays."

She continued to manipulate his knee. "The swelling is much diminished. You should be ready for surgery in a month or so—would you like me to make the necessary arrangements?"

The colour left Pike's cheeks. "Thank you, but no, not just yet. I will need to talk to Shepherd. I am not sure when I can be spared."

"Surgical techniques and anaesthesia have improved greatly in the last ten years," she said.

"I'm sure they have." He rolled down his trouser leg.

"You don't even have to have the operation in a hospital," she persisted. "I can do it here if you wish."

He looked up from the bootlace he was retying. "You? Here?"

"Home surgery is always an option. I can employ a private nurse and another doctor to administer anaesthetic."

Pike reached for his cane and pulled himself to his feet. "Thank you, Dr. McCleland, but I am in your debt as it is. I do not wish to impose further."

"Is it because I am a woman? I admit to not being a fully qualified surgeon—women are barred from the profession, you know—but the technique is a simple one. Or perhaps you do not think me capable," she said, even though her instinct told her this was not the case at all. She felt sure his reluctance had more to do with his experiences in South Africa. His demeanour, the sparkle of perspiration on his brow whenever the subject of surgery was mentioned, reminded her of Florence after her prison ordeal. Encouraging her sister to talk about her ghastly experiences had helped very much. With a man of Pike's reserve, however, it seemed unlikely he would be willing to talk—to her or to anyone—about something that he would see in himself as a lack of moral fibre.

"No, no, not at all, I know you are quite capable of operating on my knee," he said. "I have seen how you work and I am full of admiration. If I were to allow anyone to perform my operation, it would be you." He flicked her a smile that did not reach his eyes. "But now I must leave. I have taken up enough of your time."

"Wait, we still have more to discuss. Please sit down, your consultation is not yet finished."

With a murmur of protest, he sank back down onto the chaise.

"You are aware of the golf course sabotage and the arrest of three of the Bloomsbury WSPU members?"

He paused. "I am."

"And you approve, I suppose?"

"Of course. They were about to detonate a bomb. People could have been killed. They must suffer the consequences."

"Even if the consequences mean force-feeding?"

"Yes, if medical intervention is necessary to prevent the crime of suicide," he replied evenly, "but I cannot see what this has to do with my knee."

"Your knee? Oh, nothing at all." Dody smiled with contrived sweetness. "Recently you gave me the opportunity to witness something I had never seen before. You told me it would assist with my further education."

He shifted on the chaise. "Ah, the Crippen execution . . ."

"And now I would like to return the favour. I would like to give you the opportunity of witnessing something that will further *your* education. I would like you to accompany me to witness a force-feeding—medical intervention, as the legal profession euphemistically call it."

She was being cruel to a kind man, she knew it, but she wanted to shake him out of some of his rigid beliefs, and this was all she could think of. As she rose from her chair, she realised Florence and Pike were different sides of the same coin.

He gazed at her for a moment. "You are throwing down the gauntlet, Dr. McCleland."

"You have never seen a force-feeding?"

"No."

"Then perhaps it is time you did. It was your department, after all, that bribed the informer and subsequently arrested the women involved. Are you aware that the poor Treylen woman has since taken her life?"

He said nothing, but the tightening of the lines around his mouth told her his answer would have been no.

Chapter Twenty-Seven

The prison cell was no warmer than the hospital mortuary. Dody did her best to control her shivering as she sat next to Olivia on the plank bed and took hold of her icy hand.

"Must you continue with this?" she said.

Olivia squeezed Dody's hand. "Please don't waste your breath trying to dissuade me. Until all suffragettes, regardless of class, are treated as political prisoners, I will continue with this course of action—even if it kills me."

And well it might, Dody thought, looking around the cell. Dim grey light filtered through barred windows, which were high up on the walls so no view out was possible. An odiferous bucket stood in a corner. "It doesn't look to me as if you are being treated as a political prisoner anyway."

"There are inequalities for men and women in prison just as there are outside it. Male political prisoners can rent better cells, wear their own clothes, and have as many visitors as they like."

Dody touched the sleeve of Olivia's coarse blue dress, so different to the brightly coloured kaftans she favoured. "But you are not even in your own clothes."

"I soiled them with vomit."

Indeed, Dody thought, the smell hung about her still.

"How many times have they force-fed you?" she asked.

"Three times yesterday and once this morning."

"Will you let me examine you?"

"What is the point? The prison physician has already done so, and I know you have no legal power to stop them."

"But I might be able to make the process more humane."

Dody exchanged her bowler hat for a light reflector, adjusting the strap around her head. Giving Olivia no opportunity for further argument, she took hold of her jaw and turned her head towards the light. "Please, dear, open your mouth for me."

Olivia licked dry, cracked lips and complied like an obedient child. Dody caught the thin beam of light from the window and directed it into Olivia's mouth, pressing down on the tongue with a wooden blade. The throat was raw, the mucosa of the inside of her mouth dotted with purple ulcers, sections of gums still seeping blood from the morning's ordeal.

"They have only used the stomach tube?" Dody asked as she put the tongue depressor down and redirected her light up Olivia's nostrils. Thankfully these seemed free from irritation.

"Yes."

"With clamps to lever your mouth open?"

"They used a metal clamp for the first two feeds, but when they saw the damage it was doing to my mouth, they exchanged it for a wooden one."

"How considerate of them."

A fleeting smile passed over Olivia's pale features.

"Your mouth and throat are raw. They cannot continue to feed you this way. The next feed will have to be through your nose."

"And when my nostrils are destroyed, I will be fed through the back passage, and after that . . ." Olivia shuddered.

Dody flinched. The only reason for feeding a prisoner that way was to torture them. "For the love of God, Olivia, pray eat something, and then this torture will stop!"

Olivia said nothing. She had lifted her gaze to the window high in the wall, the whites of her eyeballs showing beneath her pupils and a strange gleam in her eyes.

Dody took off her light reflector and spent a moment adjusting her hat. *Olivia must be coming down with a fever*, she thought, though she had failed to notice any other sign. She raised her hand to feel Olivia's brow, but Olivia dodged her touch and clambered to a standing position on the plank bed, stretching out her arms on either side.

This parody of a crucifixion was not the plump and affable Olivia she thought she knew. She realised then that the gleam in Olivia's eye was not fever; it was fanaticism and it was far worse than anything she had ever worried about in Florence.

"Don't you understand, this is the only way to make them see reason?" Olivia cried. "If I die, I will die a martyr to the cause and then, ultimately, maybe not this year or the next, but eventually, the women of Britain will be set free!"

Dody looked around the cell. "Hush now, I haven't finished your examination—do you want the wardens rushing in?" She took Olivia's hand and urged her gently back on to the bed.

Olivia fell silent, stared at Dody for a moment, and then shook her head like one waking from a nightmare. She allowed Dody to guide her back into a sitting position on the bed and open the buttons at the back of her dress. She sat limply as Dody listened with her stethoscope to her breathing and heartbeat. Both were faster than normal, probably caused by her sudden burst of excitement, Dody surmised, but no faster than the hammering still reverberating through her own chest.

As she redid the buttons, she observed that Olivia's generous figure showed no sign of malnourishment.

"As you can see, Dody," Olivia said, speaking levelly again, "I am hardly at death's door. That puts paid to the lie that force-feeding is necessary to save lives. The doctor weighed and measured me yesterday. He said I could safely afford to lose three more stone before my life becomes endangered."

The cell door creaked open and a warder appeared with a tray of food. A tin plate of potatoes sat next to a cylindrical tin of watery soup. The rims of the containers were black with grime as if they had never been cleaned.

"As a political prisoner, you are entitled to have food brought in from the outside. I'm hardly surprised you're not eating this," Dody said, though she knew this was not the point.

"Dody, have you not heard me? I will not eat. Even if they send in venison with cherry sauce."

At this the white-bonneted warder said, "I might just as well call them in now, Doctor; get this over with. Everyone's waiting in the corridor for your say-so."

Dody gave Olivia one final squeeze of the hand and rose from the bed. "Very well, then."

The door opened and two more warders appeared, pushing a trolley holding an assortment of equipment: yards of stained rubber tubing, jugs, funnels, and enamel bowls. A tall man followed, and introduced himself with a stony face as Blake, the Holloway physician.

Dody pulled him aside and tactfully suggested he try naso-gastric feeding this time. He answered imperiously that this was exactly what he had intended to do. When she commented on the dirty equipment, he said he was at his wits' end chiding the warders about it. Dody took it upon herself to send one of the warders out for some clean tubing, as narrow as she could find. "Irrational woman, seeks her own torture," the physician muttered.

While the preparations were being made, Dody became aware of a figure slipping through the open door. Pike took up a position in a corner of the cell as far from the action as the cramped conditions would allow. He gave Dody a brief nod. The others in the cell did not glance up from their tasks, as if they had not even noticed his arrival.

Blake removed his frock coat, placed it on the bed and rolled up his shirtsleeves, took the rubber apron handed to him by one of the warders, and slipped it over his head. Taking a yard length of tubing—still too wide for Dody's liking—he coated it liberally with goose fat from an enamel kidney dish.

Holding the slippery tube up between his thumb and fore-finger, he asked Olivia, "Have you ever experienced feeding through your nose?"

Olivia shook her head.

"Will you cooperate with me?" He dangled the tube in front of her face like a boy teasing a smaller child with a dead snake.

Again Olivia shook her head. Blake nodded to the three warders. They descended like birds of prey and hauled a kick-ing and screaming Olivia from the bed, dragging her towards the chair. Once they'd got her into a sitting position, one of them sat on her knee while the others took an arm each and pinned them behind her back.

Olivia continued to scream until her voice was no more than a hoarse croak. Dody moved to stand beside her and smoothed the hair from her damp face. She indicated a tumbler on the table. "Have some water at least," she pleaded.

Olivia shook her head violently.

"Then you must be quiet in order to hear the doctor's instructions. If you do as he says, it will be easier for you."

Olivia fell silent, though her eyes darted about the cell like those of a cornered fox.

"Thank you, Dr. McCleland." Blake cleared his throat and addressed Olivia. "When I insert this tube into your nostril, you will feel it in the back of your throat. You must swallow then to ensure it passes into your stomach and not into your lungs."

"May you all rot in hell!" Olivia screamed.

Blake moved to stand between the two warders pinning Olivia's arms and indicated to the woman sitting on Olivia's knee to get off and grab her ankles. On the count of three, the woman tipped Olivia back in the chair as if it were a wheelbarrow, while Blake pulled back Olivia's head. She bucked and gagged when the tube was inserted, and the faces of the wardresses turned red with the effort of keeping her still.

Swallow, Olivia, swallow, Dody silently begged, feeling the tears begin to prick. Her eyes briefly met those of Pike, who up to now had been staring at the scene with unfaltering stoicism. She moved across the cell to stand next to him. A string of blood appeared from Olivia's nostril and mixed with the tears trickling down her face. Beads of red dropped onto the milky white of her throat.

"The tube is too wide," Dody whispered to Pike. "It's tearing the nasal cartilage." Pike nodded as he continued to watch without uttering a word.

The physician attached a syringe to the end of the tube and withdrew a small amount of fluid. "He is ensuring the tube is in the stomach and not the lungs," Dody explained.

Satisfied that the tube was in the correct position, Blake replaced the syringe with a funnel and slowly began to fill it with the contents of the jug. Olivia moaned like a dying animal.

Dody leaned towards Pike again. "Probably eggs and milk," she whispered. She felt strangely disassociated.

Then Olivia gagged and a terrible sound bubbled in her throat. Dody put her fist to her mouth and bit down on her knuckles.

The doctor leapt to the side as a torrent of liquid gushed from Olivia's mouth. "God damn it!" he cursed. "Now we will have to start the procedure all over again. Can't you see that we are doing this for your own good, you stupid woman!"

Olivia wept. The doctor prepared to reinsert the tube. Dody turned to Pike, but found him gone, the slow tap of his cane fading down the prison corridor.

Chapter Twenty-Eight

Pike took the buff envelope of photographs from his brief-case and paused for a moment, tapping the envelope against his hand. Then he spread the dog-eared photographs on his desk for one last look. He had viewed them so often during his recuperation in Hastings, he would not have been surprised to find that his vision had been playing tricks on him. Consequently he had resisted looking at them since his return.

And yet here it was again—one grainy photograph showing one policeman so different from all the rest.

He had no sooner placed the envelope in his desk drawer than Sergeant Fisher appeared in his doorway, twisting his hat in his hands.

"Good morning, Fisher," Pike said. Despite the pending meeting with Shepherd, the morning had to be good compared to the events of yesterday afternoon. He'd seen some disturbing things in his time, but they didn't get much worse than the force-feeding he had witnessed with Dr. Dorothy McCleland.

"The meeting in the superintendent's office has been changed, sir. It is now in the commissioner's office," Fisher said. "They want to see me, too."

Pike felt an ache in his stomach. Had they found out about his injury? Were they going to demand his resignation—and Fisher's, too, for his complicity?

The glum look on his sergeant's face suggested he, too, thought this the likely scenario. "Let me do the talking, Fisher," Pike said. "I'll tell them I coerced you into helping me."

"Yes, sir." Fisher's manner suggested he didn't think Pike's intervention would be of much help. He had the appearance of a man about to face a firing squad.

"Buck up, man," Pike tried to jolly him along. "You lead the way, I'm a bit slow this morning." He dreaded to think what condition he would be in after the steep climb to the top of the commissioner's tower office.

As it happened, they were kept waiting so long that by the time the commissioner's secretary had shown them into his office, Pike's knee had almost recovered. Some rare winter light reflecting off the river several storeys below struck them in the face as they entered. In front of the window Pike saw only the silhouettes of three men. As his eyes adjusted, he made out the commissioner seated behind his carved wooden desk, Shepherd swamping a small chair to his right, and Pike's friend from Special Branch, Superintendent Callan, on his left.

Pike managed to keep his surprise to himself, but Fisher's gasp was audible. His sergeant had probably never shared air with three such highly ranked officers in his life. Pike prayed Fisher would not weaken and say anything untoward.

"Good morning, Pike, Fisher," the commissioner greeted them, smiling. He commented about the weather; how nice it was to have some sunshine for a change, though at this time of year one knew it would never last. He asked Pike if he had recovered from his bout of influenza. Pike told him he had never felt better.

"I am told that congratulations are in order," the commissioner said at the end of the pleasantries.

"They are, sir?" Pike scanned the line of faces before him.

"Indeed, yes, for both of you." The corners of the commissioner's eyes crinkled, his small moustache twitched. "Sergeant Fisher has been put forward for promotion—inspector at Whitechapel."

No doubt to fill one of the gaps left empty after Pike's purge of the division. He turned to Fisher, held out his hand, and said warmly, "Well done, Fisher, you've earned it. Though I shall miss you."

Fisher did not crack a smile; indeed he did not even meet Pike's gaze. His hand, limp and sweaty, barely returned Pike's squeeze. Pike could not understand his lack of enthusiasm. The job offered better pay, would set him well up the promotion ladder, and he would finally have the money to provide his ailing wife with the nutritious diet she required.

"Collect your transfer papers from my secretary, Inspector Fisher. That will be all." The commissioner smiled again.

The door closed behind Fisher. Smiles faded. The temperature in the office seemed to drop several degrees. Pike, who had still not been offered a chair, edged closer to the warm air rising through the flue in the floor from the office below.

The commissioner studied Pike for a moment. "And now to matters of a graver nature." He linked his hands and leaned towards Pike across his desk. "I understand you believe the disorderly conduct of the police at the suffragette riot was endorsed by certain high-ranking police officers."

This was not a question. Dykins must have bleated to Shepherd about how Pike had forced the information from him. Pike straightened, placed his hands and cane behind his back. "Yes, I am convinced that is the case, sir," he said, allowing his gaze to linger on Shepherd, who stared back with hard, flat eyes.

"And you are correct," the commissioner said. "The order came directly from the Home Office. The women were to be put in their place, *with force if necessary*—those were the most esteemed gentleman's very words."

Pike took a breath. The light from the window was not so blinding now, as if a cloud had passed over the sun. "That is scandalous," he said, trying to keep his voice level. "Those orders resulted in the deaths of three women—and one of those deaths is likely to be found manslaughter at the least. The senior officers concerned"—he looked at Shepherd again—"should have realised that tactics like that would only incite the women further."

"And we have learned from our mistakes. It will not happen again. Thanks to you, the overzealous officers have been sacked and the force's reputation has been saved," the commissioner said. "The matter is over."

"Lady Catherine Cartwright was beaten about the head by a police officer whom I have yet to identify. I do not consider the force's reputation saved while that man continues to serve."

"Drop it," Shepherd said coldly. "Drop your enquiries and move on."

The commissioner frowned at Shepherd. Pike stared from one to the other and discerned the fear behind their stony masks. He took a step towards the desk. "May I hazard a guess as to what is worrying you, Commissioner? You are concerned that if I continue with my investigations, the press will get wind and the name of the man who gave those orders will be exposed. You have mentioned no names, but it is not hard to guess. He is surely the Home Secretary, Mr. Winston Churchill."

The commissioner exchanged glances with his companions and said, "Mr. Churchill is a promising young politician who does not deserve to be cut down so early in his career because of a minor tactical error."

"But it is not only Mr. Churchill you are worrying about," Pike added, as if the commissioner had not spoken. He was making waves, he was going to be dismissed, and he had nothing to lose. "Certain high-ranking police officers might also find themselves in the spotlight for giving a young politician such questionable advice."

There was silence for a few moments, broken finally by the shuffle of paper as Shepherd removed a photograph from a buff envelope and handed it to the commissioner. Pike knew what the photograph was, even before the commissioner held it up so he could see his daughter's white face staring out from the bedlam of the riot. Pike had hidden the photograph at the bottom of his locked desk drawer, to which only one other man had access: Walter Fisher.

He could not believe, did not want to believe, that Fisher

had betrayed him. But it was suddenly painfully clear: Fisher's promotion—and why he had reacted to the news as if he had been sentenced to the gallows. And why he could not meet Pike's eyes.

Shepherd had known about Fisher's dire domestic circumstances and made the sergeant an offer he could not refuse.

Pike felt a stabbing pang, like broken glass, deep inside his chest. This betrayal, more than anything else that had just transpired, broke through his defences and made him feel sick to the stomach.

He had no inclination for the charade he sensed was about to be acted out. "Before you ask, yes, that is my daughter," he said. "She was present at the recent suffragette rally. And yes, I failed to submit the photograph as evidence in fear of the consequences, for her and for me, keeping it locked in the drawer of my office desk." Pike turned and headed towards the door, not bothering to attempt to hide his limp. "I will write out my resignation forthwith."

"Wait, Pike, not so fast," said Callan, who had remained silent until now. He left his chair and guided Pike back into the room by the elbow, pulling over an empty chair and indicating for Pike to sit. "There is a way out of this, old man."

"I can't see what. I have no more desire to work with the superintendent"—he pointed his cane at Shepherd—"than he has to work with me. The situation is untenable. I have withheld evidence, which is a sackable offence. I have perverted the course of justice almost as much as those of you who suppressed the truth behind the riot—the truth being that they bribed roughs from the docks as well as the police officers to deliberately cause havoc. We are as guilty as each other."

The commissioner coughed. "Yes, well, I suppose if one chooses to look at it like that. But the men were not meant to physically harm the women, just frighten them."

Pike's anger almost boiled over. "That's like telling a pack of dogs to do no more than lick a sheep they have pulled to the ground."

"We are at a stalemate, Matthew," Callan said. "We do not want you to resign. Be realistic, man. Money is tight; you have a daughter to support who would most likely be expelled from her school if this came out."

Pike said nothing; his friend spoke the truth. Though he was wrong on one count: Shepherd would have been glad for him to resign. Pike should have been storming from the room, but instead he sat there, waiting to hear them out.

And he hated himself for it.

"There is a new department at Special Branch," Callan went on, "for which I feel you are highly suited. It is a department devoted to monitoring the suffragette activity in London. You are just the kind of man we need, quiet and nonthreatening, and you have already shown a degree of sympathy to their cause, which will put you in their favour. This is a much-sought-after position."

"I have no sympathy at all with the militants," Pike said. "I do not condone violence by anyone. But if you are referring to my visit to the magistrate yesterday to persuade him to release Miss Olivia Barndon-Brown, any man who witnessed the barbarism in that prison cell would have done the same. I recommend a visit to the cells for all of you."

Callan met the commissioner's eye and raised his brow as if to say, *What did I tell you?* "Go home, Matthew," he said, "sleep on it. Come and see me in a day or two and we'll discuss it further."

Pike got to his feet. "I will not stop looking for the officer who bludgeoned Lady Catherine," he said, breathing hard.

"Of course not, and we don't expect you to," the commissioner said pleasantly, shooting a warning look at Shepherd. "We gave you free rein to deal with those other police thugs, did we not?"

"You may have managed to play down the brutal behaviour of men like Dykins to the press, but I don't know how you can play down a cold-blooded murder—if that is what it turns out to be—of a prominent society woman."

"In fact, gentlemen," Shepherd spoke over him, "I think we can conclude that Lady Catherine tripped and fell during the riot and her injuries were caused by someone inadvertently treading on her head. The autopsy report is vague, but it does lend some support to this theory . . ."

The commissioner held up his hand. "Your devotion to the force is admirable, Superintendent, but the autopsy report, vague though it is, does not suggest this is what happened at all. Mr. Cartwright has seen the report, and the man is not a complete fool."

Of course, Pike thought, the commissioner was still under pressure from Mr. Hugo Cartwright to find his aunt's killer. If not for this, the commissioner might well have agreed with Shepherd's cover-up. What a fine line they all trod.

The commissioner turned from Shepherd back to Pike. "We want the blaggard caught as much as you do."

Shepherd crossed his arms and leaned back in his chair, giving Pike a black look. After a moment he sighed as if in great pain, and lifted up the photograph of Violet from the commissioner's desk. "Lucky chap," he said without expression. "You've been given a second chance—don't waste it." He held the photograph up to Pike, flicking it with his fingernail and producing a sharp crack of sound.

Chapter Twenty-Nine

"Dody, have you seen this?" Florence stood up from the chaise and rattled the newspaper, shattering the companionable silence of the morning room.

Dody looked up from the letter she was writing. "I haven't had the chance to read the paper today. What does it say?"

"It appears the suffragettes' golf course sabotage was doomed to fail, even if the women had not been apprehended in the act. Police scientific analysis reveals that the blasting caps used in the thwarted explosion were defective and would have been incapable of detonating the dynamite under any circumstances." Florence's voice trembled with rage.

She tossed the paper to the ground. "Derwent supplied us with those blasting caps—how foolish he has made us look!"

"But perhaps the crime will not be considered so terrible now?" Dody suggested. "If Miss Lithgow and Daisy were to say that they knew the bomb would not have gone off, perhaps they will be released earlier?" She did not really believe this but hoped the idea might placate her sister.

"I hardly think so." Florence's glance suggested that Dody knew nothing about the real world. "Oh, it is so humiliating. Look at the heading they printed: 'SUFFRAGETTES BUNGLE BOMBING: WILL THEY NOW STAY IN THE KITCHEN?'" She thrust the newspaper at Dody and strode to the door.

"Wait, Florence, where are you going?" It would be just like her sister to go and confront O'Neill, though Dody dared not say that in case she set the idea in motion. "I'm going to my room to think this through."

"Pike will be here soon," Dody said. From the moment they had learned that Pike had orchestrated Olivia's release from prison, Florence had seemed keen to make peace with him. Dody was looking forward to seeing her sister and the man she had begun to regard as her friend bury the hatchet.

"Call me when he gets here." Florence closed the door with a bang.

Dody finished the letter she had been writing to her parents and smoothed out the crumpled newspaper. She was reading it when Annie entered, saying with a grimace that the chief inspector had arrived. Dody stood, glanced in the mantle mirror and repinned some loose strands of hair. "Show him in, Annie. Then go upstairs and tell Florence he's here, and bring us some tea."

"Miss Florence has gone out, miss."

"Out? Where?"

"To see Miss Barndon-Brown, I think, miss."

Dody felt herself relax. But it was a pity her sister had not stayed to meet Pike. It was only natural, Dody told herself, to want to see the people you felt affection for get on well together.

"Thank you, Annie," she said, hiding her disappointment. "Show the chief inspector in."

The smell of fog, dank and sulphurous, followed Pike into the room. "I would have been here sooner," he apologised, "but visibility was terrible. I had to climb out of the cab and guide the driver with a lantern for some of the way."

"It was good of you to come at all on such short notice and on such a dismal evening."

He gave her a stiff little bow, barely touched her hand. "My first day back at work was not as busy as I had expected. I was getting ready to leave when my clerk gave me your message. I hope there's nothing wrong."

"On the contrary, please sit down." Dody indicated the chair nearest the fire. "I wanted to thank you personally for what you did for Olivia; she was released yesterday evening. My sister and I are very grateful. I'm sure Olivia will contact you herself and thank you when she's feeling better."

"It was the least I could do, Dr. McCleland."

She smiled. "Please, call me Dody." Away from her parents' house, she gave only a few special friends the liberty of calling her by her Christian name. Now the matter of keeping some kind of professional boundary between herself and Pike did not seem so important.

He did not appear to hear what she had said. He seemed distracted, his eyes flitting about the room as if seeing it for the first time: the inlaid writing desk near the window; a faint draught making the curtains shiver; the chaise; the deep pink velvet upholstery of the Queen Anne armchairs; the crackling fire. When finally his gaze settled on her, she could tell that his attention was still elsewhere.

Then he gave a small start, as if suddenly appreciating the

significance of her words. "Dody," he said, testing her name on his lips with the hint of a smile. "Very well, then."

Her peevishness lifted. She paused to examine him. The way he sat rigidly erect on the edge of the chair betrayed an even greater tension than when they had stood side by side in the prison cell yesterday. "Is something troubling you?" she asked.

"No, no."

"Your first day back at work did not go well?"

He took out his cigarette case. "May I?"

"Of course," she said, turning down the offer of one for herself.

"No, my first day back did not go the way I expected. I am to be transferred. They implied it was a promotion of some kind—utter rot, of course. They found out that my daughter was present at the riot. The so-called promotion is a sideways shift to another department on the condition that I remain silent about the men who instigated the violence at the march. If I don't, I'll be dismissed." He exhaled smoke. "I can't afford to lose my job."

No wonder the poor man had been so distracted. Though surely this kind of behaviour was not unusual in the police force, and Pike was canny enough to know that. There was something else bothering him; Dody was certain of it.

"Have you also been instructed to drop the search for Lady Catherine's killer?" she asked. "Are they intending to cover that up, too? If so, they shan't get away with it. If the papers don't print the letters all the WSPU women are writing, my sister has assured me the women will find other ways to make their anger known."

"I am to continue that investigation," Pike said. "My last

assignment before I am moved. Presumably Hugo Cartwright has the commissioner's ear." He continued to look troubled.

"What is it then?" Dody asked.

"Probably nothing of importance; just a strange notion I had when I was going through the surveillance photographs again in Hastings."

"They say two heads are better than one."

Pike smiled back briefly and leaned towards his briefcase. He stopped when Annie rattled through the morning room door with the tea tray, thumping it on the table before Dody.

"Thank you, Annie, that will be all," Dody said with a frown. She made a mental note to speak to the girl about her churlish behaviour at the next opportunity.

She began pouring the tea. "I'm sorry. My sister had intended on being here when you came. She was very grateful for what you did for Olivia."

"I only managed to help one woman. I'm afraid the situation is likely to continue until the law is changed."

"You mean equal rights for men and women?"

Pike touched the knot of his tie. "Actually, I was looking at the smaller picture, that of force-feeding."

"You do not believe in equal rights for—" Dody saw the exasperation in his face and laughed. "Very well, one thing at a time; I will leave your daughter to argue the case of equal voting rights with you." Pike looked relieved. Dody handed him tea, but he refused her offer of cake. "Florence and I also wanted you to convey our apologies to your sergeant for neglecting to give him back his truncheon. I thought my sister had organised its return and she thought I had."

Pike stared into his teacup. "Fisher is no longer my sergeant."

Dody was about to ask why when Pike clanked his cup down, slopping tea into the saucer.

"Just a minute—you say the truncheon has not been returned?"

"I'm sorry if it has caused such an inconvenience." Dody was surprised that he would take issue with something so trivial. "Surely your sergeant could have accessed another truncheon if he needed one so desperately?"

Pike did not answer for a moment. "Tell me again about the truncheon, from the beginning," he said.

Although she did not yet know the cause, his anxiety was infectious and put an edge to her voice that the intense scrutiny of his intelligent blue eyes did nothing to soothe. "We borrowed the truncheon from your office and then I used it on the pigs' heads. I left it clean on the hall table for Fletcher to return. Olivia noticed the truncheon there, and when Florence told her how we had managed to procure it, she was most impressed."

Pike grunted.

"Then yesterday, before Olivia was released, Florence went to her flat to get her some clean clothes. She saw the truncheon on the top shelf of Olivia's wardrobe. She later asked Olivia where she'd got it from, and Olivia said she had taken it from our hall table to play a little joke on us, just as we had on you."

Pike was frowning.

"Yes," Dody went on, "I'm surprised Fletcher never mentioned the truncheon wasn't there for him to collect. I assumed he'd returned it and he must have assumed that I had given it back to you. Perhaps that is why Florence went to see Olivia—to collect the truncheon so she can return it to you. A peace offering, I suppose. I don't think she'll be very long."

"But, Dody," Pike interrupted. "The truncheon *was* returned. By Fletcher, I assumed."

Dody paused, the thin edge of the teacup against her lips. "It was? Then what—"

Pike got up from his chair and began to pace the room. Dody had never seen him so agitated. Dread descended like a dark mantle around her, banishing the sense of pleasure she'd felt at the beginning of his visit.

He stopped pacing and returned to the table, where he delved into his briefcase and extracted an envelope of photographs. He pointed to the tea tray. "Can you clear this away, please. I have to show you something. Look at this photograph, Dody. Pay particular attention to the policeman you see in the background emerging from the alley."

Dody could see nothing but a blurry shape and the glint of a badge on a beehive helmet, and told him so.

"But what was this officer doing in the alley," Pike asked, "while his colleagues in the foreground are clearly in need of help?"

"Relieving himself?"

"In the middle of a violent demonstration? That's the last thing a policeman would be thinking about, believe me." Pike pointed to another picture, in which a policeman stood behind two others struggling to hold a thrashing woman. This time the image was slightly clearer. "I think this is the same policeman."

Dody stared hard at the picture. "You may be right. He seems to be the only one in a cape. The others are wearing greatcoats."

"Indeed, his uniform is slightly different to the others, but that's not the only difference."

Dody continued to stare at the picture. After several

seconds she said, "Yes, I see it. He is much shorter than the rest. The difference is quite remarkable."

"Exactly! Metropolitan police are required to be a minimum of five feet eight inches. That person would be five foot five at the most."

A shiver coursed through Dody's body. She suddenly saw the figure in a very different light—narrow at the shoulders, wide at the hips. "Because it's not a policeman—in fact, it's not a man at all, is it?"

"Exactly. A woman disguised as a policeman and carrying a policeman's truncheon."

Pike strode from the morning room as fast as his game knee would allow. "You have a telephone in the hall? I need to send some men over to Miss Barndon-Brown's flat."

"Olivia? Surely you don't mean that Olivia is Catherine's killer?"

"We have just deduced that there was a woman disguised as a policeman at the riot. Why else would Miss Barndon-Brown have a truncheon hidden in her wardrobe? Why else would she have lied to your sister when she found it, telling her that it was the truncheon you were using in your experiments?"

The cold of the hall hit them after the cosy warmth of the morning room. *Why indeed,* Dody thought. *And what will Olivia do when she finds Florence on her doorstep, wanting to hand the truncheon back to the police?*

Chapter Thirty

Pike slammed down the telephone receiver and glanced at the grandfather clock in the hall. "The telephone station is closed, confound it. I had no idea it was this late." He spun on his heel. "I need my coat and hat." But Dody was already staggering from the cloakroom with their outdoor things in her arms.

Pike reached for his coat and collected his bowler and gloves from the hall table. "You can't come with me, Dody. The situation is too unpredictable."

Heat rushed into Dody's cheeks. "Unpredictable? Don't skirt the issue with euphemisms. If Olivia has killed once and if she is as unstable as I suspect she is, then Florence is in terrible danger. If you think I would run the risk of my sister being injured with no medical assistance at hand, then you have to think again."

"As you wish, but I do not like it." Pike headed out the front door, but did nothing to stop her from following him into the street. Dody hastily shrugged into her wool cloak and ran to catch up with him.

"Besides," she added as he continued to pay her no heed, busy searching up and down the street for a cab, "you don't know where Olivia lives, do you?"

He swivelled to face her, abashed at his own haste.

"If we don't find a cab soon," she added, glancing around, "it will be quicker for us to walk—Olivia lives only down the road from here."

Bombarded with questions from both Pike and Dody, Olivia's aged doorman seemed to have trouble comprehending either of them.

Dody tried to calm herself. "This is going nowhere," she whispered to Pike. "The man is hard of hearing. It is important that only one of us speaks at a time—let me question him."

Pike conceded and backed down the porch steps. Dody touched the old man on his sleeve and asked him his name.

"Biggs, miss."

Looking him full in the face, she asked slowly, "When we asked if Miss McCleland was here, you said that she had been and now she was gone. How long ago did she leave, Mr. Biggs?"

"At least 'alf an hour ago, miss," Biggs said with a look of relief.

"Was Miss Barndon-Brown with her?"

"No, miss, she was on her own."

Dody heaved a sigh of relief. Florence had come to no harm. Perhaps she hadn't mentioned the truncheon after all.

"Do you know where she was going?"

"She wanted me to get 'er a cab to Whitechapel, but I couldn't find one. I think she took the tube."

"Lord, she's gone to Whitechapel on her own," Dody said to Pike. "O'Neill lives in Whitechapel."

"That's right, I know the place. Would she have any other reason to go to Whitechapel?"

"None that I know of."

"Do you have any idea why she would go to O'Neill, and at this time of night?"

"She was livid with him about—" Dody paused to choose her words, not sure how much Pike knew about Florence's involvement in the golf course sabotage. "A certain issue. It wouldn't surprise me if she wanted to have it out with him."

"We need to talk to Olivia," said Pike. "Ask the doorman to show us up."

"But surely we should find my sister first—I can't bear to think of her in Whitechapel alone!"

Biggs had caught snatches of their conversation. "Don't worry, miss," he said, trying to console Dody. "Miss Barndon-Brown went out not long after. Perhaps she was intending on keeping an eye on the young lady."

Dody felt herself sway.

"Was Miss Barndon-Brown carrying anything?" Pike asked the old man.

"Yes, sir, some kind of bundle—might've been clothes by the looks of it."

Dody gasped and Pike stepped closer to her. It was the smallest of movements, but comforting nonetheless. Despite his physical incapacity, she realised there was no one else she would rather face this awful situation with. She swallowed and made herself stand tall. She must be clearheaded if they were to succeed.

Pike thanked Biggs for his help and steered her down the porch steps. He looked anxiously up and down the street, the fog so thick even the streetlamps failed to penetrate it. "It looks like we'll have to take the tube, too. British Museum Station will be the closest."

Until now, Dody had always managed to avoid the underground railway, but she gave the matter no thought as they hurried on foot to the station. Pike purchased two tickets and they descended in the rickety lift. Within seconds she found herself standing in a chilly tunnel of tiles and soot, waiting for the arrival of the next train to Aldgate.

As they waited in silence, Dody forced herself to think rationally. Who was the most lethal of the pair? That rogue O'Neill or the suspected killer, Olivia? Then again, there was always the chance that Pike had it all wrong, that neither of them was any danger to her sister. He'd admitted to a bias against the Irish, and she'd seen for herself the prejudice he held for the militant suffragettes. These thoughts brought some fleeting comfort until they were dashed by a picture of Florence making her way alone at night across the East End, blinded to the peril of London's most notorious streets by her stubborn sense of purpose.

Pike must have sensed her thoughts, felt her tremble. He offered her his arm. The comforting warmth of his body reached her through her thick cloak. "I don't wish to sound impertinent," he said, "but how worldly is your sister? How might she cope in a hostile environment on her own?"

Dody envisaged Florence on the hockey pitch. Then she pictured the tact and insight Florence used when controlling some of the more difficult members of her WSPU group. Goodness, she'd even managed to make her way back from the golf course alone the other night and on foot. But the baser side of human nature, the causes and effects Dody witnessed day after day at the hospital—of impoverished, desperate men and women—could Florence read them? Was Florence as worldly as she liked everyone to think? And even if she was, how could she ever imagine that her dear friend Olivia was a danger to her?

She was about to answer him, to explain Florence's well-hidden naivety, when she felt the slap of hot air on her cheeks, then the rumble of rails. Soon it was impossible to hear the sound of her own voice. A monstrous light appeared at the mouth of the tunnel, the wind increased, and they were almost blown off their feet as the train screeched to a halt.

Chapter Thirty-One

Florence's angry knock rattled the door and she felt somewhat pleased when Derwent O'Neill opened it, the cigarette falling from his lips at the sight of her.

He appeared to compose himself, gave her a quizzical smile, and bent to pick up the dropped cigarette. After pinching the glowing tip between finger and thumb, he pushed it into his waistcoat pocket. "Well, well, what a sight for sore eyes. Miss Florence McCleland—to what do I owe this honour?" he asked.

What indeed? Florence stared back at the Irishman. The boiling rage that had fuelled her horrendous journey had all but dissipated. As she stood by the door, she felt the last of it fizzle to the floor and disappear into the cigarette butts and stains of the tenement landing. She took a deep breath, summoning the last of her courage. "I'm surprised you need to ask. Did you not read today's paper?"

Derwent ignored her question. He put the back of his hand against her cheek. She flinched and stepped back. "Lord, woman, you're half froze," he said. "Come in out of the cold. This place isn't much; my cousin's out of work and we're on the last of the coal, but 'tis a lot more cosy than the landing."

"Your cousin is home?"

"No, out drowning his sorrows."

Florence drew herself to her full height. "Then I will say what I have to say right here where I stand."

Derwent gave her a crooked smile, turned, and called back through the door. "Say hello to Miss McCleland, Patrick. It seems the lady does not want to be in the flat alone with me."

"Now why doesn't that surprise me?" came Patrick's voice from within. "Hello, Florence! Do come in, it's quite safe."

"Patrick's working on another draft of his play. Your dear mother said its message was too strong, so he's trying to tone it down, make it more acceptable to the English censors."

Florence felt her shoulders drop with relief. "Very well, I'll come in, but only for a moment."

Derwent bent at the waist and made a sweeping gesture to usher her in. The odour of the flat hit her first, an unsavoury mixture of unwashed clothes, alcohol, smoke, and burning oil. But the fire in the grate was bright, and the smile Patrick flashed her from where he sat writing at a makeshift desk was reassuring. "Will you pardon me if I don't get up," he said. "I'm writing a very tricky exchange of dialogue. I won't be long."

"Please, don't let me interrupt you."

Derwent cleared a crate for her beside the fire and placed a handkerchief over its splintery surface before she sat. He then took a ceramic jug from the mantelpiece and filled two glasses with black ale. When Florence opened her mouth to speak, he silenced her with a finger to his lips.

"Drink up; it's not businesslike to launch straight into things. If you want to be treated like a man, you must learn to behave like one." He lifted his glass. "Sláinte."

Florence had never tasted ale before and found it more pleasant than she'd expected. The dark frothy liquid slid down her throat as smooth as warm milk.

"I must congratulate you on escaping the force of the law. It is too bad the other three were not so fast on their feet. It must be all that hockey you play," Derwent said.

"We were betrayed; it is no joke. But Olivia has just been released after two days of force-feeding, so that is something at least."

Poor, brave Olivia. Florence pictured her friend as she had left her: sunken, dark-rimmed eyes blazing from paper-pale skin. It was the memory of those eyes that had kept her going through her arduous journey to Derwent's lodgings. Olivia had suffered so much, while she had run away. Tackling O'Neill was something she had to do—for Olivia and for Jane and Daisy, for the whole Bloomsbury group—if she were ever to hold her head up among them again.

She took a sip of ale. "You knew those blasting caps were defective, didn't you?"

Derwent flashed her an infuriating smile. "You think I'd be so irresponsible as to let loose a pile of dangerous explosives on a group of hysterical females? I didn't want your deaths on my conscience, especially not yours, charming Florence."

"Don't talk to me like that. You led us to believe—" She broke off as Derwent moved to squat before her, close enough for her to smell the ale on his breath, see the line of his unshaved neck beneath the beard.

"I led you to believe what you wanted to believe," he said silkily. In the fire's light his dark eyes sparkled. He looked intently into hers. And then the infuriating look became something else, a look she did not care to meet. "I told you when we met at your parents' house that I didn't give a fig for your little cause." He shrugged. "But who am I to deny a group of bored bourgeois women a good time—add a little excitement to their dried-up lives?"

Heat surged through her and she lashed out at him. The slap stung her hand more than it did his sandpaper cheek, but it was still powerful enough to unbalance and knock him to the floor.

At the noise, Patrick stood up and stretched. "There, I'm done," he said, eyes shining with amusement. "I told you you'd met your match with this one, Derwent."

Florence got to her feet. The consuming rage that had filled her had dissolved into a warm glow of satisfaction. She knew herself well enough to recognise that the blow had not been for Derwent alone. The poet who had tricked her out of her virginity, the police, the politicians, the magistrates, and the male doctors with their feeding tubes—that slap was for all of them.

Derwent rubbed his cheek and glared at her from where he had fallen. Patrick winked at Florence. Then a grin cracked Derwent's granite features, followed by a laugh as smooth as Tullamore Dew.

Patrick laughed, too. "You pack a fine punch, Florence, to send Derwent O'Neill to the ground. It is good to start as you mean to finish—and this one certainly needs keeping in line. I think you will make a fine job of taming him, and my mother will thank you for it."

Florence smiled uncertainly. Patrick seemed to think she and his brother had some understanding between them. She wanted to scotch the notion right then, but her head felt fuzzy. It could wait.

Derwent heaved himself up from the floor. "Well, maybe I deserved that." He dusted himself down, took the jug from the mantelpiece, and emptied the dregs into his and Florence's glasses.

"Hey, save some for me!" Patrick said.

"Too late, little brother, 'tis all gone." Derwent tipped the empty jug upside down. "Get us a refill from the White Hart. Hurry up now, before it closes. There's money in the tea caddy."

"That's Liam's money in the tea caddy, for emergency use. I'll not touch it."

Derwent sighed, put his hand in his pocket, and dropped some coins into his brother's palm. "Get yourself an extra pint and all—and one for cousin Liam, too, if he's still there."

Florence put down her glass. "And you can walk me to Aldgate Station, too, please, Patrick, before it closes for the night."

Derwent spoke before his brother could answer. "Mark Lane Station stays open longer. I'll walk you there when we've finished our chat."

Florence lifted her chin. "I've said all I wanted to say. I thought I'd made myself clear."

Derwent pouted and played the aggrieved party. "But you've given me no time to defend my actions. And besides, I have other suggestions for your campaign that might interest you."

"You've already told me that you have no interest in the cause."

"True, my own cause is at the top of my priorities. But any kind of thorn in the side of the British government suits me, no matter how small. There are several strategies we have not discussed, strategies that pose no more danger to the perpetrator than a stiff fine." He tilted his head to the door, urging his brother on his errand.

"Well, are you coming or not?" Patrick said to Florence.

Again Derwent answered before she had a chance to reply. "Be off, man. I've said I'll walk her to the station."

With a shrug, Patrick farewelled Florence, picked up the jug, and grabbed his coat. Soon his heavy footsteps on the stairs were rattling the thin tenement walls.

Florence's common sense told her to call out to Patrick, make him wait for her, but she found a heavy mist clouding her mind as thick as the fog that had descended on the London streets earlier that evening. It was the alcohol clouding her judgement, she knew, but she didn't care. *This must be how Dody's patients feel after being given an anaesthetic*, she thought. Awake yet oblivious to the operation being performed.

The room was cosy and her lids heavy. She still had plenty of time for the tube at Mark Lane, and she didn't doubt that Derwent would see her safely there. She had put him in his place, had she not? Shown him who was boss. And besides, she *was* interested in hearing what he had to say that might give the cause more publicity.

He moved to a set of rough-planked shelves in one of the room's dark recesses and returned with a half-empty bottle of Irish whiskey. Pulling the cork with his teeth, he moved to fill Florence's empty glass, but she covered it with her hand before the first drop fell. Not all her common sense had deserted her, she was pleased to note.

"You enjoyed it enough with the ale, why not try some on its own?" Derwent said.

Florence's jaw dropped. "You put that in my ale?"

"Only a drop, just to sweeten it up a trifle."

"In that case, no thank you, I've had enough," she said with indignation. *You should never mix your drinks*—it was one of the many instructions her mother had given her before her first season out, and one of the few society rules she'd ever thought worth sticking to. She had no desire to make a spectacle of herself in public.

"Suit yourself." Derwent took a pull from the bottle, shovelled a few pieces of coal onto the fire, and dragged another crate alongside hers.

She shot him a wary look.

"You wouldn't deny a man the warmth of his own—well, his cousin's—fire, would you?" He moved the crate closer still.

"No," Florence answered primly. "Provided that is all you are doing."

He made the sign of the cross. "Upon my mother's grave."

"Patrick implied that your mother was still very much alive." She let the matter drop. "You suggested you had some other ideas that might draw attention to our cause."

"Oh, yes, so I did." Derwent laughed. He'd been doing a lot of laughing since her arrival, and Florence wondered how long he'd been drinking.

"Well . . ." He paused to take another swig of whiskey, wiping his mouth with the back of his hand. "Have you thought about violating public property?"

Florence delved into her cloudy thoughts. "We pull slates

from roofs, damage politicians' cars—that sort of thing. And you know about the golf course—where rich and influential men play to the exclusion of women."

Derwent slapped his knees and guffawed. "And who in hell—"

"Language, please."

"I do beg your ladyship's pardon." Derwent began again, "Who the dickens cares about what happens to politicians' cars excepting the politicians themselves? Or the privileged few who can afford to play golf. You need to find ways to reach the ordinary workingman." He pulled his beard as he thought. "I know, how about one of yous shinning up Nelson's Column and putting a suffragette bonnet on the esteemed hero's head?"

Florence could not contain herself. The laughter began in her belly and spread through her body until she was shaking with it.

Derwent laughed, too. "Or daub some priceless work of art with streaks of white, green, and purple. Or put a corset around the waist of Prince Albert in the park—that kind of thing?"

Florence almost doubled up. Derwent slapped her on the back like he would a chum in a bar, rocking back and forth on his crate.

"Yes, very amusing," Florence said when she had recovered. "Though I cannot see how this especially affects the ordinary workingman—or woman. Did you know, Derwent, that more than eighty percent of the women in England are workingwomen? And men have the temerity to tell us we should stay in our homes!"

Derwent ignored her words. "You should take life a little less seriously, Florence McCleland," he said. "You're very beautiful as it is, but when you laugh, the world is a better place for it."

He moved towards her and at once she got to her feet. "It's time for me to leave," she said soberly, trying to restore some of her dignity. If only the room would stop spinning.

"I'm sorry. I didn't mean to upset you," Derwent said. "I'm not that sort, despite what people say. But any man would weaken if he saw your face as I did just then, glowing in the firelight." He reached for her hand and kissed it. Before she knew it, he was doing the same to her lips, pressing his body into hers, making her aware of every contour of his hard-muscled physique. Her body responded to his with a pleasant ache and a quiver she had not felt for a long time.

But since the poet, Florence McCleland had vowed never to let a man touch her with passionate intent again. No nun took her vows more seriously than Florence did the guiding principles of the cause, especially those pertaining to purity and dignity. She pushed him away. "Stop!"

He stepped back as if doused with cold water. "Florence, please—you can't do that to a man!"

"I can and I will. I will find my way to the station now, alone, thank you very much. That's twice you've proved that you are not to be trusted."

He moved to grab her, but Florence moved faster. She lunged for the whiskey bottle and smashed it against the mantelpiece. Holding the jagged remains by the neck, she feinted towards him. He backed off, his eyes never leaving the splintered bottle, and raised his palms. "Don't be a fool, Florence. A woman of your station won't survive out there on the streets alone at night."

"I made it here, didn't I? I think I've proved that I'm quite capable of looking after myself. And I'm sure I'll be a lot safer alone on the streets than I would be with you."

And then she reminded herself of the other guiding principle of the suffragettes. Hope.

Chapter Thirty-Two

Florence hesitated at the tenement entrance, peering across the yard through the grainy darkness of the alley. Damp, sooty air stung her cheeks and chilled the tip of her nose. A sleeping drunk who had been huddled in the building's doorway when she arrived was still there.

He stirred, and Florence tightened her grasp on the broken bottleneck. But after unfolding one bleary eye, the man stared vacantly at her for a moment, then rolled over and began to snore once more.

Her heartbeat calmed. She dropped the jagged bottleneck into her beaded reticule and stepped over the man and into the yard. A few brisk steps took her through the alley to the arch connecting it to the street. Once more she paused, propped her umbrella against the wall, and worked her fingers into her gloves. She gazed nervously around her. In places the fog had lifted. There was activity in the High Street, where before there had been none. *You must appear confident, even if you are not.* That was what she always told the Bloomsbury group before a mission. She turned up the collar of her coat, adjusted her feathered hat to a jaunty angle, and stepped out.

A man struggled along on the other side of the road, hunched over a barrow jammed with household items. In the dim light she made out a protruding chair back and what looked like the legs of an upturned table. The man was heading in the same direction as she, and he walked with a purpose; he did not seem drunk or looking for trouble. She would follow close behind, she decided, so he might provide protection if necessary. With any luck, she might even find a cab before she reached the station.

Her low-heeled boots clacked on the pavement.

After a few paces the man slowed and glanced over his shoulder at her. "Piss orf. I ain't interested."

"Excuse me, sir?"

"Acting the toff won't work eiver—I said piss orf."

"Oh, no, you've got me quite wrong. All I wanted to do was follow you to the station. I mean you no harm."

"Women, nuffink but pests." He spat on the ground. "Ya fink I wanna be saddled wiv anuvver when I only just got shot o' the last? You fink I'm pushin' around me worldly possessions for the fun of it? I'm lookin' for a new gaff, that's what I'm doin'. Na piss off or you'll be sorry."

How typical; the first sober man she encountered had to be a misogynist. "Ignore me, then," she called back. "I don't care. I'll just follow a short distance behind—"

Something flew through the air, cutting off her words and splattering into her face. She gagged; spat warm globs from her mouth. With the back of her hand she wiped her lips—it was fresh horse dung. "Horrible man!" she screamed after him, shaking her umbrella.

The barrow trundled on to the sound of bitter laughter. Damn him and all his kind! He would probably call in at the next public house and recount the hilarity of his encounter at her expense.

That set her thinking. Derwent had sent his brother to the White Hart. Perhaps he was still there. Patrick would see her safely to the station.

There were plenty of pubs around. Almost every street corner in this part of London sported a drinking or gambling establishment of one kind or another. But she knew the White Hart would have to be convenient for the brothers to fill their ale jug.

She doubled back down Whitechapel Road and spotted the White Hart's illuminated sign almost immediately, a white stag's head against a blue background. The pub stood among a line of dreary terraced shops on the High Street, a stone's throw from the alley leading to Derwent's lodgings.

The name of the pub, the White Hart, had been repeating itself in her mind since Derwent had mentioned it, and she couldn't think why it seemed so oddly familiar. Other than a few sheltered visits to Olivia's soup kitchen, she had never been to this part of London before, though she did know it by reputation. It was an area of the utmost deprivation and depravity, where even the police were loath to venture.

Florence needed all her wits and courage to overcome the next challenge. A group of laughing, shoving people spilled into the street outside the pub. She negotiated her way along the bumpy pavement towards them, took a deep breath, and pushed her way through the narrow door and into the smoky interior.

The Hart was a crowded, stinking place, packed with hard-ened drinkers of both sexes. As she elbowed her way towards the bar, she noticed how emaciated many of the men were, how they leered at her through hungry eyes. The women wore an abundance of paint and laughed lewdly and loudly, expos-ing gapped teeth and shuddering bosoms. It was hard to imag-ine Patrick O'Neill drinking in a place like this—Derwent yes, but not Patrick.

Finally she reached the publican, who was struggling to pull the ale fast enough to keep up with demand. He seemed the only sober person in her vicinity, his face flushed with the effort of providing for his thirsty customers and not from the liquor itself. "Excuse me," she said. "Can you help me? I'm looking for an Irishman named Patrick O'Neill."

The publican ignored Florence in favour of a woman standing next to her, as round as she was tall. "No more for you, Nelly," he said. "Not till you pay for that last one."

"Ow, come on na, Bill, give us some tick. You can't 'spect me to go out in the street on a night like this." She put a skinny, pleading hand out to the publican and Florence realised that the woman only appeared rotund because of the multiple layers of clothing she wore; perhaps it was all she possessed. "Besides," Nelly added, "ol' Jack loved nights like this—I wouldn't be safe."

The publican pressed his finger to his lips. "Hush, Nelly, talk of the Ripper don't do trade no good at all."

"Give us anuvver then and I'll keep me mouf shut!"

The barman poured Nelly another gin and then answered Florence's question.

"Patrick O'Neill, you say? He left a while back, miss." He looked her up and down, wiped his hands on his grimy apron. "Now if I was you, I'd get my chauffer to drive me straight on 'ome. Jack the Ripper 'asn't been up to 'is tricks for twenty years now, but there's plenty of others about 'opin' to take 'is place, mark my words."

Nelly cackled and nudged Florence with her elbow. "Jill the Rippers, too—watch out for them threads of yours, your ladyship, there's some out there wouldn't fink nuffink of cutting yer froat for that fancy coat. Do what Bill says, ducks, and go on 'ome."

Easier said than done, Florence thought, panic rising. And as if on cue, quick, bony fingers began to tug at the silky pockets of her sealskin coat. "Oh, please leave me alone," she pleaded, trying in vain to brush the fingers away.

I t should have been a ten-minute walk from Aldgate Station to O'Neill's lodgings, but both Dody and Pike had trouble negotiating the rutted pavements and crooked cobbles, and it was more like twenty minutes before they reached their destination. The George Yard building was a tall, red-bricked tenement accessed from the High Street through a brick arch and then a small alleyway.

They stopped in the yard outside the tenement and stared up at the dimly flickering windows. "I can't believe Florence came here on her own," Dody said, unsure which was the stronger emotion accompanying the fear she felt for her sister: intense anger or incredulous admiration.

"Who knows what words of encouragement Miss Barndon-Brown used to get her here," Pike said. "I'm afraid I cannot recollect the number of the flat. I had hoped I might see an officer from Special Branch here, but if so, he's very well disguised or hidden."

Dody noticed a man slumped in the doorway and

instinctively moved towards him to see if he needed assistance. Pike pulled her back and nudged the man with his boot. "Hey, you! Wake up!"

"Bugger off, I need me kip."

"Police! Show some respect."

It was as if Pike had lit a fire under the man. His eyes jerked open and he pulled himself into a leaning position against the wall. "Wot, wot? Ya want me ta move on, Officer? In this wevver?"

"I want you to answer my questions, that's what I want. I'm looking for a woman."

"Ain't we all, mate, ain't we all."

Pike tilted his head to Dody. "She's well dressed, a little shorter than this lady."

The drunk blearily focused on Dody. "Yeah, I seen 'er I fink."

"How long ago?"

A scratch of the head, a burp. "I dunno."

Pike cursed under his breath. "Think, man. You saw her tonight, but when? Was it dark, did she wake you up?"

"Stepped over me, she did, not too long ago, I reckon. Oi! Yer no copper, where's ya uniform?"

The frustrating discourse was brought to a merciful conclusion when the O'Neill brothers burst through the front door and into the porch. For a moment both parties stopped what they were doing and stared. The men sized each other up.

Pike spoke. "We're looking for Florence McCleland," he said coldly to Derwent. "We were told she'd come to see you here."

Derwent ignored Pike and gave Dody a low bow. "Good evening, Dr. McCleland."

"Answer the chief inspector's question, please, Mr. O'Neill," Dody said.

"Oh, for God's sake, Derwent," Patrick broke in. "There's no time for playing around." He turned to Dody. "She stormed out of here not long ago after having a disagreement with my brother. She's out there alone. We've just come out to look for her."

Pike took a step closer to Derwent. "A disagreement?"

Dody placed her hand on his arm and silently urged him to hold back. This was not the time to settle scores, not when her sister was alone on the streets, possibly this minute being stalked by an unbalanced killer.

Derwent let go a weary sigh. "I think she might have been off to find my brother at the pub—but failed on that count, as you can see. He has just come home and, obviously, did not see her. We thought we'd try and find her together."

Pike frowned under the porch light, as if he wanted to believe what the brothers were saying. Dody prayed that Pike would put aside his pride. Two able-bodied men would be a useful addition to their search party.

"Four people will be better than two," he said finally to the brothers. "We will search together."

His part in the discussion over, the drunk slipped back down the wall like a melting pat of butter.

Chapter Thirty-Three

It would have been quicker to walk, Florence mused as her gaze ran the length of the nag's bumpy backbone, but at least she felt safe with the Polish cartman, whom the publican had called Sleveski. The man's English was broken, his manner taciturn, though he did brighten briefly when the publican suggested she offer him tuppence for a lift to the station.

At last the station sign came into view. Sleveski pulled up near the underground steps and with a grunt thrust out his hand. Working her way around the broken bottle in her reticule, Florence prised out his fare and shot him a smile, but he turned his head away. Men usually succumbed to Florence's charm, and this was her second snub of the evening. Still, the Whitechapel experience had been a worthwhile, character-building exercise; one can't have it one's own way all the time. She had braved and she had overcome. As Poppa would say: the hotter the fire, the stronger the steel, et cetera, et cetera. Soon she would be home and recounting her adventures to Olivia.

In her exuberance she jumped from the cart, only to catch her skirt and petticoats on a jutting nail to the sound of ripping fabric. Lord. Now she looked no better than half the women in that awful pub: dirty face, hair and hat crusted with dung, petticoats like shredded rags. She smiled to herself as she made her way to the station steps, the clip-clop of Sleveski's cart swallowed by the noises of the street. Imagine if Dody were to see her now.

She almost stumbled into the chain barring the station entrance. The station was closed. "Damn and blast it!" she swore, her newly raised spirits crashing. She'd had enough character-building experiences for one night. This was the second time in one week her adventures had left her stranded in the middle of the night with no way of reaching home. But this was considerably further from Bloomsbury than the golf course. She pulled up the collar of her coat and clamped her jaw to stop her teeth from chattering.

Florence spun in a slow circle, trying to see past the fog and the surrounding buildings, searching for the looming silhouette of the Tower by the river where Mark Lane Station was located. She could see nothing, but in the near distance she heard a foghorn. The river wasn't too far away.

She struck out along the wide pavement of the main road, allowing her senses to guide her. Streetlamps were few and far between. There was still the chance of a cab, though in her heart she knew it was unlikely. No cabbie in his right mind would be looking for a fare here, especially not on such a miserable night. A few motorcars passed and she tried to signal for them to stop, but they travelled at such speed she doubted she was even seen. A distant clock chimed eleven. Any omnibuses would be stopping for the night now.

It began to drizzle and she opened her umbrella and forced her heavy legs to keep on moving. A drooping hat feather tickled her face. She ripped it from her hat and threw it to the ground.

After a few minutes she became aware of a group of men following not far behind. One of them whistled and called out to her to stop. Another begged for a kiss. More motorcars sped by. Just as she was contemplating throwing herself in front of one to force it to stop, she became aware of a low rumble, a jangling harness, the creak of leather, and the grind of heavy wheels. At last something slower was crawling up on the other side of the road—a brewer's dray if its bulky silhouette was anything to go by.

She crossed the road, but the horse-drawn vehicle proved speedier than she had estimated and she had to jog to keep up with it. She called out to the driver to stop, but he acted as if he had not seen or heard her, his head nodding over the reins. She discarded her umbrella and ran alongside the wagon as fast as she could, past factory walls rising like cliffs from the pavement. She was screaming out to the driver to stop, the first tears of the evening running down her face. Fear and exertion snatched at her breath and turned it into choking gasps. The group of men might cross the road at any moment, do unmentionable things to her under the driver's very nose, and still he wouldn't notice. Or would choose not to.

Then came a narrow break between the factory walls. Giving up on the wagon, she slipped into the alleyway, praying it would be a shortcut to the river.

She found herself in a narrow maze of twisting alleys, dark

tunnels, and tiny cobbled streets, the dwellings on each side almost meeting above her head in places. Her breath rasped as she ran, dodging barrels outside ramshackle lantern-lit shops and decrepit public houses, and homeless men huddled around braziers. Every now and then she stumbled into small, crooked courtyards where she stopped to catch her breath, the air rank with the smell of human waste. And each time she stopped, above the gasping of her breath, she thought she detected the ring of hobnailed boots behind her.

After the third time, she knew the footsteps weren't imagined. Fear gripped her heart. There was nothing character building about rape.

At last she broke free from the alleyways and found herself in the open grey light of the riverside. The Tower rose majestically ahead, and just around the bend on its waterside she could see the tangled forest of masts and cranes of St. Katharine docks.

Florence drew in great draughts of stinking river air—no odour ever seemed sweeter—and pushed her exhausted limbs along the embankment wall between the Tower and the river, heading for the comforting hum of traffic from Tower Bridge.

The tide was out, leaving small, clinker-built vessels stranded on the reeking mud flats. Larger ships were moored in the central river pool, dirty brown water slapping against their hulls before curdling its way on to the sea. There were no people about the place, but lights glowed on some of the ships and there were noises from the docks: the clank of chain and winch, the thump of heavy loads. Respectable noises made by hardworking men. No danger here of the catcalls and innuendos from the predators she had left behind.

Or had she left them behind?

Again she heard the clack of hobnail boots. She had no energy left; she had no choice but to turn and face her attacker. When she reached the handrail at the top of Queen's Steps leading down to the river, she sensed someone behind her. She whirled around, then grabbed the rail to stop herself sinking to the cobbles in relief. A policeman stepped out from the murky gloom.

The publican called time and Dody found herself jostled on all sides as people spilled from the public house and into the street.

Outside the White Hart, Pike finally managed to flag a hansom, waving his warrant card at the reluctant driver. Dody would have preferred a motor taxi but she knew they had to take what they could get. It was a tight fit. She was crammed into the cab between Pike and Derwent while Patrick hung on behind the driver, an unenviable position leaving him exposed to the chill wind and drizzle.

Pike thumped his cane against the roof and they were off, thundering down the Whitechapel High Street as fast as the overburdened horse could take them. The publican had arranged for Florence to be taken to Aldgate Station—they had at least managed to find out that much. For a few exhilarating seconds Dody rejoiced at the thought that her sister was probably at this very moment sitting safely on the tube—until Pike looked at his watch and broke the news that it was eleven o'clock and the station had been closed for more than an hour.

Dody felt numb. Even though the London she knew was only a few miles to the west, it was a world away from this den of poverty and vice, where gangs of cutthroats ruled the streets at night and homeless children and prostitutes slept in churchyards by day.

"We should try Mark Lane," Derwent O'Neill said. "I told her it stayed open later."

"How could you have let her go out alone? What kind of man are you?" Dody cried.

"She insisted she'd walk alone. I'm sorry I didn't insist more."

"We'll find her, Dody," Pike said. "We might still catch her on the High Street—unless she managed to flag a cab or omnibus, in which case she may be turning her key in your front door at this very minute." His words rang empty. Dody could tell by his grim face that he did not believe them.

The hansom slewed around the water pump in the square and stopped in front of the station steps. There was no sign of Florence. Patrick jumped down from the cab and stamped his legs. "Come on, Derwent," he said between chattering teeth. "It's time we swapped places. I'm frozen stiff, man."

"Ah, it's good for you, brings out the roses in your cheeks," said Derwent.

Pike leant over Dody and opened the door. "Out," he said, prodding Derwent with his cane. He turned to Dody. "I propose we head to lower Thames Street and then the river."

She nodded glumly, unable to speak anymore.

Chapter Thirty-Four

This must be a trick of the light, Florence thought, blinking her eyes. She could not believe what they were seeing. She had left Olivia only a few hours before, exhausted and recuperating from her ordeal at the prison. "Olivia, is that you?"

Olivia removed the beehive helmet and stepped under the sallow glow of a streetlamp. "Hello, Flo. I hardly recognised you, either. You're a mess. Where's your hat?"

Florence absently touched her tangled hair. "My hat? It must have blown off in the alley. Oh, I'm so glad to see you, Olivia. I was being chased, you see. I've had the most awful time . . ." She broke off, trying to make sense of her muddled thoughts. "But why on earth are you dressed like that?"

"Oh, you'd be amazed what one can get away with when one is dressed like a bobby. Unlike you, I can walk the streets of Whitechapel quite unmolested."

"You dress this way so you can walk here freely?" Florence seized and ran with the absurd notion. "To see what life is like for the women of the streets? What an amazing idea, why did you never tell me? I would have come with you."

"No, Flo, that isn't what I meant."

Florence forced an uneasy laugh. "You've been to your soup kitchen then?" *Keep her talking. Let her think you are a naïve fool*, Florence thought desperately. "But you should be resting . . . I wouldn't have thought you were well enough."

"No, Flo. No soup kitchen."

Olivia pulled the truncheon from her belt and turned it over in her hands.

"What do you need that thing for?" Florence asked, indicating the truncheon with a stiff wave, sensing there was no going back, that Olivia had seen through her ploy.

"It's very useful, Flo, believe me."

"Look, it's awfully cold, come with me to the bridge for a cab. We can talk about this over cocoa once we get home." Florence's teeth were chattering, but not only from the cold. There was something in Olivia's eyes, a fixed and feverish look, so utterly unlike her friend. And then she remembered; she had seen it before, briefly, in the street outside the WSPU breakfast. Olivia had worn that same expression when she'd attacked the man who had been harassing Daisy. Olivia had scratched his face like a wildcat. She would do anything for Daisy.

"Besides, if I had let you return it, you would have discovered it was not the one you and Dody had borrowed. Did you tell your sister about finding it in my wardrobe?"

"No, no, I never thought to," Florence lied automatically. She attempted to swallow, but failed; her mouth was too dry. "If this wasn't our truncheon, then whose . . ." She broke off and backed away to stand once more at the top of the stone steps leading from the embankment to the river.

"Come, come, Flo, you're usually quicker than this."

"I'm cold, I just want to go home," Florence said. "I don't understand why you're here." With shaking fingers, she attempted to loosen the drawstring of her reticule. At the bottom of the steps, river mud, the consistency of thickened cream, gleamed under the embankment lights and reflected their shadowy movements above.

"I followed you. Once you told me you'd seen the truncheon, there was nothing else I could do. It was I who killed Catherine. You know it. I can see it in your face. I've had the uniform and truncheon for years, bought them from a dodgy market stall. I knew they'd come in handy one day; the police are our constant opponents. I took them with me to the demonstration, and when things started getting out of hand, I changed in the alley, out of everyone's sight." Olivia slapped the truncheon in her hand and took a step closer.

"That's ridiculous, I don't believe it," Florence said, believing every word. They had been separated during the riot, and not reunited again until the evening. "You can't have killed her. It makes no sense at all. Oh, Olivia, please stop this nonsense and come home." Her fingers closed around the bottleneck.

"Think of the publicity, think how bad it would have looked—a policeman murdering a suffragette! It's unfortunate that things have not yet eventuated as I had hoped, but there's still time."

"You could never be so hard and callous. Why would you choose Catherine? She was our friend, she loved you."

"Nonsense, Catherine loved nothing but her cause. Catherine found Daisy and me in *flagrante delicto* at my house when we were supposed to be folding leaflets. She threatened to expose us, to tell you. You always said you never wanted *those* kinds of women in the group, don't you remember?" Her voice rose. "We should have the right to live as we choose." She paused, poked Florence's reticule with the tip of the truncheon. "What have you got in there? Let me see."

Florence held up her hands, praying that Olivia would not see the glinting glass. "Rules are made to be broken," she stuttered. "I wouldn't have minded. I know what Catherine was like . . ."

"She said I was corrupting an innocent young girl," Olivia said, now with a hysterical edge to her voice.

"Not if Daisy was consenting. She was old enough. Love between women is not illegal, no one cares."

Olivia raised the truncheon.

"Olivia, don't do this! I'm your friend. You are feeling unbalanced by the terrible treatment you suffered in Holloway. Come home with—"

With a splintering snap, the truncheon slammed down on Florence's arm. The bottleneck fell from her grasp and she collapsed onto the stone steps, dizzy with pain and fear. "Please, Olivia, no," Florence sobbed, clutching her shattered arm, desperately searching for a means of escape.

But with Olivia above her and the mud below, there was no way out. When Olivia descended the steps, Florence began to scream.

The cab slithered to a stop on the macadam just outside the Tower. Terrible screams reached them before they had stepped from the carriage. "That's Florence!" Dody cried, scrambling over Pike and onto the street, hitching up her skirts as she ran across the cobbles towards Queen's Steps. She was soon overtaken by Derwent and Patrick, pelting towards the figures she could now see, grappling at the river's edge.

At the sound of the men's shouts, Olivia looked up briefly. The police buttons on her uniform glinted under the lamplight. Florence took advantage of Olivia's distraction and lashed out with her elbow, knocking Olivia to her own level at the bottom of the steps. When Dody arrived, breathless at the top, it was hard to distinguish who was who as one shape pushed and the other grabbed. Then, in an instant, both figures rolled from the steps and plunged several feet down, into the river mud.

Dody moved to follow, but found herself struggling against Derwent's strong grip. "Where are they? I can't see them!" she cried.

"Stay put, woman. There's no point any of us leaping in until we can see where they are."

"Down there." She pointed into the sucking murk. "There's movement over there, can't you see it?" The mud bubbled some distance from the steps. Dody saw Olivia, struggling to hold Florence under the mud.

By now, Pike had caught up with the group at the top of the steps. "Patrick," he panted, ripping off his coat and jacket. "Run to the docks and get help."

Patrick dashed away in the direction of the lights, some two hundred yards in the distance, and Pike made for the steps. Derwent was quicker. He pulled Pike back by the collar and shoved him to the ground, Pike's cane clattering on the cobbles.

"Don't be a fool," Derwent said. "That muck's like quicksand, you haven't a chance."

Then Derwent was on the bottom step, launching himself

as far as his long legs could take him, landing waist deep in the viscous, stinking mud.

"Where is she, where's Florence?" Dody heard him cry as he waded towards Olivia, his arms outstretched. He reached out to grab her, but she slipped from his grasp.

Then a gunshot rang out in the fog.

Dody covered her mouth with her hand. "My God, she has a pistol!"

"O'Neill's still standing. She must have missed," Pike said.

The two slippery forms came together and it was unclear who had the advantage until another shot cracked the air, followed almost immediately by a high-pitched scream. Then Olivia was gone and the only sound was the gentle slap of the tide.

Derwent disappeared, too.

"It's all right," Pike said to Dody, "he's looking for Florence."

"She's been under too long, let me go, I have to try—"

"You need to stay dry and ready to attend to her when he brings her out," Pike said, holding fast to her arm.

"Please let—"

"Wait! I see her. He's got her—look."

Dody saw Derwent heaving to lift Florence, her clothes weighted down by the mud. Dody's heart leapt.

"He's struggling—he needs a hand." Pike let go of his hold on Dody and started down the steps. He lowered himself into the mud and waded laboriously out towards Derwent. He was still yards away when Derwent stumbled and dropped to his knees, holding only Florence's head above the mud.

Pike edged closer. He was agonisingly slow. If he slipped like Derwent had just done, Dody knew he would not have the strength in his knee to push himself back up.

When he was close enough, Pike thrust out his cane. "Grab this!" he called.

Derwent closed one slippery hand around the cane and hauled himself to his feet, while with the other he struggled to lift Florence further out of the mud. Dody saw no signs of life. Florence's head was flopped against her chest. Pike approached her other side and took some of the burden, and they began to make their slow way back to the steps.

Dody dropped onto the bottom step and lay on her stomach with her chest extending out over the steps and her feet towards the embankment. As soon as the sodden trio came close enough, she reached out to Pike and entwined her hand with his.

The clatter of running footsteps reached her and she knew it must be Patrick returning with help from the docks. Firm hands grabbed her ankles; someone helped her with Pike's hand. The human chain tugged and pulled until, with a sucking squelch, the pressure suddenly eased. To the sound of cheers from the men who had just arrived, Florence was dragged to the embankment and up onto the steps.

"Put her down. On her back," Dody instructed. She knelt at the side of the still form of her sister. "Please God, please God." She prayed as she had never prayed before. Pushing away clumps of mud-caked hair, she placed two fingers on the side of Florence's neck, desperate to feel the pulse of her sister's life.

Nothing.

She prised open Florence's mouth and forced her hand into her throat, scooping out gobbets of mud with her fingers. There was still more lodged in the pharynx, she could feel it but not reach it. She withdrew her hand and slammed her flattened palm onto Florence's chest. A spray of mud burst from Florence's lungs and the paroxysms of coughing that followed were the most joyous sounds Dody had ever heard.

"Get us a cab from the bridge," Dody heard Pike say to one of the onlookers. He knelt by Dody's side and tucked his coat around Florence's shuddering form, as tenderly as if she were his own daughter.

"Is she going to be all right?" he asked.

"Yes, I think so." Dody looked around at the sea of anxious faces. "Thanks to all of you. Thank you."

Pike got up and went over to where Derwent O'Neill was standing. Both men were shivering and dripping mud as they huddled together in earnest conversation. Dody wrapped her body around her sister's to infuse warmth into her and stroked her muddy face with the edge of her skirt.

After a minute or two Florence's eyes opened. She tried to speak.

"Hush, now," Dody said. "There will be plenty of time for talking."

"Olivia, where's Olivia?"

"She's dead—you don't have to worry about her anymore."

"She killed Catherine. Tried to kill me."

"She was deranged, my love."

"I think she broke my arm." Florence tried to shift her position and gasped with pain. "It hurts terribly."

"I know, darling, but I will soon have you feeling like new again."

Dody continued to stroke her hair. Florence frowned, little corrugations cracking through the drying mud on her face. "This is quite a setback to our group. But we will overcome. You know that, don't you, Dody?"

"Of course, my dear."

"The fight isn't over yet," Florence said with as much strength as she could muster.

Dody turned her head to Pike, wondering if he'd heard what her sister had said. His eyes met hers and he smiled.

Chapter Thirty-Five

Ninety-nine, one hundred. Dody placed her silver-backed hairbrush on the dressing table and steeled herself. "I'm ready now, Annie."

The maid moved behind the chair and yanked the comb through Dody's hair, indicating that Dody's one hundred brush strokes were amateurish and insufficient.

Dody drew a breath; no mean feat in her restrictive corset. "Gentle now, please, Annie, I'm a cowardly creature."

"You never used to mind, Miss Dody. It only hurts now because you've forgotten what it's like for me to do your hair." She took a "rat," a small oval-shaped pad from the dressing table and pinned it to one side of Dody's head.

And now I have been reminded, Dody thought, *I will not be requesting the service again.*

"Who would think that only two weeks ago you were

flinging yourself about in the mud with a madwoman—there's nothing cowardly about that, I'm sure."

"It wasn't me in the mud, Annie. I was just one of the many heaving from the steps."

Annie took some sections of hair and carefully smoothed them over the pad, pinning them into place. "Miss Florence is lucky to be alive, thank the Lord," she said through a mouthful of hairpins. "The mud wasn't so merciful to Miss Barndon-Brown, though, was it? Not that she didn't deserve everything she got."

Dody pictured Olivia as she had last seen her, a pathetic mud-caked figure on the mortuary slab. She had attended the postmortem conducted by Dr. Wilson, but not assisted; indeed she had scarcely spoken throughout the proceedings.

The cause of death was a gunshot wound to the abdomen, deemed to be self-inflicted, though whether by intention or accident, it was impossible to say. The O'Neill brothers had disappeared before the police arrived on the scene, and nobody had mentioned their involvement.

When Wilson cut through the skull to the brain, Dody had half expected to see a tumour, something organic to explain Olivia's monstrous behaviour. But even at the cellular level under the microscope, the portions of brain she examined had appeared normal.

"Florence's arm is healing nicely," she said, watching with awe the transformation that was taking place in the mirror before her. Annie had repeated the procedure on the other side of Dody's head and was now skillfully smoothing her long fringe into the two pads.

"Not long to go now, miss." Annie gathered up a remaining length of hair at the back, twisting it into a bun and holding it in place with an enamelled comb, the same colour as the gown she had earlier laid out on the bed. "Do you want feathers, too, miss? All the ladies are wearing feathers these days."

"No, my hair looks wonderful as it is, thank you, Annie. I don't want to block anyone's view of the stage."

"And you don't want to look taller than the chief inspector, neither, I wouldn't think."

There was still an underlying sting to the maid's tone whenever Pike's name was mentioned. If Florence could forgive Pike, surely Annie could, too? In fact, Florence had forgiven Pike to such an extent that his daughter, Violet, had been invited to spend the night as a guest in their house. Florence was even lending the girl a gown for the opera.

She could hear girlish laughter coming from Florence's room now. It was hardly surprising that they should be getting on so well, Dody reflected. Violet Pike was more of a suffragette than Dody would ever be.

"That will be all now, Annie. I can finish dressing myself. Go and see if Miss Pike needs a hand with her hair. Her father will be arriving shortly."

"Very well, miss." As Annie opened the door to leave, Dody heard giggling from Florence's room, then a snatch of a verse she hadn't heard since Florence was a schoolgirl.

Mama, Mama, what is that mess that looks like strawberry jam?
Hush, hush, my child, 'tis poor Papa, run over by a tram.

The girls fell silent. Annie must have entered the room like a cold draught. Dody returned to her dressing. Her gown was by no means the latest from Paris, but she had worn it infrequently enough for it to still look and feel new to her. She stepped into the folds of rose chiffon and fastened the close-fitting bodice, making sure the décolleté revealed plenty of the tantalising lace chemise beneath. She stared in amazement at the stranger in the full-length mirror: not a hair out of place in the mahogany pompadour, the perfect S-shaped posture, tiny waist, and she laughed at herself, the modern, freethinking career woman, secretly revelling in her own femininity.

She would make sure she dressed up like this at least once a year; it was good for the soul, if not—she struggled for a deep breath—for respiration.

P ike pulled his watch from the pocket of his cream brocade waistcoat. "We still have plenty of time, but I can't think what's keeping them."

"It takes time to create a thing of beauty," Dody said from her seat on the chaise.

Pike's eyes laughed. "Then it should have been you keeping us all waiting."

Dody felt herself colour. She had not meant to fish for a compliment. She moved to the window, hoping for a cooling draught, and pulled the curtain. White flakes tumbled from a black velvet sky. Pike moved to stand beside her. She breathed in his familiar, reassuring scent. How she had clung to him when they'd been trying to find Florence. Then it had seemed the most natural thing in the world, but now? Now she did not know.

"The first snow of winter," he remarked. "Beautiful."

"Yes, for those of us who have warm, comfortable houses."

"That is true. But if one were to always think like that,

how could one ever enjoy doing anything—even going to the opera?"

She turned to face him. "Oh, I know I will enjoy this very much."

He put out his hand and walked her back to the fireplace, where he noticed the postcard on the mantelpiece. "Greetings from Ireland?" he cocked an eyebrow.

"From Derwent to Florence, wishing Florence a rapid recovery."

"I see."

"As you should, seeing as it was you who helped the brothers vacate the country so speedily."

"Derwent killed Olivia by accident while they were struggling with the gun—we know that. But an Irish-hating judge might not have seen it that way."

Their conversation was interrupted by an offstage trumpet blast—or Florence's imitation of one—announcing the arrival of "Lady" Violet Pike.

Pike stared for several incredulous seconds. Violet wore Florence's magnificent gown of forget-me-not blue silk, which, thanks to Annie's skill with pins and darts, could have been made for her.

But at Pike's dumbstruck reaction, the smile on Violet's lips began to falter, as if she thought his look must signify disapproval.

"Go on," Dody whispered to him. "Make her feel grown-up."

"Oh, yes, right." Pike moved to his daughter, took her hand, and kissed it. "My dear, you look beautiful." He turned to Dody. "I am a lucky man to be able to escort two such beautiful women to the opera."

Florence cleared her throat in an exaggerated fashion, indicating her arm, which was still in the sling, and then to her elegant day dress as if it were made of rags. "Well, I suppose it's all right for some. Go ahead, the three of you, have a jolly good time. Bring me back a program—if you can bear to spare me a thought, that is."

Dody laughed. "Have a sherry with us, Florence, before we go."

"Oh, if you insist," Florence gave in with no hesitation. "But you must promise to take me with you next time, Pike, just as soon as my arm is better."

"Three beautiful women next time, splendid," Pike said with a smile as he handed Florence a glass of sherry.

Annie entered the morning room carrying a small silver tray with an envelope on it. She stood before Dody and gave an uncharacteristically formal curtsy as if she, too, was overwhelmed by the elegance surrounding her.

"A boy just dropped this off, Miss Dody," she said.

"Oh, who can this be from? And at this hour?" Then Dody saw the untidy handwriting and the Home Office stamp. She became conscious of four pairs of eyes staring at her, and coloured for the second time that evening. "Excuse me, please."

She moved into the hall, where she opened the note with trembling hands and read it beside the Christmas tree to a backdrop of silver orbs and miniature candles. Dr. Bernard Spilsbury had returned from his holidays. If it were convenient, he wrote, would Dr. McCleland mind joining him for a staff meeting at St. Mary's Hospital at eight o'clock tonight?

So, he was back. This was typical Spilsbury. He worked all hours himself, and would think nothing of calling a meeting late on a Friday night, giving no notice at all. *The privileges of the great*, she thought. But Dr. Eccles had said that Spilsbury was looking for an assistant, even intimated that Dody's name had been mentioned. Could this be the purpose of the meeting? She pressed her hand to her temple and felt the beginning of a headache. How could she enjoy the opera, knowing that her dream job might be on offer? Not to mention working alongside a man she respected so highly.

Her sister joined her at the tree. "Well?" Florence said, tapping her foot upon the black-and-white tiles. "It's from him, isn't it? He wants you for something right now. I can tell. Let me see it."

She took the note from Dody's hand and read it quickly. "The cheek of the man! There is no emergency."

Dody wrung her hands. "I don't know what to do."

"Go to the opera with Pike and Violet, of course. Imagine this wretched note came two minutes after you had left."

"But . . ."

"What do you want to do?"

"Both."

"Don't fib. You want to see Spilsbury, despite how guilty it makes you feel."

"I have to, Florence. This might be the only way I can get ahead with my career—you of all people should understand this."

"But what of Violet, what of Pike?"

"I'll make it up to them. Next time it will be my treat. I'll apologise in a minute, after I've changed, and I'll explain the situation to them. They won't mind . . . they both adore Miss Melba . . ." She hesitated; saw her reflection in one of the Christmas baubles—the pile of dark hair above a slightly blurred face, a dreamy hint of rose. She could have been looking at her sister.

"I know," she said, "you can go to the opera instead of me." Her voice sped. "I'm sure your arm will be fine. Just don't exert yourself, no clapping. We'll call Annie and she'll have you dressed in a jiffy."

Florence placed a hand on Dody's arm and forced her to look her in the face. "Dody, that won't work, can't you see? It simply won't work at all."

"Of course it will work. You and Violet get on splendidly."

"For someone so clever, you can be quite stupid."

Dody bristled, brushed Florence's arm away, and turned to the staircase.

"Violet's not the problem," Florence went on, following Dody up the stairs. "Can't you see? It's Pike."

Dody reached the landing and went into her bedroom, closing the door behind her. "Sensible clothes, warm clothes," she chanted as she moved to her wardrobe.

Florence knocked but didn't wait for an answer. She sat on the bed and addressed herself to her sister's back. "Dody, what are you scared of? If Spilsbury's job offer is contingent on you dropping your plans at a moment's notice on a Friday night—are they the sort of conditions you want to work under? Surely, if you are the best person for the job, and how would you not be, the job will be there for you on Monday morning."

Dody turned around with a heavy sigh, and came and sat next to her sister. She felt the cold of a tear snaking its way down her cheek.

Florence took out her handkerchief and dabbed Dody's face. "Careful, Dody, you don't want to go to the opera with a tear-streaked face. I am half convinced you are afraid of going with Pike. I think that you may actually feel something for the man and it's scaring you silly."

Perhaps her sister was right, Dody thought. True, she was desperate for the job, for some formal recognition among her peers, and her desperation was making her behave like an idiot.

As for Pike.

She sniffed. "I don't know how I feel."

"Shush, of course you don't know. But right now, that doesn't matter. You are going out to see the famous Miss Melba in a gala performance and that is wonderful in itself. Try not to think of anything else."

Some minutes later, Dody walked down the stairs, her head held high. She met Pike's quizzical look with a steady smile. "I'm sorry I kept you waiting. And you, too, Violet. There was something I needed to discuss with Florence. It is resolved now. Shall we go?"

Florence was right. If the job was to be hers, it would still be hers on Monday morning.

Pike put out his hand to Dody. She saw the unasked question in his eyes and hesitated. It was such a brief hesitation that no one else in the hall, with the exception of Florence, would have noticed it. Nor understood the significance of the squeeze that Dody gave his hand back.

The three of them walked together to the waiting carriage. It was snowing lightly. Gentle flakes brushed their cheeks and sparkled on their hats. As Florence waved them good-bye from the porch, Dody wondered when her little sister had grown to be so wise.

Author's Note

While this is a work of fiction, all of the attitudes and many of the events depicted are fact. Details of the November 1910 riot were taken from eyewitness accounts and newspaper articles. Police did behave brutally, and three women were killed. None of the women, however, were called Lady Catherine Cartwright and none were mysteriously murdered. Nor has it been proved that Winston Churchill was behind the brutal behaviour of the police, though rumours abounded at the time.

I have been unable to find evidence of a female autopsy surgeon as early as 1910, but Bernard Spilsbury did have a female assistant, Hilda Bainbridge, by 1920, so I hope the reader can forgive this ten-year discrepancy!

Dody McCleland's background is that of my grandmother's, at the time one of a handful of female graduates of Trinity College, Dublin. Much of the Fabian colour, for example the hockey match, was inspired by her memoirs.

Details of Crippen's execution were constructed from newspaper articles of the time. The force-feeding scene was inspired by eyewitness accounts—the horror has not been exaggerated.

The main characters are of my own creation, but several of the background figures are nonfiction. These include:

DR. BERNARD SPILSBURY, the father of modern forensic science.

EMMELINE PANKHURST, the founder of the militant suffragettes, the WSPU.

CHRISTABEL PANKHURST, her daughter.

LADY CONSTANCE LYTTON, a prominent victim of force-feeding.

DR. HAWLEY HARVEY CRIPPEN, hanged at Pentonville Prison for the murder of his wife. DNA evidence recently come to light suggests that Crippen might have been innocent of the crime.

WINSTON CHURCHILL, future Prime Minister of Britain.